STRENGTH
IN
UNITY

T.K. RIGGINS

How To Set The World On Fire Series:

Book 1: How To Set The World On Fire

Book 2: Money Jane

Book 3: Next Level Hot

Book 4: Outlaw OTP

Book 5: Questbeats

Book 6: Ride with the U

Book 7: Strength in Unity

Published in 2024 in accordance with Franchise Publishing.

Cover design and interior formatting by: Edge of Water Designs, edgeofwater.com
eBook Formatting: Spica Book Design, spicabookdesign.com

Issued in print and electronic formats.
ISBN 978-1-7773215-6-7 (Book)
ISBN 978-1-7773215-7-4 (E-book)

Franchise Publishing
Vancouver, British Columbia

For the real Amelia,
and the moments worth a lifetime.

Table of Contents

Prologue

The spider froze, like a thief caught red-handed. It had nowhere to go. It was too far from the edge of the bar top to make a clean escape, and so, it opted for a strategy of lying still. A fatal mistake.

Amelia Jane wound up and crushed the weak arachnid beneath her palm.

The two regulars sitting at the bar nearly jumped out of their stools, caught off-guard by the loud slap. But Amelia was more interested in the newcomer huddled at the end of the bar. He hadn't even flinched.

And he had scars, just like her.

One of the regulars, Darcy, rattled the ice in his glass. "Hey, sugar. Can I get another?" He hiccupped.

Amelia smiled, but it wasn't genuine. "Of course." She glanced at the newcomer. His water glass was still full.

"Me too," the other, Brantley, said.

Amelia wiped spider guts on her ragged black dress. She picked up a few glasses from the rack on her way to the bar well and scooped a few ice cubes into each. Her target was a dark-purple bottle. She didn't know what the mixture was called, but it was the cheapest liquor in town.

While pouring the drinks, she quickly scanned the room. With the room's open floor concept, Amelia could easily see all the wooden tables scattered about. An old piano sat in the centre of a small corner stage. Amelia couldn't play the instrument, but she loved the rare times when music filled the atmosphere.

Not that she was likely to hear any music tonight.

Although there was plenty of seating in Sugarplum, there weren't many visitors this early into the evening. Amelia liked when it was slow—it was much easier to avoid chaos when patrons weren't stumbling around drunkenly with their arms flailing. Even when seated, some drunkards still managed to knock the plates she was carrying or smash their drinks accidentally.

Of the few filled tables, the only one that warranted her attention was the table where Gerard sat. As the owner of the pub, he'd often sit with regulars to make them feel welcome and to build rapport. But the two men he was sitting with now weren't just patrons, they were part of the local Tyco gang.

Gerard had always stressed to Amelia the importance of keeping the Tyco happy, which meant showing respect to all its members. Bringing them fresh drinks before their last round was empty was the easiest way to serve them well. Right now, their pint glasses were about a quarter full.

Amelia finished pouring the drinks for the grizzled regulars at the bar, dropped them off without receiving a single thank-you, and then grabbed fresh pint glasses. She cracked open the tap of her keg barrel and filled both pints with ale. Now she hustled over to the Tyco table, but slowed when she got closer. All three men were hunched over.

"I'll have it for you next week," Gerard said.

Amelia placed the pints in front of both guests. One of them snorted before sitting up straight. "Thank you, Amelia." His chubby cheeks rose with his bright smile. The other Tyco member was glaring at Gerard.

"Can I get you anything else?" Amelia asked to break the tension. "Maybe something to eat?"

"Not now," the glarer said, without even glancing at Amelia

Gerard leant back in his chair. "Amelia, can you please grab our new pianist a bowl of stew."

Amelia clasped her hands together. "Really? You're our new pianist?" It was hard to believe the Tyco members were also entertainers, and she couldn't hold back her excitement.

The snorter grabbed his belly and laughed. "Have you ever played the piano, D'Angello?"

D'Angello finally broke his stare to look up at Amelia, but he seemed more disgusted than angry. Amelia didn't apologize.

"He's at the bar," Gerard said.

Amelia nodded. She didn't have to check; she knew the mysterious, quiet newcomer was the piano player. She wondered if they shared the same taste in music. She curled her hair around her ear, excused herself from the table, and headed for the back room.

The kitchen wasn't anything glamorous. It was a small room with a side table in one corner used for prep, and a burning cauldron beside it in the other. Gerard left the stew simmering in case anyone wanted the daily special. Amelia didn't know why he called it that. There wasn't anything special about the stew, and it was the only dish they served each day.

The vegetable stew smelled good, but it usually tasted bland. There wasn't much variety for produce in the Badlands, and Gerard bought in bulk to save money. It didn't matter much, though, because patrons didn't come to Sugarplum for the food.

Luckily for Amelia, Gerard normally stocked a jar with her favourite treat: fresh dates. She snuck an extra one from the jar as she made up the plate. Gerard allowed her to eat anything she wanted while on shift, but she didn't often take advantage of his kindness. She was grateful for the work, and she didn't want to jeopardize it.

She added a small dinner roll next to the dates, laid a full leaf of lettuce to cover the rest of the plate, and then placed a soup bowl on top. She spit her date seed into the waste bin, then took her whole setup to the cauldron and scooped a full ladle of simmering vegetable stew.

She carried the plate out of the tiny kitchen, making sure her thumb was steady at the base of the bowl so it wouldn't slide around on her short trip. Gerard stressed the importance of presentation, and even though the newcomer didn't seem fazed by much, Amelia didn't want to serve him a dish that looked unappetizing.

Amelia glanced at her other tables as she headed behind the bar. The two groups of four were too busy talking to enjoy their drinks. The table of two were shier with each other, and were drinking wine fast to hide it. An old man was taking a nap next to his nearly empty glass at another spot, and a lone woman across the room appeared, to Amelia's surprise, to be actually enjoying her stew.

The newcomer turned towards Amelia when she approached, his curious brown eyes shifting to follow her every move. He was likely Amelia's age based on his lack of facial hair. He had a cut on his lip and a bruise on his cheek. Given that and his skinny stature, Amelia doubted he'd won a lot of fights.

Gerard had told Amelia not to judge customers too quickly, but she couldn't help it. She had survived this long because she was careful who she trusted, and it carried over into her work at the pub by gauging who would give her better tips. She considered herself a good judge of character—she didn't need to follow Gerard's letter of the law on everything.

However, her judgements came not from how someone looked, who they were friends with, or how rich they were. Instead, she trusted her instincts; she felt like she connected to a person's core rather than how they portrayed themselves on the outside. Her troubled soul could recognize the likeness of another.

"On the house," Amelia said. She placed the plate in front of the newcomer, pointing the spoon handle in his direction.

The newcomer remained expressionless. Amelia's eyes locked with his. He had a confidence about him that outweighed his stature. She wondered what scars he hid. When he reached out, she saw fresh blood on his knuckles, which only intrigued her more.

The newcomer stirred the stew a few times but didn't take a bite. Instead, he grabbed a date with his free hand and popped it into his mouth.

Amelia looked down to hide her smile. She curled her hair around her ear again, but the sound of a smashing glass pulled her attention in the opposite direction.

The quiet pub went completely silent.

Over at Gerard's table, the snorter, the one with the chubby cheeks and bright smile, had his hands in the air. He looked around the room. "Just an accident," he said. He stared at Gerard. "It's crazy how they seem to happen in an instant. Without notice."

Gerard was sitting straight, but he remained still. Nobody in the pub moved except for the Tyco members.

D'Angello chugged the full glass of ale that Amelia had just delivered, set the glass on the table, and then stood. He wiped his mouth, glared at Gerard again, and then stalked out of the pub.

The snorter reached into his pocket while he stood, and then tossed a couple Aileron onto the table. "See you soon," he said to Gerard. He took another look at the bar, smiled towards Amelia, and then followed D'Angello out the door.

When the door closed behind the snorter, the other patrons returned to their normal conversations. The two tables of four were chatting again. The regulars at the bar swayed and laughed. The woman sitting alone went back to eating her stew.

Amelia glanced at the newcomer. His bloody fist was clenched tight as he stared at the door. Even though he was battered and bruised, it seemed like he was ready for another fight. She longed to use her magic to heal his wounds; they looked ready to ooze with more blood. Instead, she hustled to help Gerard.

She grabbed the broom and dustpan that were tucked beside the keg barrels. Gerard had picked up the big pieces of glass already, and crossed paths with Amelia as he dumped the glass into the waste bin behind the bar.

"Thank you, Amelia," Gerard said.

Amelia appreciated Gerard's respectful nature. Not only did he give her a chance to earn her wages rather than scrounge for them on the street, he also taught her valuable lessons in honour, respect, and hard work. She'd learned how to serve others, listen to those in need, and accept the support of her mentor and friend. She trusted Gerard because he never asked her to do something at Sugarplum that he wouldn't do himself.

Amelia swept up the rest of the glass and cleared the table where the Tyco members had sat. After she disposed of the broken shards, she served the patrons at the tables while Gerard tended the bar. They worked as a good duo, even through the commotion and drama that seemed to find its way in night after night.

But it seemed like there was a new member to their team.

Amelia watched Gerard shake the battered hand of the newcomer, who laughed and talked cheerfully while he ate up all of Amelia's stew. Gerard left his spot from behind the bar and led the newcomer to his seat at the piano. From across the room, Amelia studied their every move.

The newcomer sat comfortably on the bench while Gerard leant on the square housing that covered the hammers and strings. Amelia moved in for a closer look by pretending to wipe an empty table. The newcomer stretched his arms and fluttered his fingers like a bird stretching its wings for flight.

As soon as his fingers touched the piano keys, Amelia thought he might be an angel in disguise.

Amelia recognized the tune. She wasn't impressed by how the newcomer played the right notes, but how he strung them together so confidently. The smooth transitions, the contrast between the crescendos and sudden diminuendos; he played with a confidence that surpassed his boyish looks.

"Miss?" a soft voice sounded beside Amelia. "Miss?" the voice said louder.

Amelia opened her eyes; she hadn't even realized they were closed. She noticed a woman shaking her empty glass at the table next to the one Amelia was cleaning. Amelia rushed over to the woman and her partner.

"Ready for another?" Amelia said with a smile.

The woman didn't respond. She just held the empty glass until Amelia grabbed it.

"Another round?" Amelia asked. She nodded her head at the man this time. His drink was only half empty. He looked bored.

"Sure, why not," the man said.

Amelia smiled and danced back towards the bar. She wasn't going to let any of her dull patrons get her down. There was music in the air! She felt nervous and anxious at the same time, excited for the night to finally begin. She wondered how long it would take for people to start piling into Sugarplum now that the entertainment had begun.

Gerard was wiping glasses behind the well, and so Amelia didn't need to pour the drinks herself. He was watching the newcomer like a proud father watching his son. Even though Gerard didn't have any children of his own, he was notorious for helping youth get off the streets.

"How did you find him?" Amelia asked.

"Same way I found you." Gerard smiled. "Fate."

Gerard had found Amelia begging for change on a street corner in the Badlands. He was generous with his Aileron, so much so that Amelia decided to pass some of it on to another beggar. After secretly watching Amelia's reaction to his gift, Gerard had approached her again and offered her a job at Sugarplum.

She earned her keep; all she had needed was a chance. Gerard had provided that. He acted how the newcomer played the piano: with grace and honesty.

Amelia ordered her drinks. She closed her eyes again and enjoyed the moment. She rubbed her right hand over the scars on her left bicep. It was as if the music forced her to relive her happy memories. She wondered if Gerard noticed her enjoying the tunes, but at the same time, she didn't care how she looked.

She served the drinks to the couple, and then did the rounds of her other tables. It didn't take long for more patrons to arrive for the night's festivities. She wondered if the music filtering through the pub was reaching their ears outside, or if there was something magical about the evening that was drawing people in. Probably a little bit of both.

Time flew by. Amelia and Gerard raced around Sugarplum, tending to all the new guests, as well as those who were there for the long haul. Most were travellers to the Badlands, but a few of the local Guardians stopped by to get a few free ales. Gerard believed keeping law enforcement happy demonstrated safety in his establishment—even if the Guardians were mostly useless and corrupt.

After an hour or so, Amelia finally had time to take a break. She wiped her sweaty brow and poured herself a tall glass of water. As she guzzled it down, Gerard stopped talking to a few new regulars at the bar and strode towards her. He poured another glass of water.

"Can you take this to our entertainer?" Gerard slid the glass onto the server station. "I don't think he'd ask for it himself, and I don't want him to get too burnt out."

Amelia set her glass down and nodded. She suddenly felt nervous, but she took a deep breath and crept out from behind the bar. She moved around the tables and through a small crowd that had gathered to dance.

By the time she reached the piano, the newcomer was rattling the keys at the bass end of the piano, finishing the song. He lifted his fingers off the keys as Amelia set the glass of water on top of the square housing, next to his old empty glass.

The crowd clapped, but the newcomer seemed more interested in Amelia than the applause.

Amelia reached into her server pouch and grabbed a couple Aileron coins. She held the newcomer's stare as she dropped the change in his empty cup. The coins clanged together as they fell to the bottom of the glass.

"What is that for?" The newcomer stared at the Aileron.

"It's a tip," Amelia said. "Maybe the cheapskates around here will follow suit."

The newcomer raised his eyebrow in confusion. He reached out towards the glass. His left hand was shaking, and the cuts across his knuckles had burst open. The clotted blood was poised to drip down the back of his hand.

Amelia instinctively grabbed his wrist to help, but nerves overcame her once again. She held his arm, frozen in shock.

"How do you play like this?" She finally mustered.

The newcomer met her gaze with wide eyes as if just as shocked and nervous as she was. "I don't really notice it," he said with a shrug.

Amelia knew what it was like to live with pain. She understood the numbing feeling that often followed the initial rush. "May I heal you?" she asked. "I've been practicing my healing ability."

The newcomer didn't flinch, just nodded his head slowly. Amelia sensed that he would let her do anything to him in that moment.

Amelia held his wrist steady and reached to her neckline with her free hand. She pulled out the golden medallion that she used as her magical crutch. It had three circles etched onto the front surface with a sword, flame, and quill in the middle of each respective circle. On the back, the words *Strength in Unity* were clearly visible.

The medallion was the only thing Amelia had to remind her of her family. Her father had stressed the importance of balancing the physical, emotional, and intellectual parts of the self, and this medal was a reminder of that philosophy. It was important to recognize the skills that each part could yield, but it was dangerous to lean too much into one over the others.

Amelia needed to tap into her emotional side for her healing power to take over. She closed her eyes, clutched her medal, and crept her fingers towards the newcomer's knuckles. She took a deep breath and focused on the connection between them, creating a bridge for his pain to flow into and be absorbed by her.

She felt a tingle run through the arm that held his wrist. The prickly feeling flowed through her heart, and then seemed to ignite like a fireball. She wanted to scream, but she stayed strong. Her body tensed up, but it was a small injury. Soon she felt at ease. She opened her eyes and saw that the blood had disappeared from the newcomer's knuckles. All that was left was a beautifully faint scar.

"How does that feel?" She tried to keep her voice steady. Her heart was still beating wildly, even though she'd broken the connection to the pain.

The newcomer had stopped shaking. He looked at his hand with his mouth agape. He met Amelia's gaze, and then quickly looked away. He grabbed the glass of Aileron and quickly emptied it into his hand. He offered the Aileron to Amelia, but kept his gaze lowered. "Here's a tip," he said.

Amelia giggled. "No tip needed," she said.

The newcomer looked up. His eyes were watery. "I'm sorry, I just …" he looked away again. "I'm not used to anyone doing anything nice for me."

Amelia rested her hand on his shoulder. "No need to worry," she said. "At Sugarplum, we look out for each other." Amelia checked the rest of the pub. She should really be getting back to her tables, but she glanced back to the newcomer once more.

He stared right back at her. "Thank you," he said.

"You're welcome." Amelia blinked a few times so she wouldn't get lost in his dark eyes. "If you really want to give me a tip, maybe you could grant a request?"

"What would you like to hear?" the newcomer asked.

Amelia bit her lower lip. "Your name," she said slyly.

The newcomer grinned. "My name is Mardious Hood."

"Well, Mardious Hood, play me something slow." Amelia tucked her medal back under her garments and backed away from the piano. "Make it hurt."

Mardious' expression softened. He stretched his fingers out wide, and then placed them gently on the piano keys. He didn't stop staring at Amelia as he began his tune.

Amelia crept backwards until she was in the middle of the dance floor. The other patrons had gone back to their seats during the break, and so Amelia was by herself. She didn't feel alone though, because it seemed as if she and Mardious were the only ones in the room.

Amelia closed her eyes and focused on the melody. She didn't recognize the song, but it was everything she could have hoped for; it had plenty of soul. She felt the music flow into her heart, much like the tickling pain she had felt moments before. She swayed her hips and succumbed to the way her body reacted to the song.

Mardious had granted her wish. She felt beautifully hurt.

CHAPTER 1

Clear Eyes

Kase recognized the scent of burnt flesh. He wondered how many in the camp had been caught in the blaze. The heavy tracks leading away suggested that some of the people had either escaped or been captured. He hoped the survivors would be receptive.

"East clear," Kase whispered into his sage mirror. There weren't any Guardians around, and none of the survivors he could see were dressed like members of the Brotherhood. Those cleaning up the camp had faces covered with ash, and they walked with heavy shoulders and a slow and saddened pace.

"West clear," Lenia said. With Roman and Helena clearing the north and south, the team was ready to proceed.

"A.K., unite," Kase said. He undid the loose knot of his camouflage cape and let it drop to the ground. He dusted off the T-shaped visor of his golden lion mask, flipped the red mane away from the opening, and slipped it over his head. Due to the tint of the visor, everything now looked red.

He was always recognizable in his Dandy Lion armour, but so were the rest of his team. The notorious Unicorn Knight, with her black mask that bore a horn, purple T-shaped visor, and purple flume, had been on wanted posters throughout the realm. Kase's grandfather, Roman, wore his legendary silver bull-horned helmet. Kase's grandmother, Helena, wore a matching open-faced ram-horned helmet. Each of them wore chest plates, gloves, and boots that complemented their chosen character in colour and style.

They all met Kase on the east side of the camp before striding together down the main path. They kept watch on the surrounding forest for any signs of trouble, but their goal was to help the victims caught in the crossfire of the war.

In the year since the Animal Kingdom's unmasking of the Triple Crown, the ex-leaders of the realm had split into three factions, each claiming the title of king: Mac, dubbed the Mighty King, had drawn most of the Guardians to his side, and held onto power through this well-trained force for law and order, which he called the Marauders; Sheese traded gold, favours, and other valuables in exchange for his followers' loyalty to his New Realm Order, earning him the title of the Currency King; and Mardious Hood, the Underground King, ruled through fear, using the Brotherhood to engage in sneak attacks and collect hostages to control influencers throughout the realm.

Although the A.K. had split the Triple Crown apart, the three kings still battled for power over the rest of the realm. The Animal Kingdom—or, as Cali preferred to call them, the Anti-Kings—led the resistance against the former High Scholar, Warrior, and Wizard. It was in this small camp that Kase and his team hoped to find an ally to help them end the war.

"It's the Dandy Lion!" an onlooker from the camp yelled. He pointed and waved excitedly to others hidden in the rubble.

Kase picked up the pace. He was happy to have a friendly welcome, but the A.K. didn't want the world to discover exactly where they were in this moment. He scanned the area for any sage mirror flashes and was relieved not to see any. He removed his helmet to prevent it from muffling his voice when he spoke to the small crowd.

"Greetings," Kase said confidently. He tapped his heart with two fingers, touched his lips, and pointed to the sky. The gesture signalled his confidence to the rest of the A.K. that they weren't in danger, but it was also a salute to the fallen. "My condolences to your clan."

"Your reputation precedes you and the rest of your Animal Kingdom," the onlooker said. "We want no part in the war, but we are grateful for help in times of need."

Not everyone wanted to pledge allegiance to a particular group, and so the onlooker's claim that his camp wanted no part of the war was consistent, but with only a minority of people in the realm. Based on recent history, however, it was only a matter of time before they became desperate enough to pick a side, whether out of need for food, shelter, or safety. A burnt camp might force a decision.

"We'll help where we can, but we have an ulterior motive," Kase said. "We're looking for Sharaine Longhorn."

The dirt and ash had made the onlooker's greying hair darker, but also highlighted the wrinkles on his sombre face. He bowed his head mournfully. "Follow me." His voice quavered.

While Kase focused on their team's priority, the other members of the Animal Kingdom split up. The Bull and The Ram helped search the wreckage for valuable items that could aid the survivors, while the Unicorn Knight tended to the wounded. They also kept a lookout for a second attack.

The onlooker tried to share the events of the destruction with Kase but explained that his viewpoint had been limited as he had been knocked unconscious before the mayhem started. When he awoke, the entire camp had been burned to the ground. The other survivors had caught him up on how the Brotherhood had pillaged and plundered, but the aftermath had been difficult for him to bear. He struggled to provide Kase with any real details of the attack.

"We're not fighters, we're scholars," he said. "We were forced out of Kimroad by the Mighty King's Marauders, leaving behind our homes, possessions, and memories. We were surviving as best we could. Now, we're broken." He sniffled.

Kase thought about the devastation that he and his friends had felt when they had been exiled from the realm. "I've felt broken too," he said. "I like to believe that I'm stronger because of it, but it's still hard to live through. I hope I can help relieve the burden for you." He placed a hand on the onlooker's shoulder.

"Thank you," the man said. "Let's start with Sharaine."

The onlooker started clearing away debris from a large site at the edge of camp. Kase hauled away some of the burnt wattle that had been used to make the destroyed huts. He started to feel the despair and pain that those trapped inside would have felt.

"Was Sharaine wearing anything special?" Kase asked. "Like a bracelet or ring?" He assumed that the bodies would be burnt to a crisp, so he'd need a way of identifying Sharaine. He'd bring everyone back to life, but it would be best to bring their leader back first to keep everyone calm.

"Yes," the onlooker said. "She wore a silver necklace with an orange gemstone."

"Help me find it," Kase said.

Kase and the onlooker picked up their pace. They found three burnt corpses before stopping to take a break. One of the dead bodies was the size of a child. The onlooker shed a few tears, almost convincing Kase to bring the young one back first. However, it hadn't been the first child Kase had needed to bring back because of Mardious' carnage, so he moved forward with his initial plans.

A few more victims later, Kase found the necklace he was looking for. He dragged the body that the necklace draped around to an open spot in the camp. He knelt beside the torso, his knees slipping deeper into the mud.

"What now?" the onlooker said.

Kase usually didn't bring people back to life with witnesses around, but he wanted to act as quickly as possible to avoid another ambush. It was often confusing for people to watch him work because, although it seemed like he brought their loved ones back to life in an instant, the process felt a little longer for him. It also took a few moments for the unalived to orient themselves after experiencing their transition into darkness.

"Can you please fetch me some water?" Kase asked.

The onlooker acknowledged and raced away.

Kase closed his eyes and focused on his environment. He felt the breeze flow through his hair. He was bothered by the stench of burnt flesh, but this time he accepted the smell for what it was. He heard rustlings from the camp around him, likely from the A.K. helping the other victims of the chaos.

He touched the body, his hands glowed, and the process of his power of life began, starting with the recollection of the deceased's last moments.

Sharaine fell to her knees. She clasped her hands together. "Please," she mustered. "Don't do this." She tried not to sob, but she couldn't help it.

Mardious crouched down in front of her. He looked much older since Sharaine had seen him last. His hair was peppered grey around his ears, matching the rough stubble that had replaced his neatly-trimmed beard. He had a few wrinkles, but his eyes were youthful and filled with mischief. A female head floated out from behind his hood and whispered something in his ear. Her skin was almost transparent, like a ghost.

"This is your sacrifice." The corners of Mardious' mouth curled up like a demon's. "Save your favourite sibling, or I will choose for you." He gestured to his right, where a couple of his goons stood with Sharaine's younger brother and sister.

Sharaine softened as she stared at Bo, her ten-year-old brother, and Madeline, her twelve-year-old sister. She'd survived for so long by playing the game of politics, but what move could she make to save them? How close was Mardious to flipping his deal and hurting both instead? What about the rest of her camp?

"I'm sorry, Bo," Sharaine said. She knew he was the stronger of the two and might forgive her easier if he suffered.

Mardious chuckled. A second head curled around his opposite ear, but her eyes were dark, and she had scars on her cheeks. She smiled and laughed with him.

Mardious flicked his wrist and gestured for Bo to come forward. An older man snorted before pushing Bo into Sharaine. Tears streamed down Bo's face, but Sharaine held him tight to reassure him that he would be okay. A few tears escaped her eyes, too.

"If I don't bring you back, bring me the one who did," Mardious said. "I will unite you with your daughter once a meeting is arranged." He reached for his beltline. Sharaine noticed he was wearing a bandolier with coloured vials stored across the leather strap. He pulled out a dagger and presented it to Sharaine.

"This blade is coated in poison," Mardious said. "There are two edges, so use it wisely." The ghost-like heads that swam behind his hood disappeared. He nodded towards one of his men, who held a torch, and swiftly exited the hut.

Sharaine didn't have much time left. She closed her eyes so she wouldn't have to face her father. She slashed Bo's wrist, turned the blade to her palm, and cut herself too. Bo whimpered, but her father merely looked to the ground as he accepted his fate.

"It's going to be okay, Bo," she said. She started to see black spots.

Sharaine heard a murmur and then fell to the ground, still clutching her brother. She couldn't move a muscle. Not even her eyes could close. She watched the Brotherhood set the straw hut ablaze until the blackness took over.

Kase felt the heat burn his skin and knew that Sharaine's last moments were over. Now, as with every time he brought someone back, he had to relive his own insufferable demise. Lava burned his extremities before flowing down his throat, through his eye sockets, and melting his skin. He tried to scream, but the grip of the liquid fire wouldn't let him. He drowned in the heat, until every last essence of his body had become one with the molten pit.

Kase exhaled. He opened his eyes to meet Sharaine's fearful gaze. He wondered what else she'd accepted before agreeing to the final terms of his enemy. He needed to act calm, but still find a way to alert the others. He didn't know how much time he had before Sharaine made a move to capture him and take him to Mardious.

Sharaine pushed herself up and looked around frantically. "Bo?"

"He didn't make it, Sharaine," the onlooker said, returning with a jug of water. His gaze never left the ground.

"We can bring him back next, though," Kase said. He considered the chance that Sharaine might not be as loyal as Mardious had hoped, since she had died for his cause. Was Cali correct in assuming that Sharaine would help the A.K. instead of taking a deal with another leader?

Cali had worked with Sharaine for years before the Triple Crown had forced the A.K. into exile, but they had been competitive enemies before they were friends. Would Sharaine put more value in her workplace friendship with Cali, or would she revert to looking out for herself first? Kase was not about to ignore the desperate thoughts of a dying politician.

Sharaine glanced to the onlooker, then back to Kase. Her face softened.

"What do we do first?"

"We need to find his body," Kase said. "Do you know where he was at the time of the attack?" Although he'd seen Bo perish in Sharaine's arms, it wasn't common knowledge to the rest of the realm how his power worked. Only the A.K. were aware of his connection to the fallen through the doorway of life.

Sharaine glanced to the onlooker again. Fear crossed her face. "No, I don't."

The onlooker smiled. "Maybe the others do?" He started walking back towards the entrance of the camp.

"Yes, I agree," said Sharaine. She stood up and pressed her hand to her heart. She picked at the charred clothing she was wearing, but she avoided looking at Kase.

It seemed like both Sharaine and the onlooker were purposefully distracting Kase. Who else had Mardious threatened in an attempt to capture him? The onlooker certainly hadn't forgotten about the child's corpse Kase had pulled from the debris, which matched the size of Bo. Kase suddenly felt like he'd been played the moment he'd arrived.

Kase needed to find the A.K. Their mission was over.

Sharaine and the onlooker led Kase towards a few huts that hadn't been burned down. As they walked, he made sure to stay behind the duo. He kept looking over his shoulder, but also scanned the camp for The Bull, The Ram, and the Unicorn Knight. He noticed that the onlooker didn't say a word to Sharaine, which was surprising since she was supposed to be his leader.

When they rounded one of the standing huts, they found all three A.K. members with the small group of survivors. The Bull and The Ram were making the wounded more comfortable. The Unicorn Knight was healing a teen's burnt hand.

Kase counted fifteen survivors in total, including the onlooker and Sharaine. The A.K. were outnumbered, but they still had the advantage of a quick escape. The Unicorn Knight wore her black trident, which gave them the ability to teleport across the realm.

If Kase didn't warn her soon, she might teleport Sharaine back to the A.K.'s hiding spot along with the rest of them. He assumed that Sharaine, along with anyone in her crew, was no longer an ally, and would leak information back to Mardious Hood.

He wasn't the only one keeping secrets.

The onlooker approached a small group that the A.K. wasn't tending to. Sharaine was left to wander, pretending to search for something, but she looked out of place. If she really were the leader of the camp, why was she so unconcerned about her group? Wouldn't she be tending to the others instead of the onlooker? Instead, she seemed lost and afraid.

Kase went straight to the Unicorn Knight. He put his helmet back on. He couldn't think of any clever ways to get her attention, so he cleared his throat. When The Bull, Ram, and the Unicorn Knight looked his way, he tapped his chest twice, kissed his fingers, and pointed to the ground.

The Unicorn Knight's hand stopped glowing. She dropped her patient's arm, but he must have known what was going on. He reached into his boot and drew a knife. He stabbed the Unicorn Knight in the calf before she could stand.

Kase instinctively punched the patient in the nose, knocking him back and off the pile of straw that he was sitting on. Kase reached for the knife but hesitated before pulling it out of the Unicorn Knight's calf. Marks that looked like a red spiderweb surrounded the wound. It reminded him of when Aura had collapsed during a beach day.

Poison.

"For the New Realm Order!" the onlooker shouted.

"Let's go," Kase said. He tugged on the Unicorn Knight's arm but ended up dragging her off her perch.

"Kase, I ... can't ..." The Unicorn Knight's head drooped. The poison was quick to act.

Kase scooped her up into his arms. He looked around for The Bull and The Ram. Their shields were already up, and they were rushing towards him.

Kase felt two sharp pains, one in his back and the other in his calf. He checked his leg and noticed an arrow sticking out from just above his ankle. He instantly felt woozy and dropped to one knee.

He felt a familiar hand grab his shoulder. She also reached for the trident that tilted left of the Unicorn Knight's head. In an instant, all three of them were teleported to an empty gold mine on Jenim Island.

Lenia, still wearing her camouflage cape from her position as lookout, was focused on removing the trident from Aura's back. It was a good thing Lenia had implemented a contingency plan in case of an ambush.

Kase collapsed. Lenia slipped her trident from the scabbard on the decoy Unicorn Knight's back. Aura was already unconscious.

Lenia quickly disappeared to save the others. Kase tried to warn her of Sharaine before she teleported back, but he didn't have the strength to speak. His helmet hit the ground.

Lenia returned a few moments later with Roman and Helena. Both his grandparents were standing, and so they must have avoided the poisonous weapons. Lenia disappeared again.

Kase tried to keep an eye open. He could feel the poison course through his veins. Although he had the ability to heal himself, the poison was acting fast and stole all his concentration. He tried to push back, so that he could tell Lenia to ignore Sharaine. If Sharaine was a spy, she could expose the entire A.K. in their hideout.

Lenia teleported back, holding Sharaine's hand. Sharaine was shaking, but Lenia ignored her and quickly moved to Kase's side.

"We're safe, Dandy," she said. She removed his helmet and stroked his cheek with the back of her hand. "It's going to be okay. Stay strong."

Yes, they were lucky no one had been captured, but it *wasn't* going to be okay. For the first time in the war, they had brought an enemy to one of their safe havens. They'd made a critical error. They'd been compromised. It wasn't the end of their cause, but it was a major blow to their safe way of life.

Kase hoped he'd die soon so that he could come back and warn the others.

He'd failed. He needed to be better, or else they'd all perish.

CHAPTER 2

Life of a Langara

Instead of feeling the burning pain of lava, Kase heard a ringing in his head. He tried to open his eyes, but the sunshine was too bright. He pulled the covers over his head before realizing where he was. He shot up and checked his room.

He hadn't been back to the Kingdom of Moiras in weeks. He'd been too busy planning the A.K.'s next moves with Cali to worry about the castle sanctuary that he'd once called home. He wondered why Lenia had brought him here.

"Lenia?" He rubbed his eyes.

Kase noticed a card on the night table. The card had his name on it. He opened it up, but all it said was *Back for Dinner* in Lenia's handwriting. Kase climbed out of bed and stumbled to the window. Based on the sun's position, it was already midday.

He wondered why Lenia had brought him to the castle to rest. The others spent most of their time in their haven on Jenim Island now; he wouldn't be able to warn them about Sharaine from here. If she intended to fulfill Mardious Hood's proposal, their whole operation was in danger.

Kase stumbled around the room, hoping to find a sage mirror. He checked on chairs, under clothes, and on the nightstand next to the card. He soon felt disoriented and needed to sit down.

He'd felt this way a few times before, after being caught with poison darts, courtesy of the Brotherhood. He would have preferred to be killed because his power would have brought him back to life instantly. Taking the poison slowed him down, and he needed to regain his energy.

He took a few breaths before giving up his search and choosing another goal. He stood up from the bed, wrote a note to Lenia in case she returned early, and pushed on through the castle.

Kase doubted there would be anything fresh in the kitchen, and so he wandered outside to the garden. There were a lot of weeds, but he was able to pick some leafy greens, dig up some carrots, and pluck a few snap peas. He washed them all in a rain barrel before devouring them.

For dessert he longed for peaches. There was a grove a ways from the castle. He could run through the fields to get there. That would certainly make him feel better, but what of his langara friends? He had not seen any of them for weeks. If he caught a ride with one of them, he could find out what they'd been up to.

"Maxim," he thought. He only sent out the call once. His bond to Maxim was greater than the mere telepathy that he used to communicate with the other langaras.

He walked a little farther and connected with a few animals in the area. Towering elk grazed near the edge of the forest. Rattlesnakes hid in the tall grass, shaking their tails in warning when he came near. Water buffalo rumbled in the distance.

Kase felt Maxim flying above him. She twirled a few times, and then came crashing to the ground. Her giant paws made the ground shake, but her roar was more piercing. Her fluffy white wings stretched wide as she dipped her head down.

Kase had to cover his nose from the stench of the langara's breath. "What did you eat today?"

Maxim grunted, which was the langara equivalent of a laugh. "Seafood," she said. "From the Quarry."

"Would you mind taking me there?" Kase asked. "I'm a bit hungry myself."

Maxim crouched down, but instead of spreading her wings out wide to make it easier for Kase to mount her, she rolled onto her side. Kase scratched her behind the ear and gave her a head massage while she purred. He missed caring for his friend as much as she missed his gentle touch.

When Kase finally mounted Maxim, he grabbed a tuft of white fur on the back of her neck and held on tight. She sprinted across the field, leapt high into the air, and fluttered her wings until she was soaring above the land. The wind blew Kase's hair back, and he closed his eyes to enjoy the breeze.

It didn't take long to get to the Quarry. After gently setting Kase down near the water's edge, Maxim took the opportunity to hunt for a few more fish. Kase wandered to the peach trees neighbouring the water. He picked a few ripe ones before returning to the bank to spend time with his friend.

"We've missed you on our hunts," Maxim said. "The competition just isn't the same without you."

Kase chuckled. When he first started hunting with the pride, he'd never been able to get a kill shot in before the langaras made their move. He'd get an elk in his sights, but just before he could fire an arrow, Maxim or her mother would pounce on the prey. After discovering how powerful Kase was, though, they encouraged him to not rely so much on his primitive weapons. He'd impressed them a few times by first using his animal control magic to force the water buffalo to run in his chosen direction and then using his advanced element control to draw lightning and strike a few water buffalo at once.

"Do you have any new moves?" Kase asked. "I need to know what I'm up against."

Maxim grunted. "I should ask you the same thing." Something under the surface grabbed her attention. Her head followed the movement, then darted into the waters of the quarry. She brought her muzzle back out of the water and spit out a fish that was too small to be a meal.

"So close," Kase teased.

Maxim huffed. She retreated from the water's edge and nestled on the bank beside Kase. She leaned her head into his hand once again. "Tell me you're going to move back here soon," she said.

Kase scratched Maxim behind the ear. "I have a lot more to do still," he said. "It's the only way to keep our enemies away from this place and to keep you and your family safe."

"Do you always put others first?" Maxim asked. "What about you?"

Kase stopped scratching Maxim. He glanced at his arm and the three symbols inscribed in a mermaid design there: a quill, a flame, and a sword. It represented an old mantra from the Academy and reminded Kase of his dedication to uniting his family, friends, and everyone in the realm. "We're all in this together," he said.

"Loyalty keeps the pack alive," Maxim said. "Independence gives it strength."

Kase turned and rested against Maxim's head. "That sounds like some kind of saying."

"It's something my mother taught me," Maxim said. "Our pack may hunt together, live together, and fight together, but what would we do without each other? Can we think on our own? Can we survive? What would we do if we were forced to live alone?"

"I've never thought about that before," Kase admitted. "I don't know what I'd do if I lost everyone and everything."

"It's not just about loss," Maxim said. "What would you do if you succeed? Would you find another fight? Are you worthy of what you have? Can you be who you are instead of hunting for more? A sense of self gives the individual strength, and therefore strengthens the pack."

Kase closed his eyes. "That's a lot to take in," he admitted. "I don't have an answer."

Maxim grunted. "You don't need one right now," she said. "Just like the world outside us can change, we can change inside, too. We just need to take time for self-discovery and self-worth."

Kase was grateful for his friend's gift. She may have been young for a langara, but she carried the wisdom of her pack. What would he do if he bested Sheese's New Realm Order, Mardious' Brotherhood, and Mac's Marauders? On the other hand, what if he made a mistake and was forced to give up his power? Who would he be?

"Thank you for sharing," Kase said. "I have a lot to consider."

"Hey, you," Lenia said.

Kase tensed, surprised to hear her voice. Maxim wasn't startled at all and began to purr as Lenia stroked her behind her ear.

Kase jumped to his feet, the urgency of his warning about Mardious' threat to the A.K. rushing back to him now that he could do something about it. "Where's Sharaine?" he asked.

"She's been helping Cali the past few hours," Lenia said. "Why?"

"All morning?" Kase panicked. How much information could Sharaine have stolen from the leader of their group? "We're in danger!"

Lenia froze. Maxim picked up on the tone in Kase's voice and scanned the terrain.

"How?" Lenia asked.

Kase paced back and forth. "When I brought her back to life, I saw Mardious take Sharaine's sister as a hostage. The only way Mardious will return her is if Sharaine gives me up."

Lenia nodded, but she didn't seem concerned. "She told us," she said. "But we'll come up with a better plan. We learn from the past, adapt to the present, and grow for the future." She grabbed Kase's hand.

Kase hadn't realized he was shaking. Cali usually consulted Kase in their plans, even though he found such politics and scholar strategies hard to follow. Lenia's calmness helped ease Kase's panic, but he needed to learn more.

"Is everything okay?" Maxim asked. She was still scanning the direction Kase was facing. The corners of her lips curled up, revealing the sharp fangs that could tear through limbs like a knife through butter.

"Yes, we're safe here," Kase answered Maxim. "But the outside threats are growing."

"Since our mission was a success, I thought we could spend the night together, but … never mind." Lenia let go of Kase's hand.

Kase stopped shaking. His worry subsided to be replaced by guilt. He couldn't remember the last time they had been alone. But he had to confirm that the A.K. wasn't in danger.

"Can we check on Sharaine?" Kase asked.

Lenia's shoulders slumped. She looked down and rested her hand on Maxim's wet nose. Maxim licked Lenia's palm. "Good-bye, Maxim," she said.

"We'll—" Kase started. Lenia held Kase's arm and then teleported them to the main hall on Jenim Island, which was bustling with people preparing for the midday meal.

Their refuge was in an abandoned gold mine, one that they'd read about in the castle library in the Kingdom of Moiras. The old king, Michael, who held Kase's power centuries ago, had unearthed a fortune of gold in these mines. Since everything was gigantic on Jenim Island, the deposits of gold in the mine were greater than any in the rest of the realm.

However, the giants that occupied the island were not fond of anyone using their resources. The rest of the realm was forbidden from taking anything from the area, since the giants needed the vast amount of oversized food, minerals, and materials to survive. They chose what to trade with the rest of the realm if necessary, but the giants didn't have any need for what the realm could offer. They only wanted peace.

The mines weren't patrolled, but if the giants were alerted to their refuge, it wouldn't take long for them to punish the Animal Kingdom. If Kase's enemies knew of their location, a battle with warriors, scholars, or wizards wouldn't be the first threat—Kase would have to defend his group against an army of giants.

It was the main reason why it was important to vet all new members of the A.K.—and there had been quite a few new members in the past year.

"I'll see if I can find Sharaine for you," Lenia said. She disappeared, leaving Kase in the midst of the lunch crowd.

Kase was happy for the help, but he wanted to go with Lenia. He knew she could teleport around faster without having to worry about him, but the only time they spent together was on missions. He caught himself daydreaming about what could happen if the missions ended.

"You're back!" Ashlyn said. She rushed over to Kase and put an arm around his shoulder. In her other arm, she cradled Kase's baby brother.

"I didn't realize I'd been gone for long," Kase admitted to his mother.

"I'm glad you're safe," Ashlyn said. "Do me a favour? Take Vance so I can grab some lunch? Thanks!"

Before Kase could answer, Ashlyn shoved Vance into Kase's chest. Kase cupped his hand behind his baby brother's head and cradled him. Vance's blanket had flopped open, so Kase tucked it back so he wouldn't get cold. Vance yawned, but remained asleep, which seemed amazing in the crowded lunch hall.

"Have you seen Sharaine?" Kase asked.

"Who's that?" Ashlyn said. She rushed away before Kase could ask another question.

Kase scanned the hall. There were over two hundred refugees in their camp. At first, Kase and the others had brought only family and friends to this safe haven, one where the three kings couldn't hunt them down. But soon they were bringing in refugees of all kinds, and now this group of misfits had become a new order of A.K. members.

Everyone contributed in their own way. Since there was a relatively even mix of warriors, wizards, and scholars, there were lots of new ideas and ways to collaborate that strengthened the group.

Kase's grandparents were loading their plates with food, but his aunt and uncle seemed a little pickier. Lenia's old colleague, Professor Bright, was dishing out soup for a few kids. Aura's parents were topping up a bowl of buns that had gone empty. But where was Aura? She usually enjoyed talking with all the people in the main hall. Had the poison taken her life, or had it just knocked her out for a couple hours like it had with Kase?

The noise and mayhem around him brought his dizziness back. As chaotic as it was, Kase was impressed that his baby brother could sleep through it all.

"Two Garricks!" Curtis yelled from behind them. He slapped Kase on the shoulder before Kase could turn around.

Kase absorbed the hit so his brother wouldn't feel the jolt. Vance yawned in return.

"Oh, sorry." Curtis gently pawed at Kase's shoulder. "How are you feeling?"

"I'm still a little woozy," Kase admitted. "Where's Sharaine?"

Curtis tilted his head to study Kase's eyes. "You must still be a little out of it. Her name is Becca, and she's in line. I'm waiting until she's past the salad before I cut in, grab food next to her, and casually sit with her for lunch again."

Kase stood tall. "So, you finally asked her out?" Curtis had been nervous about chatting with Becca, a new A.K. recruit who had been with them for a couple months. But it seemed like he had made a move while Kase and the others had been searching for Sharaine.

Curtis blushed. "No, we're just flirting. Talen gave me some advice, saying that I should ask questions and then listen to her stories. I forgot how fun it is to get to know someone new. We'd been stuck here for so long, I … oh, she's almost there. I'll come find you in a bit."

Curtis hustled around a few tables, cut through the line, and posted himself beside Becca. He didn't slap her on the shoulder, but she noticed him instantly. They shared a laugh, and then Curtis helped her fill her plate.

Kase was a little jealous of Curtis. He couldn't remember the last time he'd made Lenia laugh like that. He thought about the days at the Academy when he and Lenia were getting to know each other. They'd share stories, joke around, and get close. He found himself smiling from the memories.

He looked around the room for her.

A lot of groups were sitting at the tables. Kase noticed Lenia's father, Eric, standing near the food, chatting with a few of the elders. Her mother, Grace, was on the other side of the hall, handing a plate to Lenia's sister-in-law, Gwen. A black trident head poked out from behind them.

Lenia stood, gently rocking her niece, Abigail. It seemed like she and Kase were both on babysitting duty. In that moment, Lenia seemed entirely unconcerned about anything else around her.

It had been a heartfelt reunion when Lenia arrived to take her family to safety, shortly after the A.K.'s initial attack on the Triple Crown. Although High Scholar Sheese had held the dagger that killed Lenia, Kase was the reason she had been in that position in the first place. As grateful as Lenia's family was that she was alive, after they learned of the doorway of life and his power, it was still difficult to move past the pain of those troubled wounds.

While she was dead, and later in hiding, Lenia had missed out on her brother Leland's wedding, and the birth of his first child. In exchange, they had missed out on Lenia's growth as a wizard and warrior into the infamous Unicorn Knight. The time they spent together now in their refuge helped strengthen their family bond, but it was at the expense of their freedom.

Kase tried to make eye contact with his wizarrior across the room. "Come on," he whispered, hoping for a glance. He felt giddy just trying to wish her to look his way.

He thought about flirting with her again: asking her questions, listening to her stories, or at least spending time with her without the pressures of leading the A.K. He wondered what they would do if they didn't have the responsibility of fighting for their kinship. Maxim's wise words resonated again.

What if the war stopped?

Would Kase and Lenia have more time for each other, or would they become busy with other things? Would Lenia want to return Kase's flirtations? Would Kase need to become stronger as an individual to be a better partner to Lenia? What did that even mean? Would Lenia become stronger on her own, that is, without him?

Kase's creeping worry swung to fear. Sweat dripped down his forehead. He cradled Vance in one hand while he wiped his brow. Were these still effects from the poison that had taken control of his body?

He took a few slow steps forwards. Lenia's healing touch would help him. She wasn't just the healer he trusted most. She was the strongest person he knew.

Before he could take another step, he felt a tug on his shoulder.

"Were you looking for Sharaine?" Cali asked.

Kase turned around to face his sister. She looked to Vance and smiled. She took her littlest brother away from Kase without even asking and cradled him in her arms.

Kase glanced back to Lenia, but his focus returned. He didn't feel nervous, fearful, or worried. He was back in the present and tackling what was directly in front of him.

"Where is she?" Kase asked.

CHAPTER 3

East Bay Funk

Dom's hand swivelled as he showed off his snack. "Do you know what's worse than finding a worm in your apple?" He paused but didn't wait for an answer. "Half a worm!"

Kase tried not to roll his eyes. He checked on Sharaine, who sat across from him. She scrunched her nose, looked to Cali, and shook her head.

"Tough crowd," Dom said as he took a bite.

Kase returned to his mind map. He had followed Cali's instructions, writing down the keywords of their discussion, but was disappointed to see nothing but a mess of words. Even though he could control the weather, creating a brainstorm was much harder for Kase. It was a lot more boring to write down ideas on a page than to move a thundercloud and feel lightning strike.

Thus far, most of his notes involved the source of each king's power. Deals for Sheese. Force for Mac. Fear for Mardious. Cali, Dom, and Sharaine had created intricate designs of their own in their notes, seemingly making the challenge look easy. He felt like he wasn't adding value, and hoped the meeting would end soon.

"Do you have any more?" Cali asked.

Kase's afternoon just got worse.

"Let's see," Dom said. He took another bite of his apple and flipped through his journal. His finger scrolled down the page then stopped abruptly. "What's brown and sticky?"

Kase ignored his father's jokes. He had practice. He regularly attended these scholarly sessions with his sister and father, so that the A.K. could make decisions together as a group. Sometimes they were joined by Aura, or Talen, or Lenia, but today Sharaine was the one with them.

He still wasn't sure he wanted to discuss their goals with Sharaine in the room, seeing as she had experience divulging secrets to the highest bidder. But Cali had pursued an alliance with Sharaine expressly because of that flaw, hoping that she could provide them with proof of Sheese's underhanded deals. In addition to briefly working for the Currency King's "New World Order," she had been the one to pack up Sheese's office in the chaos that followed the A.K.'s unmasking of the Triple Crown.

Unfortunately, all records and other proof had been lost in Mardious' attack on Sharaine's camp. Kase couldn't bring evidence back into existence like he could Sharaine's father and brother, but trading lives for information was a deal that the former High Scholar's aide was willing to accept. Kase didn't like using his power as a bargaining chip; it felt like something a dealmaker like Sheese would do. But he trusted that his sister's plans would help heal the realm, and they had to do everything they could to save all the fallen, not just the ones that would turn to their side.

"I knew those stairs were up to something," Dom grinned.

Sharaine covered her mouth and giggled. Kase didn't realize how well-manicured her fingernails were. She stared at Cali, and they both burst into laughter.

"Good one, Dad," Cali said. She sighed. "We needed that break."

Kase was a little disappointed he'd missed the setup. He looked over to Dom's journal, but it was quickly pulled away. Dom gave him a smirk as he hid his precious jokes.

Sharaine sat straight. "Thank you, Mr. Garrick. That was fun," she said. "Continuing on, Sheese's notes didn't just detail his deals and plans for the Triple Crown, they also included contingencies if things went wrong. Specifically, how Sheese could control Mac and Mardious in the event they turned on him."

"Control them?" Kase had felt manipulated by the High Scholar before, but he didn't think he, or anyone, could be controlled.

"By profiling both Mac and Mardious, he understood the strengths, weaknesses, and motivations behind each," Sharaine said. "Understanding their profile gave Sheese the advantage of manipulating his allies and enemies in the direction he wanted them to go."

"And it also gives us the advantage of knowing what our enemies want," Cali added. "In order to avoid further destruction, pain, and bloodshed, we have to consider giving them what they desire most."

"Well, we don't *have* to, but we should consider it as a possible solution," Dom chipped in. "Some say that war is the great equalizer because the victors need to unite to win and are left to enjoy the spoils. In certain scenarios, winners of war gain land and riches, but they also create new rules and laws that fit their ideologies. Well … until their enemies rise up again and start a new war."

"If we want to unite the entire realm, we must consider creating victories for all," Cali said. "By understanding what each leader wants and, ultimately, what the people they influence want, then we might be able to have unity and prosperity for all instead of rewards only for the winners."

Kase took a deep breath. The Animal Kingdom wanted freedoms that had been taken away from them. They all knew the consequences of having greedy leaders in power, but was there truly a way for their enemies to change rather than be conquered? The concept sounded too good to be true.

"I'll start with Mac," Sharaine said. "His motivation is simple: to eliminate all wizards. Since Mardious was the High Wizard, this has made it easy for the Marauders to hate Mardious and all those affiliated with him. Their goal collectively is domination, and the only way to reach that goal is with death."

Cali and Dom added notes to each of their mind maps, but Kase wondered how this information could possibly help them. Their plan couldn't be to give Mac what he wanted.

"Mac, like many other warriors from that time, blames wizards for running his family out of his hometown," Sharaine said. "The hardships that his town carried because of the wizards that immigrated into their community cannot be undone."

"Mac is not as heartless as Sharaine is making him sound," Dom cut in.

"History has been unkind to Mac but pushing him away into his simplistic ideology will not just hurt him, it will hurt all those around him too. What we need to do is show the realm the prosperity of union, rather than the disparity of segregation. We need to prove how much stronger we can be with unity." He put his hand on Kase's shoulder.

Kase remembered when his father had died. Dom had been pursuing one of the doorway-of-life relics with Mac. Kase knew that Mac had been different back then compared to the disgruntled tyrant he was now.

"If we talk to him, do you really think he'll listen?" Kase asked. It was easier to fight warriors in combat than to sit them down for a scholarly lecture.

"We don't create culture because of who we are, we create it because of what we do," Cali said. "Do you know why the Animal Kingdom follows you, brother? Do you think it's because you have the power of the doorway of life?"

Kase wondered if Cali was asking him a trick question. They had just made a trade with Sharaine because of his power, and it was obvious that no one would follow him if he were still just a warrior that practiced basic magic. "Everyone here has died," Kase said, looking at Sharaine, Cali, and Dom. "The reason you're here is because of that power."

"Yes, you're technically correct," Cali said. "But why does the Animal Kingdom follow you? Not because of your capabilities. We follow you because you show us that we can do it too. You give me strength and hope with your selfless daily actions. You're my younger brother, my hero, and an example for us all."

Cali had never complimented Kase in this way before, and Kase had no clue how to react. He had always looked up to her for guidance, even though they had grown up protecting each other.

Dom put his arm around Kase. "You inspire me too, son."

Kase shrugged off Dom's arm and chuckled. "Don't overdo it," he said. "How does this help us defeat the Mighty King and his Marauders?"

"We show them that we can come together and defeat a common enemy," Sharaine said. "Someone who practices magic that Mac doesn't understand but who doesn't represent all wizards: Mardious Hood."

Out of the three kings, Kase had been dreading fighting the Underground King the most. Mardious had outwitted them all in the past, and the vigilante's history of besting Kase, Cali, Dom, and Roman made him the greatest and fiercest adversary to the Garrick family.

"The Brotherhood has been oppressed for decades," Sharaine continued. "Although they have grown thick skin from living in the slums, they are all in pursuit of a better life: higher status, riches beyond their dreams, and a lavish lifestyle. However, Mardious' true motivation for the doorway of life isn't aligned with that of his following; his motivation is purely self-serving."

"All he wants is Money Jane," Cali said.

Dom looked down at his mind map and fiddled with his quill. Kase remained focused on the plan. "So we bring back Money Jane, and he will stop his terror?"

"Mardious will watch the world burn if that means he is united with the only person he's ever loved," Sharaine said. "I remember that Sheese had circled that note, the note that said that even if he gains ultimate power, or in this case wins the war, what's the point of having it all if he can't celebrate it with the one person that means the most to him?"

Kase felt a pinch in his heart. Maybe he had more in common with Mardious than he was willing to admit. The main reason Kase had pursued the doorway of life was to bring back the woman he loved the most, even if those at the table were also important to him. He felt the need to leave the table and find Lenia.

"If we deliver Money Jane to Mardious, he will no longer have a reason to fight, and it will leave the Brotherhood without a leader," Cali said. "If his following shows weakness and retreats back to the Badlands, we should be able to convince Mac to stand down by creating a scenario that's better than any deal that Sheese can offer."

"It will also give us a starting point for a fresh relationship with the people of the Badlands," Dom said. "It's an opportunity for them to develop and build their cities instead of scrounging for scraps."

"So it all starts with bringing back Money Jane." Kase wrote her name down on his mind map.

"But you need a piece of her." Sharaine flipped through her journal, combing her finger down as she scanned each page.

Kase studied Sharaine as she scribbled something in her margins. She'd witnessed him bring her family members back after Lenia had recovered their remains on a return trip to their camp. Was Sharaine recording a note for future plans? Or reminding herself of a secret she knew about the A.K.?

"I can ask The Bull," Kase said. It was a good reason for him to get out of the meeting and stretch his legs.

Kase and Cali's grandfather had led the Money Jane investigation during his time as a High Guardian, and in the end he had been the one to take Money Jane's life. That, in turn, had led to a battle with Mardious Hood, ending in his and Helena's deaths.

"No need. I know her resting place," Dom said, uncharacteristically quiet. "I can show Kase where."

"Great. Then we can get to work on a new plan." Cali turned a page in her journal and began making some notes on an empty page.

Kase huffed. His excuse hadn't worked, and now he was stuck with more homework. Instead of making a plan, Kase started doodling a sunny sky onto the page.

Sharaine broke the tense silence. "Do you think that's enough heavy discussions for one day? We can sit with our mind maps for now and plan out the more specific details later. I want to check on my family to make sure they're settling into this new environment."

"Well, I thought I saw them laughing at the mountains earlier," Dom said. "They are hill areas, after all."

Kase barely got the joke—it was a stretch, even for Dom. Sharaine scrunched her nose again.

"I can take you outside," Kase said. It was another good excuse to leave. The caves they were hiding in here on Jenim Island were a bit of a maze, and guiding Sharaine as she got accustomed to their hideout would help her eventually navigate on her own.

Cali rubbed her face but then smiled. "No, I'll take Sharaine. You two take a break, and we'll meet back here in a few hours."

Kase nodded at the team, grabbed his papers, and took off without any hesitation. He appreciated Sharaine's help with the plans, and her information was useful for the next stage of the war. He understood her sacrifice now and was glad to have an ally who was willing to look their enemy in the face to get the truth out.

CHAPTER 4

A Scorpion and a Frog

Kase stumbled through the cavern entrance and squinted at the bright blue sky. Their gold mine refuge granted them safety, but he still missed the warm sunshine on his skin. He took a deep breath and jogged towards the warrior training in session.

He had hoped to join Lenia before she started her training session—it felt like he'd spent time with everyone in their camp except for her—but it seemed he was still shaking off the effects of the poison.

Kase jogged down the path to find some warriors practicing with their long-range weapons. Giants had initially constructed the open gold mine in one of the beautiful mountain ranges on Jenim Island, but all that was left here was a desolate crater.

With no giants patrolling the area, the Animal Kingdom was able to get fresh air when they pleased. If a giant animal came too close, there were many small caverns that their crew could sneak back into for safety. Even so, when on the island Dom rarely ventured outside.

Lenia was nowhere to be seen, but Talen sat on a giant stone, fiddling with her crossbow. The weapon was smaller than a regular crossbow and was designed to fit on Talen's forearm. When Kase got closer, he noticed her sliding thin, metal spikes into the leather guard on her opposite wrist.

"Is that how a shark would do it?" Kase asked.

Talen strained her neck. She was wearing her Shark Knight helmet and could only see through the open jaws of the silver mask. Although the helmet was menacing, Talen often noted how inaccurate it was because of its tiger-striped plume; real tiger sharks weren't orange like their big cat counterparts. Kase thought the discrepancy amused her.

"Do you think this is the best place to hold my inventory?" Talen asked, holding up her leather guard.

Even though she was a scholar, Talen was committed to her training. Kase felt a little guilty. Talen had helped him so much; the least he could do was spend more time helping her train to develop her warrior skills. He was happy that she hadn't hesitated to ask him for advice.

"A shark might wear it on a fin, but I'm not sure if that's the most convenient spot for a Shark Knight." Kase said. "Can I see it in action?"

Talen tapped her heart, kissed her fingers, and flipped her wrist to the sky. She led Kase to the nearest target. The group needed to haul all their training gear in and out of the caves every day, and so the targets they had were small and lightweight. The one Talen had chosen was a normal Guardian helmet dangling on a stick.

"Since I cannot shoot very far, Lenia advised me to focus my shot on the most vulnerable areas of a Guardian's armor," Talen said. "I do not have the full setup here, but the open spaces in this helmet provide a worthy target. Only twenty-three percent of the head is exposed."

Talen loaded a needle into her crossbow. This took a moment because she had to switch hands to remove the needle and then load it. Eventually she levelled her arm at the target. A metal handle stuck straight up from her wrist. She moved her palm up to the metal handle and tucked her fingers around its edge. She took a deep breath and focused. This was a different technique, one that Kase had not witnessed from her before.

He could tell Lenia's tips were getting through.

Talen pressed the handle forwards. As her fingers moved in line with her forearm, the needle pushed the strings of the tiny crossbow back. Talen kept pressing until her fingers were down and her palm faced her. When her hand was perpendicular to her arm, the needle darted towards the helmet.

It bounced off the crown.

"Nice shot!" Kase said, impressed at how fast and straight the needle had flown.

"Did I not miss?" Talen asked.

"But your form was perfect," Kase said. "As long as you have a solid base and keep practicing good habits, you'll get the results you want. And if you keep training consistently, your skills will become second nature in battle."

"I am aware," Talen said. "With all the modifications I have been making, it feels like I discover new things with each step. It is like climbing a mountain and reaching the top, just to realize there is another mountain to climb. Aura is studying that poison that felled you both. That has made me wonder if I can add poison to this new system. I just have to find a way to store it correctly."

Kase glanced at the open mine pit as he pondered Talen's mountain metaphor. Each level of the mine was stacked on top of another. If he or Talen were to climb from the bottom of the pit when they reached the first level, they woud be at the bottom of the next.

As Kase counted the levels, he spotted a group running along one of the ridges to his left. He knew it was Lenia leading the others on a run since her trident bounced above her head with every stride.

"I can't wait to see you reach the next mountain, Tal," Kase said as he moved away from the target and towards his own goal. "Would you consider storing the needles on the same arm as your weapon? You won't have to switch hands that way."

"Thanks for the tip," Talen said. She tapped her heart twice, grazed the bottom of her shark helmet, and then pointed two fingers to the sky. "I'll keep climbing."

Kase returned the gesture, and then started running after the group.

He was used to training every day, and so even though he was still recovering his muscles felt loose, yet powerful. He decided to increase his pace. He was at least a mile from Lenia's group, but that didn't mean he couldn't try to catch up to them as quickly as possible.

Kase tried to focus on his breathing, but he couldn't help but think about his recent discussions with Maxim and the A.K. scholars. What mountaintop was he climbing towards? What would the world look like from that peak? What would be next after he reached his goal? Did the others have similar goals? What would Lenia do once the war was over?

The group had stopped, but they were still at least half a mile ahead of Kase. He spotted Lenia teleporting a few of them away at a time. Since their run was clearly over, Kase turned around and jogged back to the training area. He had the energy to continue, and he was ready to participate in whatever was next.

When Kase returned, he found Talen loading a needle into a guard on her bicep; he was more interested, however, in the warriors practicing their combat skills. About twenty warriors were paired together, swinging wooden swords and sparring with each other.

Lenia backpedalled alone into the middle of the area with her hands held high. "Okay, now that we're warm, let's try something new," she said.

Kase grabbed a practice sword from the rack and snuck to the edge of the crowd. Even though he wanted to spend time alone with Lenia, her group lessons were always interesting. He appreciated the leadership role she took with the warriors and enjoyed all her latest drills and strategies.

"There will be times in battle when we'll need to improvise as a unit," Lenia said. "Not everything can be executed by following strict orders, but if we can communicate effectively within small teams, we can create advantages in special circumstances."

Lenia puffed out her chest, but kept her sword pointed to the ground. "We!" she yelled.

"We!" Kase and the crowd yelled back.

"We are!" Lenia yelled.

"We are!" the crowd yelled back.

"We. Are. The!" she yelled, stressing each word.

"We. Are. The!" the crowd said in the same cadence.

Lenia and the crowd started with a low grumble, but they grew louder and louder as they bobbed back and forth and yelled together: "We are the A.K.!"

They all kept yelling until Lenia lifted her sword. "I need a couple volunteers to team up with me on this exercise."

Kase shot up his hand before anyone else had a chance. His heart pumped wildly. "I'll volunteer!"

The group murmured at first, but a few more hands shot up. Lenia's brother, who was a healer-turned-warrior, waved his sword eagerly. Kase wondered what he was getting himself into, but he knew by Lenia's grin that it would be worth it.

"Thank you, Dandy," Lenia said. "Curtis, Paul, step forwards."

Leland huffed as Kase made his way to the front with Curtis and Paul. Kase turned to the crowd, awaiting further instruction from the professor.

"I'll need my helmet if I'm fighting as the Dandy Lion," Kase said.

Lenia disappeared, returning a few seconds later at Kase's side. He graciously accepted his helmet from her and put it on. The red tint helped to fight the glare from the sun.

"For this exercise, we will be fighting three on one," Lenia said as she walked closer to the crowd. "To make things even, Kase will be the one fighting alone."

Kase sized up his competition. With Curtis' training as a warrior, Lenia's ability to teleport, and Paul's natural strength from working as a brick layer, Kase felt like he was at a disadvantage.

"How is this even?" Kase muttered.

Lenia shot him a sideways grin. "As a team of warriors and non-warriors, we'll need to trust each other's intuition and skills," she said. "In battle, we might naturally defer to a trained warrior like Curtis as a leader, but that puts a lot of pressure on him to make all the decisions. We need to trust each other to succeed, not wait for someone to give orders."

"What's wrong with a warrior taking the lead?" Roman said. As a former High Warrior, Roman was used to giving orders.

Lenia didn't miss a beat, even when teaching a legend. "This session is not about right or wrong. It's about adapting in battle. It's about trying something different so that we're prepared when we face a cunning adversary, one that has gotten the best of us before."

Lenia was referring to Mardious Hood, he who had killed Roman, Helena, and Lenia before. She didn't even need to speak his name. Roman seemed satisfied with her response.

"If we can beat Two Lives, we can beat anyone," Curtis said. "But do you think we really stand a chance? Even if we work together?"

Kase smiled proudly at Curtis' credit. He caught Lenia's eye and received another grin.

"Every enemy has strengths and weaknesses," Lenia said. "Haven't you seen the Dandy Lion lose a battle?"

Kase's smile disappeared at the reminder of his loss to Lenia for the A.K. leadership. He would never forget her celebrating her 'kiss of death' as the grass underneath him became coated with his blood. "That won't happen again," Kase said.

He received a wider grin from Lenia. "Let's huddle up," she said, tickling the air. "We don't want to give our strategy away. Are you sure you're ready for battle, Dandy?"

Kase backed away. He wanted to keep his legs warm as he built his strategy, and so he paced back and forth as he stared at his enemies.

Lenia was the clear threat: not just because she was the most skilled of the three, or because she was also a wizard, but because of her teleportation abilities. Kase could match her in battle technique and magical power, but he couldn't teleport. He'd need to move quickly; that way Lenia couldn't surprise him with an attack.

Curtis was the next threat, given that he'd graduated from the warrior program at the Academy. He was thicker than most, owning the name Kodiak Mountain, but he was strong and smart. He had improved his defenses and wouldn't be tricked easily. Kase would be able to overpower him with magic, but it would need to be timed perfectly to get Curtis to yield.

Curtis' brother, Paul, was the weakest in skill, but had the most strength. As a bricklayer, and now the Animal Kingdom's lumberjack, he was big, strong, and tough. He hadn't chosen an Animal Kingdom name yet, but he fit in well with the team. Kase would need to avoid his heavy swing—even a single strike with a wooden sword would be painful.

Lenia, Curtis, and Paul broke the huddle. Curtis and Paul swept wide as Lenis kept pace down the middle of their formation. They each gripped their wooden swords with two hands, but Lenia had an additional weapon strapped to her back.

"Let's go, Grandson!" Roman shouted. The rest of the crowd cheered. Did they know the nature of the assignment? Kase wondered. They were supposed to be learning from Lenia's team about how to handle a cunning adversary.

It was time for Kase to ruin the lesson.

To gain an early advantage, Kase needed to rely on his wizard abilities. He could control the weather, but a heavy wind might not do much, and lightning on a sunny day could attract the wrong visitor. He couldn't feel any animals around, but he could create one with an illusion.

Kase reminded himself of a time when he had faced Mardious Hood and had been overtaken by an army of illusions.

With Lenia creeping along with Curtis and Paul, Kase was running out of time to work his magic. He focused on his Dandy Lion golden helmet and red mane. He normally had a leather vest with a claw mark across his chest, red ribbons tied around his biceps, and golden pants. He decided to keep his wooden sword as his weapon.

Kase took a deep breath, and then set his plan in motion. He covered himself in his illusionary outfit, but at the same time created thirty other identical Dandy Lions. He shuffled around so they couldn't pinpoint the spot where he'd been before working his illusion.

The crowd awed. All three of Kase's opponents stopped. Curtis and Paul looked to each other, but Lenia stayed focused. "What do you see? How do you feel?" Lenia asked them.

Kase and his illusionary army crept forwards. He had a few of his illusory selves switch positions so he could get lost in the crowd. Between Curtis and his confused brother, the Kodiak Mountain was the bigger threat, and so Kase aimed towards him.

"Where did they come from?" Paul asked.

"It's an illusion," Lenia said. "Focus on the small details, though. Even the best wizards can miss something."

Kase hadn't missed anything, and he wasn't going to let Lenia talk him into doubting himself. His illusions would disappear once touched, and so he needed to act quickly. A teleporting warrior could make quick work of his army.

All the Dandy Lions sprinted forwards, splitting evenly to attack Curtis, Lenia, and Paul. All three warriors got into a ready stance, but Lenia soon disappeared. It was too late though, Kase was already headed towards a swinging Curtis.

Illusions started to disappear as Curtis and Paul both swung wildly at everything around them. Kase ducked a Curtis attack, and then contacted Curtis' arm with a swift swing of his wooden sword. He followed up with a strike to Curtis' leg. The Kodiak Mountain screamed, dropped his sword, and fell to the ground, playing the part of a sparring party perfectly since Kase's strikes were not deadly.

Kase picked up Curtis' sword and released his power over the illusions. Lenia was fifteen yards away to Kase's right, but Paul was only five ahead. Kase rushed towards Paul with a sword in each hand.

Instead of defending himself, Paul lowered his guard and pointed to the sky. "Bird!"

Kase dropped his arms and searched the sky frantically. If a Jenim Island bird swooped down and grabbed any of the Animal Kingdom members, they might never be seen again. Kase's power to bring the fallen back to life could only happen if he had a piece of their body; he couldn't bring them back if they were lost.

The red tint of his helmet made it easier to search the sky by blocking the sun's glare, but he saw nothing. He felt around the environment using his power to see if he could connect to the bird. He didn't feel anything—except for the blunt end of a wooden sword hitting his arm.

Kase looked to Paul. He was pointing his wooden sword at Kase's neck and grinning. "Do you yield?" he asked.

"What?" Kase said angrily. Was it a trick? Did Paul think it was clever to put everyone else's lives in danger? What would happen the next time someone gave a warning, but it was ignored because of a stupid sparring trick?

Another sword hit Kase in the back of the knee. He buckled to the ground.

"Do you yield?" Lenia asked. She also stood over Kase, pointing a sword at his neck.

Kase was disgusted. Was this their plan all along? Did the Unicorn Knight win through treachery again? His healing power was already at work, leaving his limbs tingling and feeling strong again. He was too upset, however, to keep the fight going.

"I yield," Kase said.

Lenia smiled. "Great idea, Paul." Lenia slapped Paul's rear with the flat edge of her wooden sword and strolled back to the crowd. "That's how you use the environment to your advantage. That's how you succeed with an unconventional strategy. That's how you change the game!"

"Great job, Brother!" Curtis said. He shuffled over and slapped Paul on the shoulder, then reached down for his sword, now beside Kase. He offered a helping hand to Kase, but Kase ignored it.

Kase sat up and hugged his knees as he focused on his breathing. He wondered if there were any birds around that he could control, to show the group how dangerous the threat still was. It was just practice, but they needed to treat their environment with the utmost respect—otherwise, there wouldn't be a war to fight.

Lenia had made it back to Roman and Helena, who both pointed at the sky and laughed. Some of the other warriors in training were already forming groups and splitting off to spar together. Everyone seemed to have extra energy as they ran around and started planning. Even Talen was vigorously scribbling in her notebook.

Kase took another deep breath, removed his helmet, and then lay on his back. He stared at the bright blue sky and let the slight breeze cool his temper. He closed his eyes and felt peace rush over him as he took a moment to forget about where he was.

He felt a soft hand gently grab his palm.

He shifted towards the touch and opened his eyes. Lenia was lying beside him, staring back. Her bright green eyes had a devilish joy that was both proud and sympathetic. Kase wanted to look away, but he was hypnotized.

"That was a dangerous move," Kase said.

Lenia smiled. "That was the point," she said. "Everyone wants to take the safe path; the one they know. I've challenged everyone to take the road less travelled, so they're ready for the unknown."

Kase took another deep breath. He was suddenly burdened by the thoughts he'd been wrestling with since waking up from the poison.

"Do you ever think about what will happen after the war?" Kase asked. "What you'd do if there were no more battles to fight?"

Lenia's expression softened. "Are you assuming we win?" she asked.

Kase shrugged. "Yes, I believe we'll win."

Lenia sighed. "That's a dangerous move," she said. "It feels like you're underestimating our enemies."

"We've always faced unforgiving foes," Kase said. "But lately I don't want to lose hope for a better life; one that doesn't involve training every day or hiding in a cave."

"Well, thinking about tomorrow is a luxury that we haven't had in a long time," Lenia agreed. "But if we think too much about the future, we'll lose sight of what's in front of us; what's happening today. And I've really enjoyed today . . . so far." She squeezed Kase's hand tightly and giggled.

Kase smiled. "Me too, but how many times can I fail when there's so much on the line? Seems like when I fight a dangerous adversary like the Unicorn Knight, she always gets the best of me."

Lenia giggled more. "That's not your fault," she said. "I'm sure you'll win one of these days."

Kase laughed and squeezed back. "The best part is spending time with you," he said. He was glad that they had a moment together, even if it was short-lived, and even though he wanted more. "What I'd really like is to take you out on a date once the war is over."

"Well, we don't have to wait until tomorrow to do that," Lenia said.

She rolled over and put her arm on Kase's chest. "What did you have in mind?"

Kase wanted to hold Lenia and teleport to anywhere except their battlefield. "We have a mission briefing tonight with Cali, Sharaine, and Dom. I think they'll have a plan for our next move."

Lenia's smile disappeared. "Right." She rolled back and stared at the sky.

"It seems like we always have something in our schedules." Kase heard the disappointment in his own voice.

"It was still nice to hear." Lenia turned back to Kase. "Promise me you'll ask me again tomorrow . . . if we make it until then."

Kase propped himself onto one elbow. "I'll ask you every day," he said. "If we make it until then." Kase leant down to kiss Lenia, but her hand on his chest stopped his momentum.

Lenia's smile returned. "Save it for our date."

Just then they heard Roman cheering in celebration, but he wasn't the only one yelling. Multiple groups were sparring, screaming, and having fun with Lenia's exercise. It was a great training day for all.

"I guess we should get back to it," Kase said.

"Not yet," Lenia said. She pulled Kase back down beside her. They lay together for a few more precious moments.

Kase suddenly felt like he'd won.

CHAPTER 5

Return of a Princess

The armour of the Marauders felt tight compared to Kase's Dandy Lion outfit. The metal girdle hugged his hips, the chest plate dipped outward from his belly, and even the open-faced helmet pinched the skin around his temples. Kase wondered if he'd gained any weight since the last time he'd had to sneak around.

"Are you sure we can't get closer?" Dom asked, peeking over the parapet of the inn's roof. They were four stories above street level.

Kase tried not to roll his eyes. They'd gone over the plan countless times over the past two days.

"I can only teleport places I've already been, and we have to stay within the vicinity of my trident," Lenia whispered calmly. "Without scouting what's in front of us, it's too risky to try another location."

"Right," Dom whispered. "Head down, no surveillance mirrors."

Kase was impressed with Lenia's patience, and how she had helped Dom's confidence return. He reminded himself of one of the tips he'd received about leadership: try to liven the mood to ease nerves during a serious mission.

Kase tapped Dom's chest plate with his index finger. "You forgot to wear your badge," he whispered.

"Badge?" Dom leant back from the parapet and looked down.

Kase brought his finger up, hitting Dom in the nose. "Remember to act normal," he advised. "If you're nervous, you'll likely draw attention to yourself. Marauders walk proud."

Dom chuckled. "Right. Act cocky, like the Rooster that I am."

Kase smiled in support. He liked when Dom wore his rooster helmet, but this wasn't the time for it. Being in the heart of Kimroad, they would be captured or killed if they wore anything but the dress of the Marauders.

Lenia tucked her trident away at the base of the parapet. She stared over the edge to survey the alley below.

"That reminds me, why did the rooster race across the road?" Dom asked.

"Oh, no," Kase muttered. He covered the opening of his Marauder helmet with his gauntlet so he wouldn't have to witness Dom's reaction.

"Why?" Lenia giggled.

"Because he had lots to cock-a-doodle-do!" Dom barely finished the punchline before laughing at his own bad joke.

Kase peeked through his fingers to catch Lenia staring at him and laughing. Seeing her smile was worth the terrible humour.

"Are we ready?" Kase asked.

Lenia tapped her heart twice, touched her lips, and pointed to the sky. Dom settled his laughter and nodded.

Lenia teleported Kase and Dom to the dark alley, leaving her trident behind. Her range of teleportation was about one hundred yards from her trident, but their current venture would lead them beyond the estimated boundary. It was risky to travel without the safety of teleportation, but they had other tools at their disposal.

Under King Mac's rule, Kimroad now banned all wizards from the capital city. Only warriors and approved scholars were allowed beyond the surrounding walls and gates. Although it was difficult to distinguish a wizard from anyone else, those found practicing magic could be arrested or killed on sight.

But Kase and Lenia were also notorious throughout the realm.

Their disguises as Marauders would only get them so far, which is why they took a page out of Mardious Hood's book of tricks. Both Kase and Lenia had tied potion bags to their belts, next to their Marauder swords and daggers, with enough powder to help them distract, attack, or escape.

Kase heard music emanating from the main level of the inn as Lenia and Dom led the way onto the main street. He thought about asking Lenia to dance, but their mission was more important than a date. If everything went to plan, he'd take her for a night on the town soon.

Kase slowed his pace so that he followed from about half a block away. He knew from experience that it was best to have a little space between groups in case someone got into trouble.

The main roads were well lit compared to the alleys and side streets. It was improbable that they would get ambushed on a side street, but they couldn't take that chance. The best course was to hide in plain sight and to act as the locals did. Since there was a ten o'clock curfew in Kimroad, it would be an added risk to sneak around in the middle of the night.

Two Marauders on horseback trotted down the street, but slowed as they approached Dom and Lenia. Dom swayed a bit and put his arm around Lenia. Kase cupped the sacs dangling from his beltline.

The patrolling Marauders stopped. One leant over to talk to Dom and Lenia, while the other surveyed the street. Kase couldn't stop, since he was in their line of sight. He kept approaching the group at his normal pace.

Dom flailed his arms, as if he were drunk. Kase hadn't like that plan when Dom had pitched it, and he didn't like it now. The Marauder that was talking with Lenia sat up tall and tapped his partner.

Kase opened the first pouch attached to his belt. He looked around as he focused on his element control of the powder. He didn't see any surveillance mirrors under overhangs, mounted to walls, or flashing through any windows. As the mounted Marauders came within earshot of their conversation he concentrated on the powder and used his power to send it floating towards them.

"What district do you command?" the Marauder asked.

Kase felt both Marauders inhale the powder. It was a potent sleeping potion, but it took a few seconds to take effect. He gripped the handle of his sword in case one of the Marauders moved to the sage mirrors strapped above their gauntlets.

"Six," Dom hiccupped.

"This is district six," the first Marauder said.

"Teen," Lenia quickly added. "District sixteen."

The second Marauder noticed Kase closing in and flicked his reins, moving his horse closer to Kase and getting a better angle on Lenia and Dom.

Kase stopped. Lenia looked back at Kase. He closed his palms together, moved them beside his cheek, and mimicked resting his head on a pillow.

"Stay back," the second Marauder commanded. He swayed a little in his seat.

Kase connected with both the Marauder horses. They were strong and well trained, but Kase kept their emotions steady just in case. He wanted to make sure that any sudden movements by the sleepy Marauders wouldn't cause the horses to whinny or panic.

The first Marauder moved his forearm to his chin. "Mirror . . . mirror."

Lenia grabbed the Marauder's calf. Both men flopped forwards, resting their helmets on their horses' necks. Kase rushed to steady the second Marauder. "Jump on," he said.

Lenia pulled herself up behind the first Marauder, steadying herself behind the saddle.

"Wait," Dom said. "Let's pull them off. It will look unorthodox to ride three."

"Where do we put them?" Kase asked.

"There was a small park on the side street we just passed," Lenia said. "Let's dump them in the brush there?"

"Dom, stay here," Kase said. He mounted the second Marauder's horse and sat behind the saddle as Lenia did. He didn't grab the reins; instead he used his animal control power to guide the horses away.

Kase and Lenia rode to the park and dumped the sleeping Marauders. They tucked them away but didn't bother covering them; the sun had nearly set, and it would be difficult to notice them in the dark.

After jumping back on their horses, Kase and Lenia returned to pick up Dom. Although they passed a few more Marauders, they weren't stopped on their way to the graveyard they sought. Kase noted that they should have planned for patrol horses.

"Northeast corner," Dom said as they trotted through the small graveyard's open gate. He pointed past Kase's right shoulder.

Kase stuck to the path through the graveyard, instead of trampling over the grass and short tombstones. The trees had dark leaves that covered the twilight, but the leaves also blocked anyone from seeing them from the entrance.

When they reached the northeast corner, they found, instead of a typical headstone, stone stakes in the ground with only numbers marking the graves. Kase didn't need to try to read the numbers as Dom knew exactly where to stop.

"Two, three, two, three," Dom said after dismounting. He rushed towards the stone marker and brushed the moss away. There were no flowers around any of the markers, and the grass around this section of the graveyard wasn't as well kept as the other sections.

Lenia raised her arms. "Twenty-threes!"

Kase smiled, but he had no time to appreciate the inside joke. He dismounted and stood in front of the stone marker. Lenia also dismounted and grabbed the reins of both horses. She steadied them so Kase could focus all his power away from the horses onto a different animal connection.

With Dom as a lookout for Marauders, Kase closed his eyes and focused his power on the rodents and critters that called the graveyard home. When bringing others, such as his grandparents back to life, Kase had connected with rats, ground squirrels, stray cats, and other animals to help dig up the bones of the buried. This technique was much more efficient than digging up a coffin and reburying to hide evidence of grave robbery.

Although he only needed a piece of a corpse to bring someone back to life, it was more comfortable for the risen if he recovered the entire body or skeleton. Taking only a finger would lead to bringing them back to life naked, which was always awkward for everyone involved. In this case, digging up the skeleton would allow them to dress it before she was brought back to life.

"Are we still good?" Kase asked.

"All clear," Lenia and Dom replied.

He had twenty critters burrowing to the casket. A few rats chewed away the side of the coffin while others dug a shield-sized tunnel to the surface. Some ground squirrels had gathered all the bones and rags and now began to move them to the surface. Kase even connected with a few owls for fun.

Just the sound of their hoots was enough to get Dom and Lenia to shiver, since they shared a crippling fear of birds.

Bit by bit, the critters gently transferred the skeleton to the grass beside the stone marker. To cover his tracks, Kase directed the small animals to shift the dirt back into the hole they had made. Kase then knelt and touched the dirt pile, prompting grass to regrow in the unsettled spot. When he opened his eyes, Dom's mouth was agape.

"That was amazing, son," Dom said. "I'm always impressed by what you can do, and how easy you make it look."

"You're supposed to be our lookout." Kase scanned the graveyard.

Lenia had taken her gauntlet off to scratch her cheek. Her coral ring glowed green, signalling that they were quite far from her trident.

Dom shook his head, panicked, and looked around the area. Kase thought this was the closest Dom had ever resembled a rooster. "All clear," he crowed.

A horn sounded in the distance. All three A.K. members froze.

"Do you think that's for us?" Kase asked.

"Hard to say," Lenia said. "The Marauders we hid didn't seem to recognize us, and they shouldn't be awake yet."

"Maybe we'll get lucky and some of the Brotherhood will get caught sneaking around," Dom said.

"We can't rely on luck." Lenia mounted her horse and stared at Kase. "Hurry."

Kase connected to the horses again. He knelt over the remains, pulled a sac from his pocket, and carefully collected the bones. He tied the sac tight, being careful not to break anything while he mounted his own horse. After Dom climbed behind him, they were off.

Dom pointed the way, but Kase didn't need direction; he remembered. He took the most direct line back to the inn; they didn't need to sneak around anymore. Responding to a sounded alert was an advantageous cover since no one would stop them from rushing to an apparent emergency.

When they passed the side street where the sleeping Marauders were stashed, Kase was relieved to find no one else on that block. They didn't stop to see if the dreamers were still there; it didn't matter. They were in the clear and, at the speed they were riding, they would soon be in range of Lenia's trident.

A crowd had formed a few blocks down the road from their destination. Some Marauders were on horseback, but most of the mob were shouting, cheering, and waving flaming sticks in the air.

Kase rounded the corner of the inn. He could still hear music playing on the main floor. He stopped both horses and turned to Lenia, waiting for her to grab him and Dom and teleport them to the roof.

Lenia hesitated.

"What is it?" Kase asked.

"Whatever is happening back there seems important," Lenia said. "Should we check it out?"

Kase was also curious about the mob, but he didn't want to push their luck. He reminded himself of a time when Lenia had gone too far and ended up trapped by a High Guardian *and* a High Wizard. They couldn't afford to be baited into another trap.

"What we have is more important," Kase said.

"Maybe we can see better from the roof?" Dom asked.

"Agreed," Lenia said. She teleported Dom and Kase to the roof. Since they had all been sitting, they all landed on their backsides.

"Sorry," Lenia said. She rolled onto her hands and knees and crawled to the parapet. She peeked over the edge on the side where the mob had gathered.

Dom followed Lenia's lead, but Kase went the other way and grabbed Lenia's trident for her. With the sac of bones in one hand and the trident in the other, Kase returned to the group.

"They definitely caught someone," Dom said.

"What are they building?" Lenia asked.

Kase peered over the edge. Roughly fifty Marauders had formed a circle in the street. Three people lay face down in the middle, with swords pointed at their necks.

While the mob cheered, a few Marauders in shiny armour collected tree branches, wood planks, and old furniture. The items were being positioned in three separate but equal piles.

"Are they going to burn them at the stake?" Kase asked.

"Barbaric," Dom said.

Lenia stood tall. "We should rescue them." She gripped her trident and drew her sword.

"Wait." Kase put a reassuring hand on Lenia's arm. He liked her passion, but teleporting into the middle of the crowd and fighting fifty Marauders would be risky. "We can help from here while avoiding any traps."

"How?" Lenia glared at Kase, as if she were upset that he'd challenged her. It seemed like she'd already forgotten her own lecture.

"By using our environment to our advantage." Kase fumbled past his dagger and unhooked all the sacs from his belt. He pretended to juggle them.

Dom slipped under the edge of the parapet and cowered. "There aren't any giant birds around, are there?"

Lenia laughed. "We'll need more than that. I'll be right back." She disappeared.

"How do you know about that?" Kase asked. Dom hadn't been at the training session, and usually spent most of his time inside planning with Cali.

"Word spreads," Dom said. "Lenia is a legend."

"Can't argue there," Kase said. He focused on the faint music from the inn as he positioned his sacs on top of the parapet, trying to come up with ideas on what to plan for a date with a legend.

Kase untied the knots on each sac and poured the powder into one big pile.

Lenia returned with one large sac of their sleeping potion, putting it next to Kase's pile. He wondered why he'd even bothered with his small pouches; the size difference was comical.

Instead of making a lewd comment, Kase grabbed Lenia by the waist. Their helmets almost banged together awkwardly, but he tried to remain smooth. "I haven't asked you yet today," Kase said. "Are you free for a date later?"

"I like where your head's at." Lenia pecked Kase on the cheek. "Now, work your magic before I start massacring those prejudiced Marauders."

Kase pivoted back to the crowd, slowed his breathing, and took control of the wind. The powder swirled out of the large sac and Kase's small pile, heading for the crowd.

Although he didn't know who had been captured, it was safe to assume that they were wizards. The Marauders of Kimroad were flooded with propaganda about the evil nature of wizards. If it were up to King Mac, wizards would be exterminated from the entire world, not just from the confines of their city.

Even so, Kase was cautious that this could be a trap. Although the Marauders weren't as cunning as Mardious Hood, it was highly possible that they could stage a capture to lure other wizards into the fight. Just as the stragglers had pretended to be allies in Sharaine's camp, these "victims" could be ready for an ambush.

The breeze of powder hit the outside of the crowd, filling the nostrils of the angry mob. Kase made sure to distribute the potion evenly to all Marauders just as the ones in the centre were finishing their wooden piles. Kase took a deep breath, and then crouched back behind the parapet with Lenia and Dom.

"That was a lot of Sleepy Time," Kase said.

"It was worth it," Lenia said. "Plus, it gives us an opportunity to make more. Maybe we can look for ingredients together?"

"I'm ready for another mission." Kase reached out and held Lenia's hand.

The Marauders began to fall like waves crashing against the beach. First the outer edge of the mob fell, followed quickly by the inner circle, and finally by those holding swords to the necks of the captured.

It took a few moments for the apparent criminals to understand what had happened, but they tapped each other and then bolted to their feet. They looked around like mice caught in a trap and then took off running.

Lenia breathed a sigh of relief. "That's two wins already today," she said. "Only one more left."

"Your lesson paid off," Kase said. "Even though we deviated from the mission, your quick thinking and planning saved lives."

Lenia smiled and her eyes sparkled. "It was a small wrinkle, but it worked out because we came together," she said.

"We still need to accomplish our main goal." Dom picked up the sac containing the skeleton. "It reminds me of another joke."

Kase didn't have time to respond. Lenia giggled, grabbed hold of Kase and Dom, and teleported them away.

CHAPTER 6

Easy Money

"**B**ecause he was undercover!" Dom said.

What Kase could see of Lenia's expression in the soft, pink twilight was pure confusion, which made him laugh. Dom's joke made no sense at all, but Kase was able to return the laughter that Lenia always sent his way.

"Wait," Dom said. "I screwed that up. Let me try again."

"Maybe later," Kase said. "Let's finish our mission, go home, and get ready for our date."

"I'm thinking a candle-lit dinner," Lenia said. She bumped into Kase.

"Maybe a nice, relaxing thunderstorm," Kase said. "I'll bring some fresh fruit to make a few drinks, with extra—"

"Slurp-a-lurp?" Lenia asked excitedly.

Dom grabbed Kase's arm. "This is the spot."

Kase had been enjoying their moment, but Dom looked serious as he knelt in the sand and pulled some clothes from his sac. He laid out the black pants and robe, and then tucked a handkerchief into the hood.

Kase removed his helmet, chest plate, and gauntlets before kneeling beside Dom. Dressing as Marauders might send the wrong message.

Like putting together pieces of a puzzle, Kase began assembling the skeleton of Money Jane within the clothing. Lenia helped. She knew anatomy better than Kase, but he didn't really know how accurate they needed to be. He'd never brought anyone back to life that ended up with misplaced bones, misaligned features, or incomplete body parts. He didn't understand exactly how the magic of the doorway had worked, but it always seemed to bring souls back from the dead into their perfect form, whether they were person or beast.

Given that Money Jane was a notorious criminal from years ago, Dom and Cali had thought that bringing her back in the same spot where she had died there on the shoreline of the Pink Lakes would help her cope with all she had lost. And it was important their group connected with her before they reintroduced her to Mardious Hood. They wanted peaceful talks with their enemies; they did not want to merely grant them their deepest wish: having Money Jane back alive.

Kase wondered if Money Jane would also have a list of demands that they'd need to accommodate, but he focused on the task at hand. Like the mission before, they could pivot if they needed to. Considering how wild Money Jane had been in the past, they needed to be ready for anything.

He looked over his shoulder to get approval from his team. Dom, still dressed in his Marauders gear, stared blankly at the skeleton. Like Kase, Lenia had removed her helmet and chest plate. Her braid dangled around her neck, and she struck a strong figure as she held her trident in one hand. She glanced around and gave him a nod.

Kase checked his beltline. His dagger and sword were tucked away in their scabbards. He took a deep breath, placed his bare hands on the clothed skeleton, and connected to the most notorious criminal in history.

Amelia slowed. She was exhausted. Sand flew from her footsteps. She heard a thud and couldn't help but look back. Mardious had dropped his sac. His face was planted in the sand, but he didn't appear injured.

The lone, bull-horned Guardian was on the top of the short hill. Amelia had expected to see the bearded, persistent warrior 'princess' that had caught them at the bank, but this warrior was young. The bull-horned helmet barely fit on his apple-sized head, unlike her tiara. He held his bow firmly, but his arrow had already released.

Before she had time to react, she felt the cool tip of the arrow pierce her neck. Her body went cold. She reached for her throat and collapsed.

"No!" Mardious yelled. "Amelia!"

Amelia started choking, but she felt no pain. Everything seemed to slow down and speed up at the same time. She felt like she was dancing, but she didn't hear any music. She stared up at the inviting twilight. It started to get blurry. She reached out for Mardious.

Mardious put his hand behind her head and held her in his lap. Amelia's arm fell to her side. Her own blood warmed her neck and pooled down her chest. Mardious applied pressure to her wound.

It wouldn't matter.

Amelia felt a sense of peace rush over her as she stared up at Mardious. A white hue seemed to surround his silhouette. She heard him play her favourite song. It was beautifully painful. Where did he get a piano from? His fingertips danced on her body in tune with the music. She felt her head sway to the rhythm even though she had no control over her movements.

She focused on the tune. It gradually became softer and slower. The breeze around her tingled less and less. Mardious' embrace was loosening. The song ended with a welcoming darkness.

Kase felt the heat of the fire burn his skin; it was hotter than he'd felt in a long time. It seemed like the longer someone had been dead, the more it hurt to bring them back. The intensity was unbearable, and the length of time the pain lingered made it even worse. Kase wished for the fire to end, but the lava burning his throat made it impossible to scream.

His eyes were wide open when the pain finally stopped. He rested on his knees and held Amelia in his arms, just like Mardious had. But even the sadness that lingered from her passing could not quench the rage that burned within him. He felt like he was in the same dance that Amelia had experienced. She might not have recognized the warrior with the oversized bull-horned helmet, but it was easy for Kase: the warrior was a youthful Dominic Garrick.

"Babe?" Amelia blinked at Kase.

Kase hesitated. Why had Dom been there? Why hadn't he said anything through all their planning—or ever? All the stories had pointed to the great Roman Garrick ending Money Jane's terror, not Dom. Why keep it a secret?

A shadow slowly crept towards Amelia, shading her bright, curious blue eyes from the twilight. Those eyes widened, and her peace turned to panic in an instant. She curled into Kase, pulling the dagger from the scabbard at his waist.

"Watch out!" In one motion Amelia stood, shielded Kase, and drove the dagger into Dom's stomach. Dom fell back with a groan.

Kase fell forwards, onto his hands. After such a lengthy resurrection, he barely had enough energy to keep himself steady. Instead of looking back, he stared at the ground. Black spots formed in his vision. Kase shook his head and took a few breaths, trying to find his strength. "Wait," he said.

Amelia stumbled backwards in the sand. She waved the bloody dagger with both hands, changing her focus as she pointed it from Lenia to Kase. "Babe? Where are you?"

"Please, drop the weapon." Instead of reaching for her sword, Lenia held up an empty palm. "We're here to help you."

"Babe!" Amelia shouted. Her head swivelled, but her grip remained tight on the dagger. She took a few more steps backwards towards the pink lake.

Kase found his strength and stood tall. "Mardious isn't here," he said.

Amelia pointed the dagger at Kase and kept stumbling backwards.

"But we can reunite the two of you," Lenia added.

Amelia pointed the dagger back towards Lenia but stopped retreating. Amelia looked to Kase, then back at Lenia, and then back at Kase. Her eyes softened.

Kase took a deep breath. Lenia reached towards him and rubbed his shoulder. Kase met her reassuring eyes with a nod and smile. He knew she worried about the pain he felt when bringing someone back.

Amelia dropped the dagger and sprinted away from Kase and Lenia. Sand kicked up as her heavy steps carried her away slowly.

Lenia took a step forwards, but then looked back to a groaning Dom. "I'll grab her. Don't let your dad die again."

Before Kase could respond, Lenia teleported down to the lakefront, landing right in front of Amelia. After a few steps, Amelia screamed and stumbled, but kept on running, now away from Lenia.

Dom groaned again. He was lying on his side, holding the gash in his belly. His hands were soaked in blood.

Kase took a few steps and knelt beside his father. "She got you back," he said. He reached out and pressed his right hand into Dom's midsection. Dom yelped from the pressure that Kase applied.

"You could see me?" Dom asked.

"Why didn't you say anything?" Kase checked on Amelia. She was still stumbling in the sand to avoid Lenia, who had teleported in front of her again.

"I …" Dom groaned as Kase pushed harder.

Kase didn't want to torture his father, but he did want the truth. "It's not like it would have changed anything."

Dom took a few hard breaths. "I'm responsible for the whole mess," he admitted. "I created Mardious Hood."

"That's not true," Kase said. His hand glowed. "Mardious Hood created Mardious Hood."

"Thank you, son." Dom's breathing slowed once his body was fully healed. "I understand the ramifications of my actions, and your grandparents paid the price for my mistake. I'm trying to be a better person now, and I hope that I'm on a path to rectify my past errors in judgement."

Dom glanced down the beach. Amelia was kneeling in the sand, while Lenia stood above her with her arms crossed. It seemed like Amelia's energy had run out.

"We're in this together," Kase said reassuringly. He left Dom and jogged through the sand. He felt his lungs struggle for breath after a few strides, and wondered if he was tired from using his power, or if it was because he hadn't been training as much. He needed to join more of Lenia's group exercises.

"I'm not a demon," Lenia said sternly.

"Exactly what a demon of the afterlife would say." Amelia had rolled her sleeves up, and her fingers traced lines on her unblemished skin. She looked oddly sad.

Kase knelt on one knee next to Lenia. Part of it was to be on the same level as Amelia, but it was also because he was still tired. "Maybe introductions would help, Amelia." Kase tried to slow his breathing. "My name is Kase. This is Lenia. The man you met with your blade is my father, Dominic Garrick."

Amelia stopped fidgeting. "Where am I?"

"You're at the Pink Lakes," Kase said. "You perished here on the beach a long time ago, but I have the power to bring the fallen back to life, which is why you're with us now."

Amelia reached to her neck and massaged where the arrow had pierced her skin. Now, there wasn't even a mark. Her fingers dipped into her collar, and she straightened. She quickly patted down her chest. "Where is it?" she panicked.

"Where's what?" Kase asked.

Amelia covered her face with her palms and shook her head. "You're dreaming right now, Amelia. Wake up. Wake up!"

"Time for Plan B?" Lenia asked.

The plan was to teleport Money Jane to the dungeon in the Kingdom of Moiras if she wouldn't cooperate. While imprisoned, the A.K. would be able to keep a close eye on the criminal and figure out another method of achieving their goal.

But Amelia didn't seem like a notorious criminal; she was fragile, lost, and alone.

Kase met Lenia's gaze and shook his head. He took another deep breath, reminding himself how difficult it was for those that had passed to accept their new surroundings. It had happened with all his family members, and even with Lenia herself.

"Can you take Dom back home?" Kase asked. "He's done enough already." Kase wasn't impressed with Dom's secrets, and he didn't need for Amelia to feel threatened by her killer.

"What does that mean?" Lenia asked, noticing Kase's tone.

"Ask him." Kase bobbed his head towards Dom, still huddled in the sand where he had been stabbed.

Lenia nodded and then disappeared.

Amelia didn't seem to care. Her hands still covered her eyes as she shook her head back and forth. Kase thought about how he could connect with her.

"I felt lost, too," Kase said. He reached down with his left hand and drew some circles in the sand. "Only I was the opposite of you—I never wanted to wake up from my dream. It was so real. And wonderful. I got to attend a party with the woman I loved, where we laughed and danced all night. But when I awoke, it was back to living my life without her. Even though I had other friends around me, I didn't care; I wanted to fall back asleep so we could be together again."

Amelia peeked from between her palms. "She died."

Kase nodded solemnly. "Yes."

"And you?"

"I died too," he admitted. "So I know how it feels. The power of the doorway of life can bring people back, but it's still disorienting."

Amelia's fingers slowly glided down her cheeks. She stared at Kase's arm. "That's quite the scar," she said. "Is it a feather?"

Kase realized his mermaid design was facing Amelia. He extended his arm to show the entire work, trying to capture the remaining, twilit light off the lake so it would stand out. "It's an old emblem from The Academy," Kase said.

"Strength in unity." Amelia curled her hair around her ear. "You have good taste, Demon."

Kase smiled. He'd finally connected with Amelia. He got the feeling that she was misunderstood, just like him. "I had it etched on my skin permanently by a mermaid friend of ours," Kase said. He rubbed the design. "She—"

"Mermaid?" Amelia seemed to regain her energy. "There are mermaids in the afterlife?"

Kase noticed Lenia had teleported beside him. She gripped her trident tight. Kase wondered if she'd show off the flame of her trident, but she wasn't paying attention to them. Instead she scanned the terrain. It was a good reminder that they shouldn't stay at the Pink Lakes any longer than necessary.

"Would you like to meet one?" Kase asked.

"Is that possible?" Amelia asked in wonder. "I thought their singing voices were so beautiful that they hypnotized sailors into crashing against sea rocks. Then they'd eat their brains."

Kase's eyes widened. Lenia chuckled, but Kase didn't want to look at her in case she made him laugh too. "Yes," he said instead. "It's possible. I don't know of any mermaids eating brains, but we've met one that has a beautiful singing voice—and a terrible memory. Lenia thought she wanted to kiss me."

Lenia scoffed. "She just talked too close to you." Lenia put her palm to her nose.

Amelia giggled. "I definitely want to meet a close-talking, singing mermaid." She looked at her bare arms again. "And get a mermaid scar."

"We'll try to arrange it, but we should probably change and get cleaned up," Kase said. "Are you hungry?"

Amelia jumped to her feet. "Sure, now that you mention it. What kind of food do you serve here?"

Kase stood and suddenly felt famished himself. It had been a long day, and time was running out for a date with Lenia. He looked to his supportive Unicorn Knight, who stood ready with her trident.

"Depends," Kase said. "Do you have a favourite food, Amelia?"

"Do you have any dates?" Amelia asked.

Kase thought about the stash of food that the A.K. had harvested. "We might have dates that the giants on Jenim Island eat," Kase said. "They're about the same size as you."

Amelia's mouth dropped open. "I love this place!"

Kase couldn't help but smile at Amelia's enthusiasm. He was relieved that her attitude had completely shifted, which gave him faith that their plans might work. They could work on the whole 'demon' mix-up. He looked to Lenia, whose shrug signified the same reaction.

He stood and extended his hand to Amelia. She studied his mermaid design again and reached out, but then she hesitated. She looked around the empty shoreline, to the lake and the forest that bordered the lakefront. She nodded and grabbed Kase's hand.

Lenia was third to join the embrace and then, instead of teleporting them to the dungeon, she teleported them away to the kitchen of the Kingdom of Moiras.

CHAPTER 7

Yield

Kase heard a rustling in the corner of his castle bedroom. He peeked his eyes open. The castle was shrouded in darkness, but he could make out Lenia struggling with her boots. He quickly sat up and swung his legs over the bed.

"Sorry, I didn't mean to wake you," Lenia said.

"I'm glad you did." Kase now fumbled in the dark for *his* boots. "I was thinking, since we never seem to get time at night for a date, why don't we move our dates to the morning, before everyone wakes up?"

"A mornate." Lenia giggled. "A daning? What did you have in mind?"

"Well, I don't think we would do the same things as a proper date," Kase said. He found his first boot and felt around for the second. "It's a little too early for dinner and dancing."

"I agree." Lenia slipped over to Kase.

Kase found his other boot and quickly put both on. "But if we get in some training before everyone else wakes, it will give us a chance to spend some time together before we do something really special." He stood to receive Lenia's soft embrace.

"I love it." Lenia wrapped her arms around Kase, nestled her head into his chest, and then tilted her chin up.

Although Kase felt like telling Lenia how much he loved her, he chose to show her with a kiss instead. As their lips locked, Kase felt the morning breeze on his cheeks.

Lenia broke the kiss before Kase wanted it to end. "Try to keep up."

She pushed Kase away and raced off.

Kase smiled and chased after Lenia. He was happy that his plan had worked. The fresh air and sunshine of the Kingdom of Moiras was nice, but training with Lenia was going to be the best way to wake up in the morning.

Lenia had teleported them to the castle garden, where she left her trident behind so she could run faster. She led Kase away from the castle grounds, through the grasslands, and to a quiet trail. She didn't even speak, but Kase could tell she was enjoying their time together, too.

They stopped when they reached Lenia's second favourite waterfall. They took a break to cool down and splash around, but they didn't waste too much of their training time at the watering hole. They continued on their run, but soon turned around and ran back to the castle, faster even than when they had started out.

As they crossed the perimeter wall, Lenia slowed. Kase sped past her excitedly, but then stopped when he recognized Lenia's worried look. She stared at her turquoise ring.

"Is it broken?" Kase asked. Lenia's ring was connected to her trident. The brighter it became, the closer she was to it. When she held her trident, the coral was transparently white.

"You don't think . . . " Lenia made a fist. "Did Money Jane steal it?"

"She's probably not even awake yet." Kase checked the rising sun over his shoulder. "We gave her enough Sleepy Time to last until mid-morning."

"Did we?" Lenia asked. "Or did you not put enough into her tea?" Lenia extended her hand and slowly waved it in front of herself. When her hand moved away from the castle and towards the open field, the ring's hue brightened slightly.

"So you think she shook off the effects of the potion, stole your trident, and escaped?" Kase asked. "I think you overestimate her."

"I think you underestimate her," Lenia said. "She is a world-class criminal, after all."

Kase thought about last night and how Amelia had acted so differently than he expected. She was supposed to be a notorious and dangerous thief, but she was also caring, scared, and innocent. Or was that one of her tricks?

"Would you like to bet on it?" Kase asked. He followed Lenia as she started moving away from the castle and along the path brightened by her trident tracker.

"Absolutely I would." Lenia started jogging.

Kase ran after her. "If Amelia stole your trident and is on the run, I will make you breakfast."

Lenia remained serious, but she couldn't hide the twinkle in her eyes. "And clean up afterwards," she added.

"It's a bet," Kase said. Even if he had underestimated Amelia, at least he was able to keep the mood light. Besides, it wasn't like Amelia really had a chance to escape.

The plan was to keep Amelia in the castle of the Kingdom of Moiras. It meant Mardious Hood couldn't find her on his own, since he wasn't aware of the kingdom's location. It also gave Talen a chance to help teach her some world history, since so much had changed since Money Jane had been alive. Without the distractions and all the new faces at their gold mine hideout, they could spend more one-on-one time with Amelia.

The kingdom wasn't a paradise, though. There were a lot of things that could trample, poison, or eat Amelia if she strayed too far from the castle. Kase hoped she was still sleeping, but he picked up the pace anyways.

Lenia raced across the open field, checking her ring on her way. She veered left towards the treeline but slowed, her palm still held out ahead of her. Her ring had become white, but there wasn't anything around that seemed out of place. Lenia finally stopped and knelt.

She pulled her black trident up and held it tight.

"No Amelia," Kase said.

"Maybe not." Lenia rested the end of the trident on the ground and stood like a proud warrior. "How did it get here?"

Kase took a deep breath and focused on his surroundings. He felt a few rodents scurrying about. A bird rested on a branch in the forest, but he didn't want to alarm Lenia. He didn't feel anything that could have dragged a trident all the way here from the castle.

Kase wondered if there were any langaras in the area, even though they weren't typically early risers. "Maxim?"

"I don't see any tracks." Lenia knelt where her trident had lain. "No broken twigs, no hair or threads, no blood."

"Should we check Amelia's room instead?" Kase asked. "Make sure she's sleeping."

"We might have a bigger threat on our hands if Amelia wasn't the one to steal my trident," Lenia replied.

"You're right," Kase said. "Let's . . . " A passing shadow shaded him from the sun for a second. He looked up. Maxim's mother, Raiden, was flying towards them.

Raiden landed gingerly on the grass near Kase and Lenia, and then slowly pranced closer. Amelia gripped Raiden's black tuft, laughing as she bounced along for the ride. Raiden stopped and knelt, but she wasn't scowling or baring her teeth, which seemed strange to Kase.

"Hey, Demons!" Amelia said.

"What happened?" Kase asked Raiden telepathically.

"Your prisoner escaped," Raiden said.

"Looks like I won our bet after all," Lenia said.

Kase didn't know which smug reply to answer first. He decided to show respect to the one with the biggest fangs. "Thank you for bringing her back in one piece," Kase said to Raiden.

"Come on, Demon Beast!" Amelia slammed her heels into Raiden like she was riding a horse. "Let's get out of here!"

"She's not as threatening as you thought," Raiden said, referring to the conversation she had held with Kase prior to them bringing another guest to the langara's kingdom. "She laid down her weapon, bowed to me, and respectfully submitted with honour and grace."

"Should I grab her?" Lenia asked.

"Yes," Kase said to Lenia. Everyone seemed calm now, but any situation involving a notorious criminal, a deadly mythical beast, and a teleporting warrior was a volatile one.

"I'm glad she didn't cause any stress," Kase said to Raiden. "We hadn't prepared her for life outside the castle just yet."

Lenia teleported onto Raiden's back and then back to Kase. Amelia sat on the ground between them, her head whipping back and forth wildly. "Hey!"

"She's a curious one," Raiden said. "But she smells like you, so I'm not too worried." Raiden turned and strutted in the opposite direction. She took a few powerful strides, flapped her wings, and flew away.

Amelia huffed as she stood. She took a few steps away from Lenia and waved after Raiden. "Wait! Come back, Demon Beast!"

"Her name is Raiden," Lenia said.

Kase wondered what Raiden had meant. He knew langaras hunted by using all their senses and by searching for prey and judging their kills. Amelia was wearing clothes from the castle, and so it made sense that she'd smell like Kase. Or did they both smell unclean? Kase checked his armpits and realized the quick dip from their morning run hadn't washed away his body odor.

"You can't fool me anymore, Demon," Amelia snapped. "I'm ready to explore the afterlife, not just listen to you lecture me about it."

"Well, you can't fool us either." Lenia gripped her trident. "Once a criminal, always a criminal." Lenia smirked at Kase.

"You win," Kase said to Lenia, but he also meant it for Amelia. "We're not here to lecture you. Where would you like to go? What would you like to do?"

"Just leave me alone," Amelia said. She walked away from Kase and Lenia without turning back.

Lenia shrugged. "Ready for breakfast?"

"We can't just leave her," Kase said.

"She wants to spend time alone," Lenia said. "I'm sure Raiden can bring her back to us when she's done."

Kase didn't want to abandon Amelia. She was in a new world and, even though he had a responsibility to try to connect with Amelia to fulfill their plan, he also understood what it was like to miss those one was closest to. She was a criminal, but she didn't deserve to be treated like an outcast. Her quality of life was just as valuable as everyone else's.

"Can I make you breakfast tomorrow instead?" Kase reached out his hand but didn't grab Lenia's just yet.

Lenia looked up at Kase and smiled. "We can save it for our next mornate," she said. She took Kase's hand. "But only if you double the bet."

"Two breakfasts?" Kase asked. He let go of Lenia's hand and draped his arm around her shoulders. He kissed her forehead, getting a whiff of his sweaty armpit in the process. He hoped Lenia didn't notice. "Deal."

Amelia looked back, but then quickly turned away again. Her shoulders seemed to slump forwards a little lower. "Stop following me!" she shouted.

"I'm still hungry though," Lenia said. "How about I grab some snacks for us and our guest?"

"Thank you," Kase said. "Hopefully a morning hike and snack will help Talen get ready for her history lesson."

Lenia hugged Kase, and then disappeared from his grasp.

Kase took a deep breath and followed Amelia. His legs were still warm from the morning training, but it didn't really matter; Amelia wasn't walking very fast. He tried to think of common ground to share with her.

"I've never ridden Raiden before," Kase said. "What was it like?"

Amelia turned her head slightly but kept marching forward.

"When she was with child, she had some complications with the birth," Kase continued. "My aunt and uncle helped her deliver her daughter, Maxim. Without their help, both Raiden and Maxim wouldn't have made it."

Amelia spun around. Her eyebrows were furrowed, and her lips were pinched together.

Kase stopped.

Amelia strode towards Kase. When she got close enough, she brought her hands up in front of her. She shoved his chest, causing him to take a step back. She brought her hand up, as if she were going to slap him next. "Leave me alone!" she yelled.

Kase put his hands up to signal defeat. He didn't want to press further to make Amelia angrier, even though he felt like pushing her back. He wondered if she was upset that Raiden had left her with him and Lenia, or if she just didn't like getting caught stealing the trident.

"I know you can handle yourself alone," Kase said. "But it doesn't have to always be like that. Strength in unity is more than just scholars, wizards, and warriors coming together. It's about trust, respect, and love for others. It's also about trusting, respecting, and loving yourself."

Amelia's eyes softened, and her hand dropped. "Good," she said. "Go love yourself."

As Amelia walked away, Kase lowered his arms. If there wasn't a way to talk through a connection like scholars, maybe he could share a feeling like a wizard. If she liked Raiden, Kase knew she'd fall in love with Maxim.

"Maxim?" Kase called out telepathically.

Nothing.

Kase followed Amelia at a distance again, even though she'd told him not to. He kept repeating Maxim's name, but he also tried to connect with other animals in the area. Maybe Amelia would be fascinated by elk, water buffalo, or snakes? How good was she at animal control? Kase hadn't seen Mardious Hood utilize that skill in any of their battles.

How would Mardious Hood approach an angry Amelia?

The former High Wizard had loved to use illusions in battle. Kase wondered if Amelia would appreciate a good illusion. He thought about what animals she might like, and which ones would be common in a grassland habitat. He took a deep breath, excited to try something new.

Kase created a cute, brown bunny rabbit to Amelia's right. The illusionary rabbit hopped a few yards away from Amelia, inching closer into her line of sight. She noticed it and stepped away. She didn't seem alarmed, but the cute bunny was not invoking any interest. Illusion failed.

Was the rabbit too dull? He thought about distinct animals from Amelia's home of the Badlands. He hadn't travelled there much, but when he was in Camptown, he'd heard barterers try to trade a variety of rodents and bugs. He remembered researching 'assassin bugs' after a trip there. They weren't very flashy looking, but they were recognizably ugly.

Kase focused again and now created an illusion of a dull, grey assassin bug.

He set it in Amelia's path, hoping she would stop and appreciate something from her home.

Amelia stepped over the bug without any interest, not appearing to recognize it at all. Illusion number two failed. Kase needed something bigger.

Since Amelia seemed to like menacing, black langaras, Kase decided to kick up the terror in his illusions. The biggest illusion he'd ever created was of a purple dragon named Billy Do-Dance. It had scared some warriors, but not Mardious Hood. Even if Amelia recognized the dragon as an illusion like Mardious had, it would certainly be harder to miss compared to an assassin bug and a bunny rabbit.

Kase focused on the dragon's entrance. He placed the dragon high in the sky, flying from behind him and Amelia. He took note of where the sun was located and then created an illusionary shadow to make the dragon more realistic.

The dragon flew past Amelia and banked down in the distance until it was in view of Amelia's path. At least it got her attention. She stopped dead in her tracks.

The dragon turned towards Amelia and flapped its wings. It sped forwards as it got closer, but slowed as it landed in the grassy field. It fluttered its wings, gripped the earth with its massive claws, and dipped its head low as it roared. The sun glistened off the dragon's purple scales and sharp white teeth.

Kase was proud of his illusion. Thanks to practice and amplified power, it was more realistic than his last attempt. Even the roar was louder and deeper than before.

Amelia dropped to the ground and cowered away from the dragon. She saw Kase standing behind her and crawled over to him. When she got to his boots, she slid around his legs and gripped his ankles tight to put him between her and the dragon.

Kase marched the dragon forwards a few steps. Amelia gripped Kase's ankles tighter. The dragon reared its head back as a glowing fireball formed in its throat. Kase wondered what an illusionary fireball should look like. If the flames were too long and touched Amelia, the illusion would disappear. He might have stopped the dragon too close to them.

"I'm here," Maxim said.

Before Kase could answer his friend, the langara swooped in from behind Kase and attacked the dragon illusion. Maxim went straight for the neck, but her claws hit the illusion before she could take a bite. The illusion disappeared. Without a massive dragon to break the speed of her dive, Maxim went crashing to the ground, tumbling into the grassy field.

Kase ran towards Maxim, breaking free of Amelia's grasp in the process. "I'm sorry," he said as he rushed to Maxim's side.

Maxim rolled over with a whimper. "What was that?"

Kase touched Maxim's closest limb—her left paw. Before he could complete an evaluation, his hands glowed and his healing power took effect.

"It was an illusion of a dragon," Kase explained to Maxim, who had sprained her right paw and had a few cuts and bruises from her hard landing.

Kase didn't feel much pain as he healed Maxim. Even though she was much larger than him, the pain was still the same. He transferred the pain in her paw and other injuries to his body, absorbed it, and then filtered it away with his magical power. The glow from his healing touch disappeared.

"Is it gone?" Maxim asked.

"Well, it was never real," Kase said. "I was just trying to show Amelia some magic to spark her interest."

"You're weird sometimes," Maxim grumped, giving him a langara laugh. "But it seemed to work."

Maxim's large eyes were fixed on Amelia, who stood a few feet behind Kase. Amelia wasn't interested in the langara, however. She was staring at Kase in awe.

"You healed a Demon Beast?" Amelia asked.

Kase nodded. He pet Maxim's paw, but she soon nestled her nose into Kase's touch. Kase was proud to have finally done something to get Amelia's attention back. "Have you healed before?" he asked.

Amelia reached for her collar but then let her hand drop. She took a few steps forwards and cautiously rubbed Maxim's nose like Kase had. Maxim gave a reassuring purr without Kase needing to ask for a favour.

"Did you leave a beautiful scar?" Amelia asked.

After dinner last night, Amelia had argued that she couldn't be alive because she didn't have her scars. She had seemed pretty upset about it when Kase explained they had been healed when he brought her back to life. He thought about the times when others had healed him, allowing him to learn from the experience so that he wouldn't get hurt again.

"No," Kase answered honestly. "But not all scars are skin deep."

Amelia looked down and reached for her collar again. "Can you heal those scars too?"

"Not by myself," Kase said. He felt like Amelia was leaving a door open for him to reach her. "But I'd like to try."

Amelia smiled and tucked her hair around her ear. She met Kase's gaze but then shook her head. "No. I'm not falling for it again, Demon. You say all these nice things and promise to take me to meet mermaids and ride lions. But then you poison my tea and lock me in my room."

Hearing Amelia call him out made guilt twist in his stomach. That day he had brought Amelia back to life had been a long one, and so, just to get some rest, he had agreed to spike her tea with some Sleepy Time. He hadn't thought she'd notice, since he had been oblivious when Lenia, Cali, and Aura had done it to him.

"I'm sorry," Kase said. "It took a lot of effort to bring you here. Yesterday wasn't a long day for you, so I thought giving you a sleeping aid would help us start our journey on the right foot today. It was wrong to leave you out of that plan."

Amelia stared at Kase. He tried not to flinch. He hoped Amelia was studying his words instead of reacting purely on emotion like she had before.

"Terrible plan," Amelia said. "But what now?"

"Well, that's up to you," Kase said. "What do you want to know? What would you like to see? I want to help guide you through this new world, but which direction we go is up to you."

"Okay . . ." Amelia looked back at Maxim, who had her eyes closed as she enjoyed the petting and warm sunshine. "What's in it for you?"

"I'm hoping that we can trust each other," Kase said honestly. "But where I come from, trust isn't a reward for a job well done. Trust is earned."

Behind Amelia, Kase saw Lenia appear in the field right where'd she left. She looked over his way and then teleported closer. Amelia was still focused on petting Maxim and hadn't noticed.

"I still don't believe you, but I'm willing to see you try." Amelia looked over her shoulder at Kase and smiled. "I don't know where to start, though."

Kase returned the smile. "How about we start with breakfast." Kase nodded to Lenia, who had done more than just gather a few snacks. She had cleaned herself up, changed clothes, and braided her hair.

Amelia looked to Lenia and into the basket. There were some buns, strawberries, and peaches. "Any dates?" she asked.

"Not here, but I can get some from the castle," Lenia said.

"No, I'll get them myself." Amelia scanned the horizon, but the castle was out of view.

"How about we ride back together," Kase said. He scratched Maxim's chin, and she turned her head so he could reach behind her ear.

Amelia smiled and nodded. He helped her mount Maxim, and then he climbed up and sat behind her. Lenia had the basket, and so she didn't join them on the ride. She teleported back to the castle while Kase and Amelia travelled with the 'White Demon.' Kase was relieved that Amelia was heading back with them, but he trusted that their journey was only just beginning.

CHAPTER 8

Earning Reconciliation

Amelia stretched her fingers out and tugged on the edge of her white silk gloves that reached all the way to her elbows. Of all the clothes she could have picked from the castle wardrobe, Kase found it odd that she was most satisfied with her accessories, especially since her gloves and dress were a sharp contrast to normal Badlands attire.

Kase was curious about Amelia's background, but he didn't want to talk about her past without Talen and Cali present. They all needed to respect Amelia, and not pressure her into discussing sensitive information. Cali called it 'Dignity by Example,' but Kase understood it as something that would help them to build a better future.

How else could they move forwards without making the same mistakes of the past?

"How much longer do we have to wait?" Amelia leant over the tabletop and rested her cheek on her arm.

They were sitting in the main library in the castle, waiting for Lenia to return with Talen and Cali. Kase was bored. He remembered when Lenia and Talen would pass the time during their school days.

"Have you ever played Flapdragon before?" Kase asked.

Amelia shifted in her seat, disinterested. "I don't think so?"

"It's pretty fun." Kase glanced around the library for supplies. A side table had some materials for element control experiments. He quickly grabbed his black fire starter, which had a trident engraved on its face.

Amelia shifted her position and twirled her hair as Kase flicked his fire starter. Kase sat beside Amelia and reached across the table for her bowl of dates. Amelia snuck a date out of the bowl after Kase moved it into position.

"You're a natural," Kase joked. His fire starter sparked, and he moved the flame to the bowl. The entire rim ignited with a flame as high as Kase's chin. Kase snapped his head back for effect. "Now, try it with fire."

Amelia studied the bowl and held her palm up close to it. She didn't seem worried about the heat; maybe her gloves were offering protection. "What's this fire burning on?"

Kase let the flame fade. "I'm controlling it. Haven't you ever practiced element control?"

"Practice my . . . I can't do demon magic," Amelia said.

Kase noticed the concern on Amelia's face. "It's not . . . I'm sorry," Kase said. "I shouldn't have assumed. Lots of wizards can manipulate fire, but not everyone. It takes discipline, patience, and practice."

Kase reduced the height of the flame so that it barely flickered above the edge. He reached into the bowl, grabbed a date, and popped it into his mouth.

Amelia reached towards the bowl again but then stopped. She clasped her hands together near the centre of her chest. "Does it hurt?" she asked.

Kase thought he heard hopefulness in Amelia's tone, but he reasoned that amplifying pain might not be the best thing to encourage right now. He thought about his lessons from Lenia when he first started to control the elements, and wondered if Amelia was taught similarly.

"I use everything inside of me to control the elements," Kase said truthfully. "Happiness, excitement, and love, but also despair, sadness, and heartbreak. My power is an extension of my life, good and bad, but I wouldn't say that it hurts to use it. Element control is a little different from healing."

Amelia turned away. Her hair fell across her cheek, and so Kase couldn't tell what her reaction was. He was about to put his hand on Amelia's shoulder, but just then Cali, Talen, and Lenia appeared at the desk in front of him. Kase released his power over the fire, diminishing it completely.

"Good morning, Amelia," Cali said. "I like the dress you've chosen. It suits you well."

Amelia, arms crossed, slowly turned towards Cali. She leant over the table and grabbed another date. "New demons," she said as she ate.

"Told you," Lenia said. "Good luck," she added before disappearing.

Kase would have liked to help Lenia gather supplies for the A.K. instead of being stuck in a lesson with Amelia, but he had a job to do, too.

"My name is Cali Garrick," Cali said. "I'm Kase's sister. I recognize that you're alone and scared, but you've been brought back into a new world, and I'm here to help you prepare."

Amelia nodded while looking Cali up and down. She turned towards Talen. "And you?"

Talen stared back at Amelia, but not like she was studying anything. Kase thought maybe Talen wasn't paying attention, but that wasn't like her; Talen always took note of every detail in a conversation, lesson, or environment.

Cali tapped Talen, seemingly knocking Talen out of her trance.

"My name is . . . Talen Sparwood." Talen looked down at the plate she was holding. "I made some horsebread for you, from a recipe I found in an old Badlands cookbook." Talen set the plate on the table next to the bowl of dates.

"Horsebread?" Amelia asked. "I don't eat that garbage. Isn't this a castle?"

Talen backed away. "Sorry," she said. "I . . . should have . . ."

"It's symbolic of our intent." Cali slid a chair in front of Amelia and sat down. "By breaking bread with each other we are offering openness, peace, and friendship. I tasted Talen's recipe before we came. It's actually quite good."

Cali broke off a piece of the horsebread. It looked stiff and old. Even though it didn't seem fresh and appetizing, Kase was willing to try some, knowing that Talen would have followed the recipe precisely. He didn't see any butter on the plate, though.

"If you wanted to be my friend, you should have brought wine." Amelia leant over the table but didn't reach for the bread.

"My mistake," Cali said. "I assumed that since you just woke up that—"

"—I know where it is," Talen interrupted. She put her notebook and quill on the edge of the table and hustled out of the room.

Amelia watched Talen cross the library, then turned back to Kase and

Cali. "I like that demon," she said. "No tricks, unlike you two."

Cali smiled but leant on the table to match Amelia's aggressiveness. "This isn't a game," she said. "We genuinely want to learn more about you and where you're from. Wouldn't you like to learn more about us, too?"

Amelia reached for the bread but then dipped her hand back into the date bowl. She leant back in her chair, smiled at Kase, and popped a date in her mouth. "I love scars," she said. "Do you have any, Cali Garrick?"

"Scars? No, but I've been through some ups and downs," Cali admitted. She took a deep breath. "I was dead, just like you. Mauled by a langara. Thanks to my brother, I'm alive and healed. I might not have any scars, but I still can't escape my nightmares."

Kase looked down. He remembered Cali's death. She was running away, afraid of the beast that she couldn't escape. At least the langara had made quick work of her; he hadn't felt too much pain when he brought her back.

"How did you die?" Amelia asked Kase.

"The first time?" Kase joked. "I fell into a pit of lava. I don't have any scars either, but that's also because I'm able to heal myself now."

"You can heal yourself?" Amelia smiled and leant closer to Kase. "I don't believe it. Can you show me?"

Cali gave him a pleased look. He pulled a dagger from his belt line and draped his forearm onto the table. Amelia peered closer as he rolled up his sleeve.

Kase slid the dagger blade across his arm, making a small cut just above his mermaid design. He flinched a bit but felt the tingling start in his forearm almost instantly. His wound healed a few moments later, and without leaving a mark.

Amelia slipped off her glove and touched Kase's forearm. She traced a line where the cut had been, and then rested her hand on Kase's mermaid design. She looked up at Kase dreamily and then pulled back. "What do you feel when you heal yourself?" she asked.

Kase had never been asked that question before. The ones that would understand knew how healing felt, and the ones who couldn't heal weren't interested. "You know that feeling you get when you get goosebumps? It's like that, but only in the area I'm healing."

Amelia scrunched her nose. "Too bad." She traced a line on her own forearm. "When I healed, I felt the pain of my patient through my whole body. It was the best part." Amelia giggled. "Scars were a nice reminder of those adventures."

Kase raised his eyebrows and turned to Cali, but his sister seemed more intrigued than alarmed. Any revelation Amelia gave about her past was a win, even if her healing process was different than Kase's.

"What kind of adventures did you like the best?" Cali asked.

Amelia pulled her glove back on. "Why do you care?"

Cali reached into her sac and pulled out a notebook. "I wrote a paper on Money Jane while I was at the Academy." She flipped to the first page. "Some of her adventures are well documented, but others are shrouded in mystery. I'm hoping that the source can provide insight into which ones were most memorable and why."

Amelia curled back further into her chair. "Am I on trial, Demon?" she asked.

"Not at all," Cali said reassuringly. "This isn't about rights and wrongs of the past; it's about how we can build a better future. Kase and I lead an alliance that is trying to unite the realm once more so that scholars, wizards, and warriors can live in harmony instead of under the corrupt rule of the Triple Crown."

"Strength in unity." Amelia looked at Kase's mermaid design. "I didn't think the Triple Crown was part of this world, too."

"They are still around, but things have changed since you were alive," Talen said. She had returned holding a wine bottle and three glasses. "Maybe a diorama would help to explain our current state? If Kase has been practicing."

Kase nodded. Talen had challenged Kase to express his political views in art form. Kase wasn't much of a painter, or meticulous enough to build a small-scale model, so instead he had practiced expressing himself through elemental manipulation. He liked making shapes out of fire, water, and dust, but he wondered what Amelia would like to see the most. Wine might be a good option.

"I can try." Kase straightened in his seat while Cali flipped to a new page in her book.

Talen set the three glasses in front of Cali, Amelia, and Kase. She poured Amelia's glass of wine first, and then followed with the other two. Before Kase could use his element control on each of their wines, Amelia grabbed her glass and took a sip. Kase focused only on his drink.

"The Triple Crown was represented by a High Scholar, High Wizard, and High Warrior in an attempt to have equal representation of the realm," Kase said. He used his power to move the wine out of the glass, like a snake slithering through the air. "The High Scholar wins their position by election but appoints the High Wizard and High Warrior as they see fit."

"More demon tricks?" Amelia asked.

"Wizard skills," Kase said, but didn't break focus.

When all the wine hovered above the table, Kase turned the shape into a pyramid, and then split the pyramid into three sections. The bottom section was in the shape of tiny people casting votes, the middle layer was shaped like a castle, and the top layer showed the three members of the High Authority.

"The Triple Crown provided governance for the people, but they also bent the laws to service their own agendas," Kase continued. "Their abuse of power gave them access to information, gold, and artefacts at the cost of the lives of the people they swore to protect."

Kase made droplets of water rain down from the High Authority to the bottom of the pyramid. He also created a secondary unit that looked like a treasure chest. He was running out of wine, and so he borrowed some from Cali's glass to make a few corpses around the chest.

"But some of us fought against that tyranny." Kase manipulated the liquid corpses to rise up and march towards the castle. "We exposed the Triple Crown for what they were, causing chaos and destruction for the whole system."

The droplets formed into a dragon, which blew fire and destroyed the castle, causing the High Authority to flee.

"Wait," Amelia said. She took another sip. "You're telling me that your army of demons destroyed the Triple Crown?"

"Yes, we caused the Triple Crown to split. Now there's a war," Cali said. "Each self-appointed king has a following, but they only want what's best for themselves. The only way for them to get power back is to destroy each other."

Kase manipulated the wine into three different armies. The scholar army was the biggest, followed by the warrior army. Mardious' wizard army was the smallest, which was currently accurate.

"We're trying to stop the fight," Kase said. "Instead of the war producing a winner and two losers, and a hierarchy that would favour the victors, we're proposing something new. If we can broker peace between the former leaders, and have them agree to a new government, then we can save countless lives. We could create a world of inclusion where everyone supports each other, rather than a world where people are put down to boost others up."

Kase combined the armies together to form a ball. The ball spun so that people on the bottom of the ball would rise to the top, and then fall back to the other side.

"Instead of relying on three leaders to make all the decisions for the realm, we could put the right people in positions that reflect their expertise and communities," Cali said. "Wizards could make decisions about magic. Warriors could improve upon laws to further public protection. People of the Badlands wouldn't have to be segregated. We could—"

"Wait." Amelia leant forward in her chair. "You think the realm would, all of a sudden, include the Badlands in their plans for the future? How strong is this wine?" Amelia looked at her glass.

Cali looked to Kase, but he shrugged in return. He couldn't think of a way to include the Badlands in his presentation without mentioning Mardious Hood. Cali had warned him that Amelia might not accept their proposal if they spoke negatively of the Underground King.

"The Badlands are already part of the fight," Cali said.

Amelia scoffed and took another sip of her wine. "It sounds like the world has become the Badlands. Chaos, fighting for power, common people suffering; that's the Badlands."

Kase returned the wine to his and Cali's glasses and released his power. Cali took a big gulp, and then searched her notes. Amelia tilted her glass towards Kase's and pointed inside. Kase obliged, moving the wine from his glass into hers. She smiled, happy, it seemed, that they were on the same page, but Kase was discouraged.

"Why did you give your spoils back to the people?" Talen asked suddenly.

Amelia shrugged and took another sip of her wine. "Why not?"

"If I believe stereotypes, then the old leaders of the Triple Crown are acting like the people of the Badlands because they are selfish, close-minded, and ruthless," Talen said. "Yet you risked it all to distribute more wealth to a less fortunate community in a compassionate, open-minded, and selfless manner. Why?"

Amelia smiled at Talen wickedly. "Maybe I'm built different." She took another sip of her wine.

"So are we," Kase said. He moved the last bit of his wine to Amelia's glass.

"Since we have a smaller following than the Triple Crown leaders, we've had to consider all forms of victory," Cali said. "That includes thinking outside the norm, adding value with diverse and equitable ideas, and presenting solutions that include benefits for the *entire* realm, rather than only a certain group."

Amelia still stared at Cali, her face scrunched up in a look of disbelief.

For some reason, Kase was reminded of what Maxim had asked him about the war. "If you had stolen everything in the realm and given it to the Badlands, what would you have done afterwards?"

Amelia stared at her glass. "I don't know," she said. "I've never had the luxury of planning for the future."

"Not even with your partner?" Cali asked.

Amelia smiled wickedly again. "We loved each other," she said. "What else did we need?"

Cali looked to Kase and nodded. "What if I told you that Mardious Hood was the High Wizard?" Cali asked.

Amelia looked to Kase, then back to Cali. "Mardious is here?"

"He's not in the castle," Kase said. "We don't know his exact location; he and his army are causing havoc all over the realm. We were hoping that we could help you find him."

Amelia smiled and curled her hair around her ear. "He's here," she whispered. "But why would you help me?"

"Because you're different. You're like us," Cali said. "We believe that a small group can set the world on fire. By thinking outside the box, testing new theories, and coming up with solutions that remember the past to improve on the future, we can have a positive impact on the realm that serves everyone. That includes the commoners, the dreamers, and even the misunderstood."

Amelia smiled. "I don't trust you, Demon." She turned to Kase. "What do you get out of it?"

"I have the power to bring the fallen back to life," Kase said. "But what's the point if our quality of life suffers because of war? If we reunite you with Mardious, we could arrange for peace talks as a first step to end the war and improve life for everyone."

Amelia laughed. "If the world is like the Badlands, then war *is* life," she said. "Especially if Mardious is in charge. This is like a dream come true!" She took another gulp of her wine.

"Well, how are we going to change things if we don't try?" Cali asked. "Even a little difference can have a great impact. Want to know who I learned that from?"

Amelia chuckled again and giddily stared at her wine glass.

"Money Jane," Cali said.

Amelia looked to Kase and softened. "Don't believe everything you hear," she said. "Our riches might have given hope to a few, but we lost others who helped us to the Tyco. Poor Gerard." Amelia shook her head and toasted her glass.

Cali's eyes widened as she fumbled through her notes. "Who's Gerard?"

"He took me in, gave me work, and put a roof over my head," Amelia said. Her words were starting to slur. "It was my fault that he was burned alive."

Cali stopped fumbling and looked to Kase. He hadn't realized that Amelia had enemies in the Badlands, but considering she was known as a hero to some and a criminal to many, it was possible that those closest to her had suffered.

"Would you like me to bring him back to life, too?" Kase asked.

Amelia laughed. "This day keeps getting better and better!" She downed the last of the wine. "Do you have any music here?"

Amelia got up from her seat and swayed back and forth as if she were dancing. She moved around the table and grabbed the wine bottle. She popped the cork, took a swig, and then grabbed Talen.

The situation seemed to mesmerize Talen and she played along. She danced awkwardly with Amelia as Kase and Cali looked on.

"What now?" Kase asked Cali.

"This isn't really going as planned, but it's leading somewhere," Cali said. "Talen is much more of a help here than with the A.K., but let's see how she does with Amelia."

"Come dance, Favourite Demon." Amelia grabbed Kase's arm and tugged him out of his seat.

Kase stood next to Talen and copied her awkward moves. He found it difficult to dance in a quiet room, but Amelia was enjoying herself. Out of all the possibilities following their first meeting with Money Jane, dancing together was not the most predictable outcome. Was this the future of the realm? Was drinking wine before noon and dancing without music the ultimate goal?

How reliable is our plan? Kase wondered, if it all hinges on someone who isn't interested in taking the future seriously.

CHAPTER 9

She's a Black Sheep

Lenia took two more quick steps and ended with a twirl. "How was that?" she asked. The afternoon sun made her green eyes sparkle.

"What song were you thinking of?" Kase asked. "Amelia moved to a slower rhythm, but I couldn't think of anything to match her moves."

Kase tried to imitate Amelia by moving his hips in a circle. He ran his hands through his hair, closed his eyes, and thought about the slow ballads he knew. Just then, Lenia's laugh interrupted his concentration.

"It might be easier with a partner." Lenia stepped forwards and wrapped her arms around Kase.

Kase lost his rhythm, but swaying together was much better than dancing alone without music. It was a little awkward for Kase to hold Lenia, since her trident was strapped to her back. To make the trident look like a pitchfork, they'd used some leather material that smelled old and musty. Kase rested his cheek on Lenia's head and looked the opposite way. Even though the odor was unpleasant, he hoped he could stay in the dance forever.

"Or maybe you need some wine?" Talen suggested. "Although . . . Amelia does not strike me as a person who needs liquid courage to express herself in a room of strangers. She is wild and free." Talen scribbled something into her notebook.

"I wonder if she's still passed out," Cali said. She squirmed as she watched the moving image on her sage mirror. King Mac was screaming about another wizard attack in Kimroad.

"I'll go check on her," Lenia said. She squeezed Kase tight, and then disappeared.

Kase sauntered back to his seat and plopped down beside Talen. They had spent most of the day in the library planning their next move. "What do we do if she can't find him?" Kase asked.

"Delivering Amelia directly to Mardious is the only option," Cali said. "If she's out on her own, and Sheese or Mac capture her instead, they'll use her as a bargaining chip to fuel the war, not end it."

"Do you think Amelia would make a good member of the A.K.?" Talen asked. "What animal would she be?" She tapped her quill on her chin.

Kase noticed that Talen was doodling instead of writing. Was that a cloud in the centre of her doodle? Maybe, but it was hard to tell as animals dressed as people covered it.

Lenia reappeared in her former spot. "She's awake, but groggy," she said. "She needs a few minutes to clean herself up."

Kase took a deep breath. He could use a few extra moments, too. They were headed back to Camptown; he hadn't had much luck before, and now they were returning into the belly of the beast. Their plan was for him and Lenia to keep a watchful eye over Amelia, but would Amelia disappear? Would she set a trap for them or help protect them?

Lenia slid over to Kase and sat on his lap. "If everything goes to plan, do we have the rest of the night to ourselves?"

Kase checked his outfit. "I don't know where to take you in the Badlands."

Lenia giggled. "I was thinking of something a little less dangerous. Would you be interested in fighting dragons with me?"

Out of all the dates that she could have planned, this one surprised him the most "Why?" he asked.

Lenia hugged Kase. "Lots of reasons." She stood and slid her scabbard over her shoulders. She gripped her trident like a warrior and pointed the prongs at Kase. "We wouldn't risk being seen by anyone. It would be a good workout. And it would give us a chance to test our skills. I could teleport and bait them into position for you to practice your lightning strikes. We could test how hard their scales really are, and if the scales would be suitable for A.K. armor. Plus, I want to see if I can use my trident to block dragon fire, the way you did during the Quest Series."

Ah, the Quest Series. How had he done it? Kase still didn't know, but somehow, he had deflected a spray of dragon fire while holding Lenia's trident. That had also been the only time he had teleported on his own. He had to admit, as crazy as it sounded, Lenia's plan would be a good way for him and Lenia to understand each other's power a little better, and on their own terms instead of in an ambush or unforeseen battle.

"I'd love to," Kase said. "Should we—"

"Ready!" Amelia burst into the room. She was still wearing her red dress and white gloves, but her hair dangled over her shoulders, brushed and shining.

"I thought you were going to change," Lenia said.

"Why?" Amelia grabbed her dress. "Is this one not pretty enough?"

"It might be too pretty," Kase said. "We're trying to blend in with the people of the Badlands until we find Mardious. If we are spotted too early, it might make things more difficult."

"I put some suitable clothes by your bedside," Lenia said. "Did you not see them?"

Amelia seemed puzzled. "I thought those were cleaning rags."

Lenia and Kase shared a look. "They're like this." Kase pulled the fabric of his rugged shirt. "They're probably the most accurate outfits we have, consistent with what everyone wears in the Badlands. Right, Tal?"

Talen was too preoccupied with staring at Amelia to respond.

"You act like people in the Badlands have a uniform," Amelia said with a chuckle. She looked Kase up and down. "If you try to blend in with the locals, you're going to stand out even more. Just be who you are, Demon."

Kase was reminded of the fancy clothing he'd seen a couple Brotherhood members wear. He added 'dress like you belong' to his mental list of Amelia advice that included 'dance with no music.' It sounded easy but, for this mission, he'd still rather dress like the masses than stand out from the crowd.

"I happen to like these clothes," Kase said, trying to boost the confidence of his team along with his own. "They're a lot looser than my Dandy Lion vest."

Amelia perked up. "You have a vest made of dandelions?"

Lenia giggled. Even though she had helped create his nickname, Kase appreciated that it still made her happy, even if it was at his expense.

"No," Kase replied. "I have a uniform that resembles a lion that is dandy. We all have uniforms based on animals. Lenia's is a unicorn. Talen's is a shark."

Amelia looked Lenia and Talen up and down, but her brows were furrowed as if to envision them.

"What would your animal be?" Talen's voice was soft and cautious.

"Sorry, Demon," Amelia said. "I don't belong in your group. Can we go already? I want to see Mardious."

Talen wrote a quick note, and then turned the page in her notebook. "Good luck," she said.

Kase and Lenia tapped their hearts twice, kissed their fingers, and pointed to the sky. Amelia studied Kase and Lenia's gesture but didn't participate. Lenia clutched Amelia's wrist, held Kase's hand, and teleported the duo to the edge of Camptown.

Lenia had already warned Kase that the main city of the Badlands had been abandoned, but Kase still hadn't expected to see such darkness. From the ridge that overlooked the city, there were a few flames visible in open windows, but they didn't provide much illumination. The stars and bright moon made it a little easier to see, but Kase was worried that the shadows were stirring.

"Is this the right spot?" Lenia let go of Kase and Amelia.

"I thought you were taking me home," Amelia said. She rubbed her arms as if she were cold, even though it was a warm night.

"We don't know where that is," Kase said. "And the ultimate goal is to find Mardious, wherever he may be."

The plan was to follow Amelia into Camptown. Since Lenia had done some quick scouting before this mission, she was confident that Mardious Hood wasn't in the area, but that the Brotherhood still often patrolled Camptown. Therefore, Kase and Lenia would either follow the Brotherhood members and Amelia to Mardious Hood or wait for Mardious to come back to the Badlands to meet her.

"Aren't you supposed to protect me?" Amelia looked around nervously in the dark.

What could she be scared of? Kase put a reassuring hand on her shoulder. "Things might be different now, but there's no need to worry. You're—"

"I'm worried that things are still the same." Amelia clutched Kase's torso. "Please walk me to my door, Demon. I can't afford to get caught by the Tyco."

Kase tried to lean away. He noticed Lenia take a long look at Amelia, and then look to him. The moonlight couldn't hide her scowl. "If you had given us an address, you'd be home already," she scoffed.

Amelia clutched Kase harder but managed to point to the edge of town. "There's a housing complex that my old boss used to own. The Tyco burned his bar to the ground, but I'm not sure where their carnage stopped."

Kase knew the area. He and Lenia had recovered her trident from a building on the edge of town once, even though it had been a trap. At least they knew what might be awaiting them this time.

"We can probably get closer, right?" Kase asked Lenia. He smiled gently, trying to show empathy, but he doubted she could see his attempt at softness in this darkness. He hoped she'd sense it.

"Let's see," Lenia huffed. She disappeared.

Kase rubbed Amelia's shoulder. He wondered how she'd react when she found out that Mardious was the leader of the Badlands gang that she considered such a threat, and that Mardious was the person everyone feared the most. Although Mardious had changed their name from the Tyco to the Brotherhood, it seemed that fear was still their weapon of choice.

Lenia returned. "No activity in the area. Not that I could see."

"Hopefully everyone's asleep," Kase said.

"It's not that late." Amelia let go of Kase and wiped her eyes. "Does that mean you're coming with me, Demons?"

Lenia stood strong. She pointed to Kase and Amelia, and then made a walking motion with her two fingers. She pointed to herself and waved her hand above her head. Kase knew exactly what she was saying.

"I'll come with you," Kase said. "Lenia will have our backs."

"Thank you, Demons," Amelia said. "You're a good team."

Kase had to take a step back. It felt like Amelia was finally accepting them, and he was a little sad their time together was coming to an end.

Lenia reached out her hands for Amelia and Kase to grab. After Amelia's white glove wrapped around Lenia's ringed hand, Lenia transported them to the complex that Amelia had described and then left them alone.

Kase wanted to tell Amelia that he was familiar with her home, but he remained quiet. He didn't want to draw any unnecessary attention from the shadows. He focused on what he could control. He felt the cool breeze around them and noted that no animals were in the immediate area.

Lenia had teleported Kase and Amelia away from the complex, outside of the sixth door. Amelia turned to the right and led Kase to the very last door. Kase noticed that the doorframe had since been repaired after he had kicked it the only time he had been here: the door was now able to be closed fully shut.

Amelia didn't hesitate. She turned the shiny doorknob and slowly entered the room. The hinges must have been newer, too, because they didn't make a creaking sound.

The pitch-black room smelled like a family of skunks lived there. Kase looked over his shoulder before pulling his fire starter from his pocket. He flicked it and quickly used his power to split the flame into four, spreading the fire around the room as he enhanced its light.

An old, heavyset man was sleeping in the bed in the middle of the room, but he didn't seem to notice the light.

Amelia clenched her fists and strutted to the head of the bed. She stomped on the torn shirt that rested on the floorboards, ignoring the sword that rested in the corner of the room. She slapped the shoulder of the sleeping man, but it wasn't enough to wake him up.

"Hey!" Amelia shouted repeatedly, shaking the old man until he faded out of his dreamland.

Kase stayed at the entrance in case the noise drew any neighbours.

The old man blinked a few times while he sat up. "Who are you?" he said groggily.

Amelia scoffed. "I own this place. Who are you?"

"I, um . . . " the old man looked past Amelia and met Kase's gaze. His eyes were completely black, which meant he had likely ingested a potion.

The old man blinked a few times and then turned his attention to the small flames that floated around the room. "Magic? What … "

Amelia slapped the man, but her gloves must have softened the sting; his head barely moved. "Stay with me," she said. "Where is Mardious?"

The old man's head dipped as if he were about to fall asleep. He snapped his chin back up. "Dragoon!" he said.

Kase turned his attention outside, but he didn't see anyone striding out of the shadows. Was the old man a Marauder? Or was he worried that he was under attack? Did he think Kase and Amelia were there to arrest him?

"No. Mar-Di-Ous," Amelia slowed her words.

"Dragoon is the salute of the Guardians," Kase said to Amelia. He decided to slow his speech like Amelia did, to help the old man understand. "It's okay, sir. We're not with them. We're looking to reconnect with the Brotherhood after being lost. Can you tell us where the leader is?"

"Where is the leader?" the old man said slowly. He shook his head as if dizzy. "To the party!"

The old man tossed his blanket off his legs and swung his feet over the side of the bed. Even though his shirt was off, he still wore his pants and boots. He stumbled past Amelia towards the door. Kase took a step out of the way before the old man could barrel over him.

"This way!" The old man pointed into town and stumbled down the street.

Amelia snuck out the doorway and watched the old man try not to fall down. Kase noticed scars across the man's back, like he'd been sliced and stabbed multiple times by a thin blade. It was consistent with how the people of Camptown lived.

"Should we follow him, or wait until Mardious returns home?" Kase asked.

"Mardious *is* home." Amelia patted Kase on the shoulder. "I thought you knew what that felt like, Demon." Amelia grabbed her dress so it wouldn't drag in the dirt as she followed the old man. The back of the dress still dragged along.

Kase smiled. He did know what that felt like. Kase checked the complex again, but all he saw were shadows. He looked to the sky as he waved his palm over his head, made a walking motion with his two fingers, and gave an Animal Kingdom salute. He wondered if Lenia would return it.

Amelia and Kase followed the old man at a distance to not disrupt his concentration. He didn't seem concerned with them anymore, focused as he was on getting to the party.

Kase ran through the precautions he'd need to take, depending on how many Brotherhood members there were. It was risky enough accompanying Amelia to see Mardious, even if Mardious were alone, but how would Kase fair against a Brotherhood army?

Lenia would help. With her, they could make a clean getaway. That was the best option.

The old man turned down a side street. Kase had spent some time in Camptown with his task force and remembered the general layout. The old man didn't seem to be heading to the main strip.

They soon came upon the first building that had light shining from its windows. The building took up the whole block and had bars on every window. It seemed like the old man was leading them to jail, but Kase had a feeling that it wasn't as it seemed.

"Mary Angella," Amelia muttered.

Kase remembered volunteering with an old woman by the same name. She tended to refugees from the Badlands, but her facility was in Kimroad. The Mary Angella he knew was trustworthy, gracious, and kind. She was also the appropriate age of someone that Amelia might have known while she was alive.

"Is she a friend of yours?" Kase asked.

The old man had reached the stairs to the front entrance. Kase and Amelia stopped trailing him, and watched as he crawled up the stairway like a toddler.

"She helps run this shelter," Amelia said. She clasped her hands together. "I can see why Mardious would be here. He has such a big heart."

Amelia took a few steps forwards, but Kase grabbed her arm. A second later, he was standing with Lenia and Amelia on a roof across from the shelter. Kase relaxed, knowing that he and Lenia were on the same page.

"Why did we—" Amelia started.

"The man said he was taking us to a party," Kase replied. "We should consider the possibilities before we go in there. Would Mary Angella host a party like this?"

"A party like what?" Lenia asked.

"The man's eyes were pitch black, like yours were when you were under the influence of The X potion," Kase said. "From my experience with Mary Angella, she was trying to help people overcome their addictions, not fuel them with more supply."

Amelia peered over the edge while the old man struggled with the door handle of the shelter. Kase and Lenia followed her gaze.

"Addiction affects everyone in different ways." Amelia reached for her collar, but then looked down to her empty hand. "Some have epiphanies, some act out violently, and others escape reality completely. He likely doesn't know what he's saying. But if there's anyone that can help our delusional friend, it's Mary Angella."

"Are you sure you're not walking into a trap?" Lenia asked.

The old man fell back and almost tumbled down the stairs as two others exited the building. The two laughed and hugged the old man and then helped him enter the shelter.

Amelia tugged at her white gloves, ensuring they were both the same length on her forearms. "Trust me, this is a safe place. No party."

Kase wasn't convinced. Entering a shelter with multiple floors was quite different from standing in the doorway of Amelia and Mardious' old home. If they had more time, they'd be able to scout the building and see who entered and exited. That way, if Mardious and his army were there, they could make a plan to corner him.

But if Mardious and his army weren't in the shelter, it would help eliminate a location so Cali could plan their next move.

"If there's danger inside, we'll go dark," Kase said. Judging by the light coming from the building, the rooms were likely lit by lanterns. Kase knew he could dim the flames as needed. "I'll flash a light only in the room we're in."

"I'll try to watch you from up high." Lenia rested her forearms on Kase's shoulders and pulled his hood up for him. "I don't know how good of an angle I can get, though."

Kase stared at Lenia. The darkness made it difficult to see her bright green eyes, but he felt lost in the search for them. He wanted to dance, even though there wasn't any music playing. He wondered if this was because of Amelia, or if it was an effect of being in the Badlands.

"Ready?" Lenia's hand slipped down Kase's chest as she looked back at Amelia, but Amelia didn't appear to be paying attention.

Kase and Lenia both checked the entrance to the shelter. A second later, Lenia had teleported Kase and Amelia to the front porch and disappeared back into the night. Music wafted faintly from inside.

"Do you know this song?" Kase asked. He grabbed the handle and nudged the door ajar to peek in. The hallway was clear. The old man must have made it to the party.

Amelia started to sway. "No. Do you?"

Kase held the door open as Amelia entered, scanning the street behind them before he followed. He needed to stay focused and keep Amelia safe so that she could reach Mardious. He didn't want to be distracted by music.

"No. I don't know any Badlands songs," he replied. He crept through the hallway, but there still wasn't any sign of danger. The rooms they passed didn't have any doors. From the broken crates scattered about, Kase guessed that these rooms were used for storing goods.

"This isn't a Badlands song," Amelia said. The music was getting louder. "It has no heart. No soul."

Kase tried to focus on the melody. The strings were light and lively. The drums were deep but struck with purpose and rhythm. Although the words were mumbled, the singer had a beautiful voice that flowed with the music. Kase wondered how much better the song would be if it had this heart and soul that Amelia spoke about.

Kase and Amelia came to a stairwell. The music was amplified by the conical pattern of the stairway. There were no windows. Kase and Amelia climbed the steps to the third floor where two considerably drunk women met them.

"Pretty dress," one woman slurred.

The other woman reached out, but Amelia swatted her hand away. "Touch with your eyes," Amelia said. Her steps grew quicker.

Kase kept his focus on what awaited them. Multiple doors lined each side of the hallway, but the rooms were dark. A couple stumbled out from one of the doorways, but quickly went back in. Light emanated from a central common area that had noticeable barred doors on the far side of it. The singing was more audible, and now the hoots and laughter of the crowd added to the jovial setting.

Kase pulled his hood a little further forward and kept his head down as they entered the central room through an open gate. Amelia stepped to the balcony and leant over as she took in the party.

A couple hundred people enjoyed the festivities. Some were leaning on the balconies of the floors above; others danced near the main stage a few floors below. The prison went down below ground level, but that wasn't the scary part. Three nooses hung from the arch in the middle of the stage. Below the nooses the musicians played as if oblivious.

Kase remembered the mob in Kimroad. Would the Brotherhood use the same brutal tactics in revenge? Or was this a Marauder hideout? Both armies were ruthless and resourceful but to destroy an army there were better options than hangings.

"Do you see—" Kase started.

"The piano!" Amelia exclaimed, pointing to ground level. "He's there!"

Kase had no time to look where the piano was. Amelia bolted to the corner of the balcony where steel stairs corkscrewed downwards.

"Wait!" Kase yelled as Amelia slipped past swaying drunkards that blocked Kase's path. A few looked Kase's way as he rushed past towards Amelia.

He stumbled down the stairway, but Amelia was already a floor lower on the stairs. As Kase passed the opening to the lower floor, he felt a push from behind.

He didn't have time to react. He rolled down the stairs, his head slamming against the metal rail.

Black spots clouded Kase's vision. His left arm and right arm were tingling. The music blended with the sounds of people yelling. He felt the vibration of the metal stairs as footsteps pounded towards him. Someone grabbed his left arm, and pain shot up through his shoulder. He winced.

"Don't move!" a deep, grumbled voice shouted.

Kase couldn't make out the man's face. The black spots in his vision were blending with the shadows. He hoped his self-healing power would help his vision soon.

Someone shoved him down, grabbed his hands, and held them behind his back. The clinking of shackles was a nice accompaniment to the music.

He didn't fight his imprisonment. Being captured by the Brotherhood in their den was inevitable. He should have been a little more careful.

"Hey!" Amelia shouted. Her red dress stood out, even with his black-spotted vision. "That's my demon!"

"Her too!" A voice shouted from higher up the stairs.

Kase wanted to interject, but he couldn't find the words. He shook his head to try and shake the black spots away, but it only made his head hurt even more. He took a deep breath to try to kick-start his recovery.

"Hey, get your hands off me." Amelia's white gloves flashed in Kase's line of sight, but Kase focused instead on the tingling feeling rippling from his forehead, down his neck, through his shoulder, and down his leg. His healing process had started.

Kase and Amelia were pulled down the rest of the stairs to the main level. By the time they reached the stage, Kase had regained his focus. Now they were led past the dance floor to a lounging area. Kase recognized the warrior sitting in a throne-like chair, but it wasn't who he was expecting.

Jax's eyes widened in fear as Kase and Amelia were shoved to their knees. Amelia huffed, but she didn't seem hurt. Jax stood from his makeshift throne, his hand gripping his sword hilt.

"Look who we found!" The man who had cuffed Kase said proudly.

"What have you done?" Jax yelled. He spun and looked at the balconies. "Stop the music! Archers! Stand guard!"

The musicians stopped playing, but everyone else was still enjoying the night. Kase's captors changed their tune. "We're sorry, boss. They just wandered in. The bounty on the Dandy Lion's head is more than enough to—"

"He can summon dragons!" Jax yelled. He drew his sword. The entire crowd went silent.

Kase remembered the last battle he'd had with Jax. In that battle, Kase had brought a dragon back to life from its scales, but since Jax didn't know how Kase's power worked, it must have seemed like Kase had conjured the dragon out of thin air.

"I come in peace," Kase spoke up. His vision was clear, and his body was now healed. He tried to remember everything he knew about Jax and his team of mercenaries. It didn't really matter why they were in a shelter in the Badlands. He knew they must have been led here by the only thing they cared about: Aileron.

Jax was breathing heavily. Everyone in the room looked at him as he searched the balconies.

Kase turned to Amelia. She was also looking around the room where Jax was.

"Why?" Jax asked. He took one long look around the room, and then stared at Kase. His hand shook as he gripped his sword.

"I heard you were for hire," Kase said. "Do you take payment in gold?"

Jax tapped his foot nervously. "I'm listening," he said. He checked the balconies again.

"We're looking for Mardious Hood," Kase said.

Jax smirked and gave Kase another long look. "He's looking for you, too."

"I want to find him before he finds me," Kase said. "Name your price."

Jax's hand stopped shaking. He studied Amelia, and then smiled at Kase.

"The Underground King's bounty is one million Aileron," Jax said. "It doesn't look like you have that on you."

How much gold was still available at the castle in the Kingdom of Moiras? More than enough to pay the bounty, Kase thought.

"Why do you think I brought my negotiator with me?" Kase turned towards Amelia. "Would you pay one million Aileron to find Mardious?"

Amelia stared back at Kase. She bit her lower lip, and then looked at Jax. "I would, Demon King," she replied. Her curious stare turned to a glare. "But not to this lowlife."

Jax laughed. Kase hoped Jax didn't take it personally and change his mood. Kase's bluff needed to succeed, or else they'd be in for a fight.

"It's not just for Jax," Kase said. "It's for the whole crew." Kase lifted his chin to the balconies. Everyone was watching intently, even if most of them had been partying before. They were all thirsty for a big score.

Amelia followed Kase's gaze. "Still . . . I don't see a single fighter here; only cowards pretending to be tough."

The crowd erupted. A few profanities were shouted. Someone threw a glass at Amelia but missed. Amelia giggled when the glass shattered in front of her.

Jax tried to calm the crowd down, but Kase knew an onslaught was inevitable. He'd lost his bargaining power, and now there was only one way this night would end. Kase concentrated, connecting with the flames lighting the old prison. He briefly flared those in their room, then extinguished all the lights.

The darkness provided a moment of silence, but then the crowd roared again. His captors would not take long to find him and Amelia in the dark, and so Kase would have to buy them time for Lenia to notice his signal.

He felt relief at her soft touch. She must have been watching from one of the windows.

He expected Lenia to teleport them away instantly, but instead he was lit from behind by the flickering fire of Lenia's trident. The light stretched just far enough to reveal Jax's angry expression.

Kase craned his neck, wondering what Lenia was waiting for. Amelia also stared at Lenia in awe, but Lenia was glaring back at Jax. Above her shoulder, the head of her trident was ablaze.

"Get them!" Jax yelled, pointing his sword.

Lenia smiled, but she didn't draw her sword or attempt to free Kase and Amelia for a battle. Instead, she teleported them away.

CHAPTER 10

Full Hearts

Amelia shook her head in disbelief. "You're worth three million Aileron?" Kase finished counting another ten coins and dropped them in the open sac. It was difficult to count any higher with Amelia talking the whole time. He made another tick on his sheet.

"So is Lenia," Talen said. She was sitting on the floor with Kase, but on the other side of the sac. She scooped her coins into the sac and marked her sheet.

"The Demon Queen?" Amelia said in shock. She picked up a necklace with a giant blue gem in the centre of the flower-shaped pendant, then tossed it aside. "But I thought you were the only one who could bring people back to life."

"You don't think she's worth it?" Kase asked.

Amelia studied a different necklace. This one was covered in rubies. She considered it a bit longer than she had the flower pendant, but then dropped it too and continued to count coins. "She's a lot more guarded than you," Amelia said. "Her scars lead to a secret world that no one is allowed to find."

Talen stopped counting and looked at Amelia. "Are they comparable to your old scars?"

"Easy, Shark Knight." Amelia chuckled. "The deep scars are the hardest to explain. The best way to understand them is to live through them together."

Kase thought about the battles that he'd fought with Lenia: the tests in the Quest Series; the training sessions they'd had; the fight for their lives at the hands of the Triple Crown. Thinking about them made him happy, sad, and angry all at the same time.

"That's deep, even for sharks," Talen replied.

"The depths are where the deep things are." Amelia had stopped counting coins and was dragging her fingers along her forearm. "Scars can take you there, if you survive the fight. We lash out, and we take hits, but the scarred grow stronger while the weak die off."

"I'm sorry I took yours away from you," Kase said.

Amelia chucked again. "I still have those scars, Demon King," she said. "I was a little sad before, but now I have an opportunity for more! Want to give me my first new one?" She grabbed a gold-handled dagger that rested on a pile beside her. She flipped the blade and offered the handle to Kase.

"Is that why you tried to start a fight with Jax?" Kase asked.

Amelia scoffed. "He doesn't deserve any scars from us," she said. "But I wanted to see you in action. Did you really summon a dragon out of thin air?"

Kase dropped another ten Aileron into his sac. "Not exactly," he replied. "The dragon was dead. I merely brought it back to life."

"Could you bring one back to life for me here?" Amelia asked.

"Well …" Kase tried to think of a better way to explain himself. He was reluctant to tell Amelia how his power worked, but he didn't want to lie to her and break the trust that he'd built.

Talen's quick thinking saved him. "If you want to meet a dragon, it would be easier to visit them in their home," she said.

"That's true," Kase said. "Have you ever been to Skyland before, Amelia?"

Amelia slumped over and went back to counting. "Are you promising to take me there, Demon King? Just like you promised to show me the mermaids?"

Kase had forgotten about his offer to meet with mermaids. Since they had to wait for Jax to reunite Amelia with Mardious, he wondered if there was an opportunity to spend more time with her. "I'd rather visit mermaids, but it turns out we don't know where they are," Kase said. "Seems like they don't want to play favourites in the war."

Amelia shook her head while she tossed coins into her sac. "Empty promises …"

"That's not entirely accurate," Talen said. "We happen to know where one mermaid is, since she's trapped. Right, Demon King?" She glanced to Amelia, whose attention was now caught by a circular medallion.

Kase looked at his forearm. Anastasia had given him his mermaid design as a token of friendship, but in their group effort to recover the last piece of the doorway of life, Anastasia had given them her greatest gift: sacrificing herself so they could succeed. Now she couldn't leave the Leviathan Triangle because of the magical barrier surrounding the cache.

Amelia perked up. "Is there a 'but' somewhere?"

"Just a small one," Talen replied. "There's a chance we could get eaten by a leviathan."

Amelia put the medallion down and faced Kase and Talen. "What's a leviathan?"

Kase was the only one in the room to have seen the giant ocean beast. It fed on whales, but it could easily swallow a ship whole. A single person wouldn't even be an appetizer; still, it would likely attack anything that entered its limited territory.

"Imagine an underwater dragon, but ten times bigger and with more teeth," Kase said.

"So we'd have to sneak past it to reach the mermaid?" Amelia asked.

"No," Talen said. "The hard part is getting there, because both the leviathan and the mermaid are in the middle of the ocean. We flew there last time, but we don't have any more magic magma to fuel our platform."

Amelia shook her head. "Sounds complicated. Wouldn't it be simpler if the Demon Queen just teleported us there?"

"Lenia can only teleport to places she'd been," Kase said. "She wasn't there last time."

"I thought she only got out of menial tasks," Amelia said. She picked up a coin and tossed it in her sac. "Like counting coins for lowlifes."

"She was dead," Kase said. He tossed his latest coins in and leant back. He needed a break.

Amelia perked up. "So she missed out? Like me?"

"It wasn't a fun adventure," Kase said. He doubted Lenia would want to see a leviathan, but she'd probably want to visit Anastasia. All mermaids were pleasant, but Lenia valued Anastasia's friendship more than she valued the friendships of the other mermaids.

"There are different circumstances this time," Talen said. "I still have coordinates for the location. If you could identify a way to get there, Lenia could likely teleport you back."

"Shark Knight, you're the best!" Amelia clasped her hands, then looked down in deep thought.

Talen's mouth curled up as she made a note in her book.

"You don't think we should actually go, do you?" Kase asked Talen.

"After we drop off this bounty, we will have some time to kill." Talen flipped back to a few pages in her notebook and revealed the map she'd made to get to the Leviathan Triangle. "Were you not looking for date ideas earlier?"

Kase regretted telling Talen of his plans with Lenia. She wasn't helping in the way he thought she would. He was looking for answers, but all she came up with were more questions. "I don't think a death trap like the Leviathan Triangle is a good date idea," he said.

Amelia giggled. "A dangerous adventure is my kind of date," she said. "Do we need the Demon King to make the trip, Shark Knight?"

Talen met Amelia's gaze, but quickly looked away and made another note in her book.

Kase thought about Lenia wanting to fight dragons as a date. Was there much of a difference between fighting dragons and swimming with leviathans? If they could get there, Lenia would be able to teleport away at any real threat.

"Fine, let's pretend this is a good idea," Kase said. "What would we need to prepare?"

Amelia turned to fully face Talen and Kase. She leant her elbows on her knees and supported her chin with her palms. Her eyes seemed to glitter.

"We need a ride," Talen said. "How we get there will dictate what else we will need to pack. Since we no longer have a levitation platform, would we make a new one? Or do we have something else that can take us there?"

"What about Raiden?" Amelia said. "You can ride Maxim."

"The langaras don't travel outside of their sanctuary." Kase tried to think of other options, but only one friend came to mind. "We don't have the supplies for a levitation platform, so it could take a while to build. I think our fastest route is with Turanus."

"I love it," Amelia said. "What's a Turanus?"

"He is a unicorn," Talen said. "Does his teleportation not work the way Lenia's does? Do you think he has been to the middle of the ocean before?"

Kase shrugged. "If not, he can fly us there. He can drop us into the water, and teleport away. At the first sight of a leviathan, Lenia could bring us back."

"If there is swimming involved, I will pass," Talen said. "Plus, I believe Turanus can only take three at a time."

"So, I'm going to ride on a unicorn and meet a mermaid?" Amelia asked. "This is going to be the best date ever!" Amelia went back to counting, but filled her sac faster than before.

Kase continued his counting too. He tried not to let excitement cloud his decision, but it would be fun to see Turanus and Anastasia in the same trip and, with Lenia's ability to teleport them out of harm's way, it was safer than their trip into the Camptown shelter.

The priority was still getting Amelia to Mardious, but to what extent would bonding with Amelia help their cause? Would doing something nice for her help her to convince Mardious to end the war? Would it at least stop her from calling Kase the Demon King?

It was worth a shot, and it was definitely more exciting than staying cooped up in a castle waiting for the potential meet-up.

The trio continued counting until they had filled three sacs. The coins were branded with the old emblem of King Michael, and they weren't accepted around the realm like Aileron was. However, since the coins were made of gold, they would hold some value with mercenaries. Hopefully they would buy them a meeting with Mardious.

There would also likely be more than just Mardious' presence at such a meeting. Poisonous darts, dragonmite bombs, and illusory armies were all in Mardious' bag of tricks. His power could not be underestimated, but Cali,

Dom, and the rest of the Animal Kingdom leaders were already planning for the potential hazards.

The trio finished counting just in time for dinner. Talen left a note on the sacs before they settled outside for an evening picnic. Amelia's favourite spot was near some black rose bushes. She liked how the flowers looked like the night sky.

Kase thought Amelia had fixed way too much food for herself, but it turned out that she had made a special sandwich for Maxim. It wasn't enough to sate Maxim's appetite, but it was a nice gesture. Indeed, Maxim seemed to appreciate the extra scratches around the ear more than anything. Talen even cracked a smile when Amelia laughed with the langara.

When Lenia showed up, she seemed exhausted. Was it their late night and early morning, or was she pushing her training too hard? The quick meal perked her up, but it didn't seem to boost her excitement to visit Anastasia.

"If the other mermaids won't talk to us, why would Anastasia?" Lenia fell back onto the picnic blanket. Kase joined her.

"We share a bond from the adventure that helped bring you back," Kase said. "Even if we don't see her, your presence in the water will alert her that we succeeded."

"Assuming she didn't find a way past the magical barrier," Lenia said.

"That is an interesting point." Talen grabbed her notebook and quill and started scribbling. "We know that only the unalived can pass through the shield, but that's about it. I had made a note to see if there was anything in the library that shows how King Michael made them, but I've been unsuccessful so far."

"Either way, we can leave if there's no response," Kase said. "The harder part will be convincing Turanus to get us there."

"Are we going to keep talking, or are we going to get a move on?" Amelia asked.

Kase craned his neck, expecting to see Amelia impatiently waiting for the rest of the group, but she was still giving Maxim an ear massage.

Lenia sighed. "As much as I enjoy resting in the sunset, it will be nice to actually do something for a change. I'll go take care of that final errand first."

She squeezed Kase's hand, and then disappeared.

"Are you ready?" Kase asked. He sat up and gathered the empty plates from the blanket.

"I can take care of those." Talen put her notebook down and helped Kase clean up.

"What do we need?" Amelia skipped back to the blanket, leaving Maxim lying in the grass.

"Good question." Kase moved to the edge of the blanket and folded it while Talen stacked the plates. "Tal?"

"Take whatever you want," Talen said. "I'm going to stay at the castle library. You reminded me of the magical barriers, and I think it would be useful for us to figure out how King Michael made them. I also need to make a list of supplies for levitation platforms."

"Shouldn't the Shark Knight come on our underwater adventure?" Amelia asked. She reached out for Talen, but Talen nervously pulled her dishes away.

"If there were sharks around, I might consider it." Talen forced a smile. "I will have fun here at the library. It is a nice break from the hustle and bustle of the Animal Kingdom chores."

"All done," Lenia said from behind Kase. She wrapped her arms around his waist and peeked over his shoulder.

"I still can't believe you paid those cowards." Amelia flattened her lapel and smoothed out the sleeves on her summer dress.

"Didn't you give money to the people of the Badlands?" Lenia quipped.

Kase wondered the same thing but held his tongue.

"That's different," Amelia said. "The people I helped fought battles every day but had nothing to show for it. You're rewarding lazy mercenaries for doing nothing. This demon world is upside-down sometimes, giving glory to those that don't earn it."

Kase had to catch himself from dropping his jaw. He was surprised by how Amelia could be so wise and vulnerable at the same time. He didn't think they were doing anything wrong by paying for Mardious' location, but it did seem backwards compared to what Amelia had done. Yet she was the criminal.

"It's a means to an end," Kase said. "When the war is over, we'll have plenty of riches to distribute to everyone so that the unfortunate or oppressed don't have to fight those battles any longer."

"I hope that promise isn't empty," Amelia said. "Are we going to see some mermaids now, or what?"

Kase was impressed by how quickly Amelia pivoted. She was wise beyond her years in one moment, and then ready for a simple escape the next. He wondered if she ever considered the dangers behind her actions, whether she was stealing to help those close to her, or journeying into an unknown abyss where they could get eaten alive.

"Let's go find Turanus," Kase said. He grabbed Lenia's hand and turned towards her, then reached out for Amelia.

"I have an idea of where to find him." Lenia smiled at Kase, tapped her heart, kissed her lips, and pointed to the sky. She extended her hand towards Amelia.

Amelia furrowed her brow and looked to the darkening sky, but then quickly grabbed Kase's and Lenia's hands. It wasn't the date with Lenia that Kase had expected, but they were getting closer to something like a date at least.

CHAPTER 11

Unicorn Nights

For some reason, Kase thought that a unicorn meadow would be filled with rainbows, waterfalls, and pixie dust. Maybe it was different at night?

"Beautiful," Amelia said.

Kase heard no sarcasm in Amelia's voice, and he couldn't make out her expression in the dim starlight. He wondered what she was feeling.

They were far east of the Kingdom of Moiras, and here the sun had fully set. He wondered what might be lurking in the darkness, and so he used his power to try to connect with any nearby creatures. He sensed only rodents and resting birds.

"Interesting, I've never seen them eat lupine before," Lenia said.

"Do they eat purple plants because they're purple?" Amelia asked.

Kase squinted at the meadow, but it didn't help. He didn't see any moving shadows or feel any magical beasts. He was looking in the same direction as Amelia and Lenia were, and yet he couldn't make out the colour of the lupine at all.

"I don't see them," Kase admitted. He knew that unicorns remained invisible until they chose to reveal themselves to those they deemed worthy. He'd been grateful to see Turanus and Luna, even though he hadn't done anything special. Was he different now?

"New friend?" Turanus asked from behind. Kase heard the unicorn's voice in his head, and in the same way that he heard the voices of the langaras. What was different, however, was that Turanus could understand Kase's spoken words.

Kase turned to see Turanus' glowing golden horn. The unicorn's black coat blended in with the darkness, and so Kase was relieved to know he wasn't completely missing things in the meadow. "This is Amelia," Kase said.

Amelia glanced up at Kase in confusion, but then turned in awe when she noticed Turanus. "What scars do you have, Demon Horse?" she asked softly.

Kase was amazed that Turanus had instantly allowed Amelia to see him, since everyone else who met Turanus had to earn the unicorn's trust first. Even Lenia hadn't seen Turanus when Kase had first tried to introduce them.

Turanus teleported to right in front of all three of them. Amelia giggled and clasped her hands together. Turanus kept his distance.

"Sorry to show up like this, but we were hoping you could help us out again," Kase said. He didn't know how long Turanus would stay with them, and so he thought it best to get the inquiry out as soon as possible.

Turanus kept staring at Kase. It was always hard to tell the intentions of the stoic unicorn, but with his golden horn as their only source of light it was even more difficult.

"What are you afraid of?" Turanus asked.

Kase blinked a few times. It wasn't like Turanus to ask about what kind of help he'd need to give, or why they hadn't seen each other in a few months. Kase felt like asking Turanus what *he* was afraid of.

"What happened here?" Lenia asked.

"What do you mean?" Kase asked. Should he be afraid of something? Rather than pretending to scour the darkness, he tried to feel his surroundings again.

"This is where Turanus kept my trident safe, when I was ..." Lenia trailed off.

"Sorry, I was asking Turanus." Kase grabbed Lenia's hand. "He asked me what we're afraid of."

"No, not them," Turanus clarified. "They are fearless. You used to be like them, but something's changed."

"What's there to be afraid of when we're already dead?" Amelia asked.

Maybe Kase was closer to fear than he would admit. Although everyone's experience was different when he brought them back to life, there were common emotions felt by all; fear was one of them. Had he collected enough fear to alter his appearance?

"He clarified that it was just me," Kase said. He let out a deep sigh. He stopped trying to reach out to his surroundings; instead he turned his energy within.

"But you can't die," Amelia said. She turned her attention from Turanus to Kase.

Lenia squeezed Kase's hand. "He's died the most," she said.

"She doesn't need to be burdened with how my power works," Kase said, making sure his secrets weren't spilled. Their plan was to return her to Mardious Hood, after all.

"Is that what you're afraid of?" Turanus asked.

"I'm sorry, I didn't mean to . . . " Lenia tried to pull her hand away, but Kase kept a firm grip.

"It's okay," Kase said. "Death is something I can handle. I am the Demon King, after all." Kase smiled at his own joke, but he didn't hear any laughter. He turned his attention back to the glowing unicorn, partly because Turanus's face was the only one he could see clearly.

"But if Turanus is looking for an honest answer, the thing I'm afraid of most is losing those I love." Kase squeezed Lenia's hand again. "Maybe birds are a close second."

This time Lenia giggled. She pulled herself closer to Kase and draped her arms around him. "Bird fear is contagious."

"That's closer, but it's not quite it, is it?" Turanus said.

"Turanus isn't buying it," Kase said.

Amelia finally took a step forward. She reached out and touched Turanus' snout. He stood stock-still but, surprisingly, he didn't teleport away.

"What is the Demon Horse afraid of?" Amelia asked.

"You can tell her that I'm afraid of a lot of things." Turanus grunted, but Kase thought it was maybe a laugh. He'd never heard Turanus tell a joke before. "But I acknowledge my fears, and don't allow them to stop me from my purpose: my duty to connect. What is your purpose?"

"He says he's afraid of a lot, but left out the specifics," Kase said.

"I don't believe it," Amelia said. She stroked Turanus' snout. "He's not afraid. He's worried."

"Are demons allowed to be worried?" Lenia asked. She held Kase tighter.

"I also feel more worried than afraid," Kase admitted. He thought about his purpose, which varied depending on how far he looked into the future. "I'm worried that Turanus won't help us on our journey, or that we're underestimating the difficulty of the Leviathan Triangle. I'm frustrated with the state of the realm and concerned that our plans will lead to a forever war. And if the war *does* magically end soon, I don't know what I'll do after; assuming we don't lose everything and everyone in the process." Kase squeezed Lenia tighter.

"You're focused on a future that doesn't exist, so much so that you can't see what's right in front of you," Turanus said.

Turanus was right. Kase couldn't even see the other unicorns in the meadow. But seeing unicorns and worrying about the state of the realm were on completely different ends of the scale. Did the weight of one future threat weigh more than all the other little moments in Kase's life?

"You're not alone." Lenia said. She kissed Kase on the cheek. "Maybe we should ask Turanus for our favour: to eliminate one of our worries."

Kase leant his head on Lenia's. He noticed the purple unicorn appear in the distance. She looked his way as she chewed on a lupine. Her blue horn glimmered against her purple coat.

Kase turned his attention back to Turanus and outlined their plan to travel to the Leviathan Triangle. Turanus stood still the whole time, even with Amelia gently combing her fingers through his coat. When Kase finished, he felt a little relief at accomplishing such a small task.

"I will help you," Turanus said. "First, I need a few moments to check on a hunter. I find him concerning. He wears a scorpion medallion that allows him to see unicorns." Turanus disappeared.

Amelia's hand fell. She looked around frantically. "Where did he go?"

"He does that," Lenia said. "Should we go introduce ourselves to his friend?" Lenia pointed towards the purple unicorn.

Amelia didn't acknowledge Lenia's words but, nonetheless, she started off towards the unicorn. Lenia followed a half step behind, but Kase walked at a slower pace.

"He's checking on a hunter," Kase said.

Lenia and Amelia both looked back at Kase and slowed their pace.

"Who would want to hunt a unicorn?" Amelia asked.

"Someone who isn't that smart," Lenia said. "Unicorns can cloak themselves with invisibility as a camouflage against those that might want to cause them harm. A hunter with impure intentions, and someone that Turanus already identifies as a threat, won't ever find a unicorn."

"This one wears a scorpion medallion, apparently," Kase said. "Did you find anything like that in the castle, Amelia?"

"Gross," Amelia said.

Turanus reappeared in front of the group before they made it to the purple unicorn. He knelt and spread his wings in a gesture that invited Kase, Amelia, and Lenia to mount him. The trio accepted Turanus' invitation. They did not ask for an explanation, nor did they ask a single question.

Amelia sat closest to Turanus' head while Lenia secured herself in the middle. Kase wrapped his arms around Lenia, resting his head on the shoulder that wasn't blocked by her trident. As far as date nights were concerned, holding Lenia while riding a unicorn under the stars was better than anything he could have planned. He tried to take Turanus' advice and enjoy the moment instead of worrying too much about the future.

Turanus teleported to the coast, but it was a different starting point than where Talen had led their first journey to the Leviathan Triangle. She'd also calculated the time it would take for them to reach their target based on the speed of the levitation container they'd used for travel. For this trip, however, it was useless information since they didn't know how fast Turanus flew.

This trip was simpler, given they were aiming for a giant leviathan habitat instead of one small portal gateway. As long as Turanus headed in the right direction, they could guess where they needed to be dropped. Kase also believed he'd be able to connect with the leviathans. For one, his power was stronger now. For another, leviathans lacked the cloaking capabilities of unicorns.

The most interesting part of their journey was experiencing Turanus fly. He didn't flap his wings like a bird, and he didn't take a running start like Maxim. Turanus simply opened his wings and galloped into the night sky. It was like riding a horse that moved up and down instead of just side-to-side, and led by a glowing golden horn that pointed the way.

Amelia was surprisingly quiet the entire trip. She swayed a little bit, enjoying the peaceful, moonlit ride as much as Kase and Lenia were. At one point she bounced her shoulders a little bit, as if she were dancing while seated. Kase wondered what music she was imagining for the unicorn trip, but he didn't want to ask and ruin the mood.

After flying for a few hours, Kase felt something in the water below them. It was not just a calling: it sent a tickling feeling straight into his gut. They must have been a hundred meters above the surface, but the connection was strong. "We're here," he said.

"You're sure?" Leina asked.

"How do you know?" Turanus added.

"I don't feel the leviathans, Anastasia, or the boundary. I feel the portal," Kase said.

Kase had visited all four magical portals that King Michael had created to keep the pieces of the doorway of life safe. He hadn't felt this connection with any of them before. So why now? Was it because he was focused on the moment, instead of worrying about the future?

"To the portal!" Amelia said and pointed.

"We don't need to reach it," Kase said. "We're over the Leviathan Triangle, so if we glide down—"

Turanus dropped suddenly, diving for the water's surface. Amelia screamed with joy, but Kase gripped Lenia tighter. Kase tried to yell at Turanus to slow down, but the rush of air into his open mouth made it impossible to speak.

"Thank you for allowing me to help you on your journey," Turanus said. He pulled back up in a loop-de-loop. Everything paused for a split second.

"Thank you—" Kase started.

Turanus disappeared.

Amelia shrieked as Kase, Lenia, and Amelia dropped head-first into the ocean.

Kase splashed about, trying to reach the surface. Which way was up? All he saw was blackness. He reached around for Lenia. He felt the cold water engulf him. Some of it flowed down his throat, like the all-too-familiar lava. For a moment he panicked. A sudden shift from cold to warm water caused him to cough and gasp.

Anastasia's trident lit the surrounding water.

"Well, this is a surprise!" Anastasia exclaimed. She hugged Lenia while her tail gripped her golden trident.

"Sorry to drop in like this," Lenia said. She gave Anastasia a hug in return. It was genuine, and not at all like the awkward tap she usually gave her friends.

Amelia was clutching Lenia's trident, dragging her free hand over her lips as she opened and closed her mouth. She focused on Anastasia's flowing hair, and now reached out to touch it.

"Are we safe?" Kase asked. He held Anastasia's trident, but he still couldn't see into the darkness beyond the trident's light.

Anastasia disengaged from Lenia and swam backwards before Amelia could touch her. "Of course!" Anastasia said. "We're far enough from the boundary that no other mermaids can hear."

"Other mermaids?" Kase asked. He didn't know why they'd be a threat. "I meant safe from the leviathans."

"We feared them, yes, but that was before I got to know them. They're actually quite pleasant," Anastasia said. "Would you like to meet them?"

"Absolutely we would," Lenia said.

"Are you sure it's okay?" Kase asked. "We're not . . . "

Anastasia's trident glowed, lighting the area around them. Behind Anastasia was a sunken ship with stencils of different sea life covering the wood of the hull. It was like looking at Anastasia's mermaid designs displayed in an art museum instead of on the skin.

"Look behind you," Anastasia said.

Kase, Lenia, and Amelia turned. An eyeball twice the height of Kase was practically within arm's reach. The iris was golden like the sun, but at this distance Kase couldn't tell if there was any bloodlust behind the stare. The leviathan was so big that the darkness shrouded its razor-sharp teeth on one end, and its tail and powerful, scaled fins on the other.

"Nice to meet you, Mr. Leviathan," Amelia said.

"Their name is Bubbles," Anastasia said. "Interesting fact about leviathans: they are parthenogenetic, meaning they don't require a male and female to reproduce. This allows them to control their own numbers and live in a balanced ecosystem within their territory. Bubbles is the younger of the leviathans."

"It's strange to think how peaceful the Leviathan Triangle is compared to the land above," Lenia said.

"Well, you should see what happens when a kraken makes it in here," Anastasia said. Bubbles grunted, which sounded like a pack of horses galloping on the ocean floor. "I did collect some nice ink, though."

Anastasia brushed her hair back to show off a new mermaid design on her shoulder. The ink glimmered like a sunrise dancing on the shores, creating the illusion that the two leviathans were swimming.

"That's the most beautiful scar I've ever seen," Amelia said.

"Would you like one?" Anastasia asked. "I've been experimenting with the designs of the new treasures I've found on the ocean floor." Anastasia waved towards the ship. Upon a closer look they saw that not just ocean creatures were drawn on the hull, but many items from the surface as well.

Kase knew that Anastasia didn't offer mermaid designs to just anyone. Was it because Amelia had been brought to the depths with Lenia and Kase, or did Anastasia see what Turanus did? Did Amelia have a way of hiding her criminal past?

"I'd love one," Amelia said. "But not like yours or the Demon King's."

"I have one too," Lenia said. She hiked up her pants and pulled her boot down so that Amelia could see the turtle design on her ankle.

"That's nice," Amelia said. She didn't even look at Lenia. Her eyes were scanning the ship. "Can we get closer to that hole? The right side?"

Anastasia pulled Amelia, Lenia, and Kase towards the ship. Bubbles stayed where they were, but the unblinking eye seemed to study their every move. Kase wondered if Bubbles was curious, or cautious. He also wondered where the bigger one was.

Amelia helped Anastasia guide them towards a design of a scale. There were weights on either side, with the load on the right being heavier than the left. Amelia rubbed her wrist just below her palm, tracing a spot for her design. Anastasia disappeared, and then quickly returned with a vial of ink.

"Is there a story behind your choice?" Anastasia asked. "I'm always curious about the world above and the details that accompany the treasures we hold dear." She opened the vial and used her magic to apply the ink to Amelia's wrist.

"I don't know if there's a particular story about using a scale," Amelia said. "It's more of a symbol. Where I come from, the poor are tossed aside. There was a time where I was able to help some of the unfortunate and give them the opportunity to afford luxuries that seemed out of reach. I was balancing the scales by taking from the rich and giving to the poor. It . . . got me into some trouble, but I would do it all over again if I could."

Anastasia placed her trident on Amelia's wrist. "Thank you for sharing," she said. "I feel like I know a little more of the world above, and it's nice to hear stories of a fellow treasure hunter. Now, this might hurt a little bit."

"All scars do," Amelia said with a smile.

Anastasia's trident grew bright as she pressed it hard into Amelia's wrist. The ink appeared to wrap itself around the middle prong before it seeped back into Amelia's skin. Amelia shrieked, but then started laughing. Anastasia pulled her trident back, and the glow diminished. Amelia's wrist remained bright like the sun.

"That might be my best one yet," Anastasia said.

"Do you say that to everyone?" Lenia asked.

"Maybe," Anastasia said. "But it's also true. I added a little extra feature with this new ink. Amelia, tilt your hand left and right."

Amelia bent her elbow and stared at her palm. She dipped her thumb left, and then turned her hand the opposite way. As she moved, the balance of the scale favoured whichever way her hand pointed.

"That's unbelievable," Amelia said.

"I stand corrected," Lenia said.

"I hope it helps you find balance, in all parts of life," Anastasia said.

Kase wondered how Amelia would find balance in her future. Would she and Mardious return to stealing from the rich and giving their treasures to the poor? Or would they become better? He thought about what Turanus had said about living in the moment, and tried not to worry too much about scenarios that may or may not happen.

Although, a second opinion couldn't hurt.

"Do you ever think about the future, Anastasia?" Kase asked. He felt Lenia grab his shoulder.

"Of course," Anastasia replied. "I think about what new treasures I might find, what Bubbles and Pookie might eat for the day, and what creatures might find their way into the Triangle."

"Do you ever think about getting out?" Kase asked.

Bubbles grumbled a little louder. Kase looked over his shoulder, but still couldn't tell how the leviathan felt based on their unblinking eyeball. He pushed away the temptation to connect with the great beast.

"You have a way out?" Anastasia's voice dropped to almost a hush.

"Not exactly," Lenia said.

"There's a trick with the barrier," Kase said. "In theory, only the unalive can pass through. The three of us have all died and been brought back to life." He gestured to himself, Lenia, and Amelia. "With my power, I could do the same to you, allowing you to come in and out of the Triangle at will."

"But I would have to die first?" Anastasia asked.

Bubbles grumbled louder. This time, Kase connected with the leviathan, and helped calm their anger. He didn't feel the other leviathan around, though, and wondered where they would be.

"Be a demon, like us," Amelia mumbled.

"It's an option," Lenia said. "We didn't come here to make it happen.

We came here to visit, have Amelia meet you, and provide you with the information. You don't have to decide today."

Kase was glad that Lenia understood Anastasia's mood. The mermaid was obviously cautious, and this type of conversation was difficult. Kase didn't even know if his magic worked the same on all creatures, but the research they had done didn't indicate anything contradictory.

"Thank you for your truth," Anastasia said. "If I may be honest, I've been enjoying my time so much in the Triangle that I haven't even thought about leaving."

"Really?" Kase asked. "You don't feel imprisoned?" He felt the guilt release from his shoulders.

"It's so peaceful down here," Anastasia said with a smile. "I'm the first mermaid to report on all my findings in this part of the ocean, and without having the responsibilities of anything else. It's like a vacation that allows me to get some work done, but most of all I get to search for new things and work on my designs. It's like a dream!"

Kase felt Bubble's mood change. He released his power and heard a softer grumble from the leviathan's direction.

Anastasia smiled brightly. "I appreciate the gesture, Kase, but I'm going to have to reject your offer for now," she said. "I hope that doesn't mean you won't visit me anymore."

"That's not what he means at all," Lenia said. "We'd love to continue to visit you, but I must admit, I don't really know where we are. It's easy for me to teleport up above, but I'm lost under the sea."

"We just need to find you the right reference point," Anastasia said. "Unfortunately, there's no land in the Triangle."

Kase thought about the reference point he'd felt when they were on Turanus. "No, but there's a doorway," he said. "I don't know how shallow the water is above it, because I had the helmet create a whirlpool last time."

"I remember," Anastasia said. "You won't be able to stand on it, Lenia, but I know how to create another whirlpool without the helmet."

"Really?" Kase asked.

"This is such a treat!" Anastasia exclaimed. "Bubbles, are you ready for a race?"

Amelia was wearing five different necklaces, and yet her mermaid design had her complete attention. She kept tilting her hand back and forth, making the scale dance on her wrist. "How much longer?" she asked.

"You're welcome to help," Lenia said. She finished flipping through another book and tossed it to the ground. She reached back to the shelf and slid out the next book in the row.

Kase dropped his book too. It was filled with useful information on what types of bait worked best for certain fish, but it wasn't anything new. They were more interested in finding lost secrets about King Michael that might offer insights or lessons from ancient times, but none of the passages they'd found so far were different from any they'd found at the castle.

"Can we get something to eat first?" Amelia asked.

Kase was famished too. After their flight with Turanus, adventure with Anastasia, and curious search through the Leviathan Triangle cache, it had been a long time since they'd eaten. But they didn't want to waste their opportunity to learn something from the past that might help them grow for the future.

"Once we leave, we won't be able to return unless Anastasia, Bubbles, and Pookie help us again," Lenia said.

"Can't you teleport some lobster to us?" Anastasia asked. "Add some butter, maybe some fresh biscuits, and a few bottles of white wine . . ."

Kase's stomach rumbled. He scanned the bookshelves they hadn't searched yet and wondered if they needed a better plan to review the information. It suddenly seemed like they'd need another trip if they wanted to be thorough. Maybe they could bring Talen to the source, rather than pick something out for her?

"My power doesn't work like that," Lenia said. "I can't summon objects out of thin air or travel directly into caches." The portals made it too difficult for Lenia to pinpoint her location. Of all the caches they'd visited, this one seemed like the most magical.

It felt like they were in a cavern wrapped in seaweed, but instead of rock walls, there was an invisible barrier that kept the water from pouring in. Giant stalks of seaweed drifted slowly back and forth, but the blue light from the water filtered through the magical plants to illuminate the area.

Unlike the caches in the Eidolan desert, Jenim Island, and Skyland, the stairs inside this cache led upwards from the portal entrance to platforms above. Water had crept in through the open portal gate before it closed but drained out the sides to what seemed like a black abyss of nothingness.

Kase, Lenia, and Amelia had started on a circular stone platform at the bottom level and then taken a spiral staircase up to an empty platform where the piece of the doorway of life had likely sat. The third level held jewels, gold, and fashionable necklaces that Amelia had combed through meticulously. She was torn between her favourites, but Kase liked the one with a black jewelled sheep on it.

The fourth and final level held bookcases filled with journals, logs, and maps. The platforms were large, and yet their edges did not nearly reach the spherical seaweed walls of the magical cache.

"Maybe there's a spell in one of these books that can create some dates for you." Lenia flashed a page from the recipe book she was holding. The page showed an illustration of a chicken pot pie.

Amelia sighed. She pushed herself up from her cross-legged position on the floor. "My order was lobster with butter and biscuits," she said. "If you really want dates, then I'll summon some here for you." She stumbled to the opposite end of the shelves from where Kase and Lenia had started.

"Should we tell her you're allergic to seafood?" Kase asked. He tossed his fictional story about pirates to the floor and picked out a thick, brown, leather-bound book from the same shelf Lenia that had taken her book from.

"I don't want to dampen her motivation." Lenia tossed her recipe book to the floor. "But if she succeeds and provides a lobster feast, just make sure you don't kiss me with any spare seafood on your lips."

Kase stopped flipping pages and turned to Lenia. He wrapped his arms around her and gave her a quick peck. "I'll be careful," he said.

He thought Lenia would appreciate their kiss in the cache, and so he was surprised to see her jaw drop. She was looking past Kase. Now she grabbed his hand to pull him towards Amelia. A glow surrounded Amelia's arm. It was similar to the glow that Kase had first felt when he crossed the barrier to the Kingdom of Moiras.

"Are you stuck?" Lenia asked.

Amelia pulled her arm back. She stretched her fingers and turned her hand from side to side as she studied it. "I thought it was a bubble, but it isn't wet," she said.

Kase and Lenia both rushed to the bookcase and reached out at the same time. Their fingertips dipped through the shield barrier. There were only five books in the entire bookcase, which is why they had ignored it in the first place. Kase grabbed the lone book from the fourth shelf, while Lenia grabbed one of the two from the third.

"Is this more demon magic?" Amelia asked.

Kase studied the cover of the book he had picked out. There were hieroglyphics pressed into the leather, but he didn't know what the symbols meant. One had squiggly lines, another had a moon with three dots inside of it, and one was a head of an angry goat. The symbols reminded him of the first cache in the desert, but he wondered now if it were a sign of something evil.

"I don't believe it," Lenia said. Her book was wide open as she filtered through the pages.

"Are you sure we should be reading these?" Kase asked. "This is the same shield that keeps the leviathans and Anastasia separate from the rest of the realm. Only the unalived can access this shelf, but why?"

"Because it contains the knowledge to make these barriers," Lenia said excitedly. She flipped her book towards Kase, which showed a sketch of a king standing under a blue semi-circle while a war was being fought around him.

"Does that mean we can go eat now?" Amelia asked.

Kase chuckled. He was glad that Lenia and Amelia both had their priorities straight. Lenia and Kase grabbed the other books on the magical shelf, and they teleported out of the cache clutching these precious books, the most valuable souvenir they had found. They had definitely earned their dinner of lobster and white wine.

CHAPTER 12

Lies Beneath

Kase finished pouring the rest of his and Lenia's potion. They'd followed the instructions in King Michael's journal perfectly, which turned out to be fairly easy, since most of the items were common: apple seeds, the bark of an oak tree, wilted rose petals, rainwater, and sheep's wool. The only tricky item was the blood of the unalive.

But the Animal Kingdom had plenty of blood to spare.

"Are you sure you mixed it right?" Kase's uncle, Eowin, asked.

"The notes didn't mention a reaction," Lenia said. "It's so … sneaky! It looks like sludge, even though it contains incredible magical properties. You can feel it, right, Dandy?"

"Get back," Kase said. He didn't want to jinx it by getting involved in more 'what if' scenarios. He and Lenia had agreed to consider the time spent preparing the mixture as part of their morning date. And it had been fun, but now he needed to focus. He pushed his uncle away with the hand not holding the potion bottle.

"Where should I stand?" Eowin asked.

"Come with me, Uncle Eowin," Lenia said. She gently tugged Eowin towards the centre of the circle that Kase had made with the potion.

Kase stretched out his arms, concentrated on the bloody mixture, and took five deep breaths. He remained calm as he waited for the tingling to begin. He noticed Lenia do a scan of the field, which made him feel safer.

Cali had been ecstatic about their discovery of King Michael's journals, and Talen had wasted no time going through them. Not only did they discover how the magical boundaries were made—through a powerful potion—they also learned the locations where King Michael had used them. The Leviathan Triangle and the Kingdom of Moiras were the two locations Kase was familiar with, but there were other intriguing spots on Skyland, in the Centaur Mountains, and within the Anaconda Rainforest. Kase wondered what treasures King Michael was protecting, or what kind of beasts he had trapped within the boundaries.

New adventures would have to wait; for now, Kase needed to focus on creating a boundary on his aunt and uncle's farm: the potential meeting spot with Mardious Hood.

Kase sensed the mixture seep deeper into the ground. It felt like he was bringing a garden back to life. The roots of the mixture dug into the soil, and a magic barrier rose to the surface. He couldn't see the barrier, but he could feel it grow.

Unlike how plants would normally reach for sunshine on their own, Kase was able to control the shape of the barrier. Talen had instructed that the strongest shape for this plan would be a dome, but Kase wasn't able to limit it that much. He ended up creating an entire sphere with one half of the barrier covering the surface, and the other half cutting into the earth below.

Kase opened his eyes. "I think that's it," he said. He couldn't feel his power working anymore, but he could still sense the boundary's existence.

"Just one more step," Lenia reminded him.

The barriers prevented the passage of the living in one direction only. This was how carnivorous beasts, such as the leviathans, could be contained on one side, while the beast's prey could enter their cage from the other.

The barriers could also be turned outwards, preventing anything living from entering rather than leaving. To set the direction, Kase, as the creator of the boundary, would have to be the first to cross.

Kase stepped towards the edge. He did not slow his pace, nor study the magical sphere before he slipped through. He barely noticed the blue tint surround him as he passed through the invisible shroud.

Eowin's staff fell forwards, but he caught it just before dropping it.

"Amazing," he said.

"You're up, Uncle." Lenia slapped Ewoin on the back.

Eowin gripped his staff tighter. "Does it hurt?" he asked.

"It's not like bringing someone back," Kase said.

"I meant for me." Eowin laughed nervously, his staff still gripped tight.

Lenia patted Eowin on the shoulder. "Let me go first." She stared at Kase, but her eyes shifted left as a smile crept onto her lips.

Lenia stretched out her arm and walked towards Kase. Her pace slowed in front of the boundary. Could she feel its presence? Before Kase could ask, Lenia broke the threshold, and a blue glow enveloped her fingertips.

Lenia's arm shook vigorously. She stopped dead in her tracks and let out a scream.

Worry flashed across Eowin's face, but Kase had seen this act before. Lenia had made the same joke when she had once found her lost trident a few years ago. Seeing the look on Eowin's face made Kase appreciate how funny it must have been when Kase reacted the same way.

Lenia finally broke down and laughed. "Sorry, Uncle Eowin," she said. "I couldn't resist." She brought her arm down and danced through the barrier, hugging Kase when she met him. Kase squeezed her tight.

"Good one, Lenia," Eowin said. He didn't seem convinced, but he understood the assignment. He cautiously stepped forwards, approaching the boundary the same way Lenia had.

Eowin didn't joke around with his passage. When a blue hue first enveloped *his* fingertips, he was able to yank his hand back through after touching it. He took a step so that half his body was through. He was then able to take a step back again. Finally he made it all the way through and then reached back, but the boundary blocked his entry.

Eowin looked approvingly at Kase. "Well done, Super Wizard." Eowin tapped the boundary with his staff, but not even that made it through.

"Nice nickname," Lenia said. She squeezed Kase, and then broke back towards Eowin. She took Eowin's staff, and then walked back through the boundary with staff in hand.

Everything seemed to work perfectly so far, but Kase had one more test. He walked up to his uncle, grabbed his hand, and entered the sphere. To his surprise, his uncle's arm came through. With Kase holding onto his uncle, Eowin was able to enter the boundary from the opposite side.

"You didn't reverse the direction of the shield, did you?" Lenia asked.

Eowin stood proud. "I'm on it." He strolled back through the boundary, pivoted like a marching soldier, and then smacked his forehead on the dome as he tried to enter. He and Lenia both laughed.

"This changes everything," Kase said. "We can go back and help Anastasia without having to unalive her!"

"Maybe," Lenia said. "But it also exposes us to our enemies. We've brought some of them back already, and if they help others to cross the boundaries, they lose their effect."

Kase's mood shifted. "And we're giving our greatest enemy a trusted, unalived ally who still considers us demons," he said.

Lenia grabbed Kase's hand. "We're vulnerable, but it's okay," she said. "Your protection isn't foolproof, but it still gives us an advantage. All we can do now is stick to the plan and figure out the rest if it gets off track. Stay in the moment."

Lenia craned her neck and puckered up. Kase kissed her deeply.

"Okay . . . I know this was a mornate for you two, but I do wish this boundary wasn't see-through," Eowin said.

Lenia broke off the kiss and chuckled. Eowin had his back to Kase and Lenia.

"Sorry, Uncle," Kase said. "Let's get ready for the next phase."

An hour before the appointed meeting time, Kase, Cali, Sharaine, Dom, Lenia, and Amelia gathered at the farm, secure behind the new magic barrier. They didn't have confirmation that Mardious Hood would show up, or that Jax had even contacted him, but they were prepared for a standoff.

Kase felt relieved to have a trick up his sleeve when facing Mardious. It was better than solely relying on Lenia for a quick escape. Still, he wasn't going to allow himself to underestimate his adversary this time.

"Have you worn this before?" Amelia asked. She sniffed her A.K. helmet.

"No. Does it smell?" Kase asked. He reached for the white lion helmet with the green mane. Talen had made it for him as an alternate, but he always stuck with his golden mask with the red mane; he liked the colours better.

Amelia pulled the helmet close. "It doesn't . . . I just assumed it would smell like you, Demon King." Amelia flipped her hair back and put her helmet on. "How do I look?" She twirled in her white dress, extending her arms as she modelled her outfit.

"Maxim would be proud," Kase said with a smile.

Amelia's dress was a little oversized, but that didn't seem to bother her. The bottom fringe was already dirty, a few loose threads dangled at the shoulders, and a small tear was visible in the side. The rough edges suited the honorary Dandy Lion, and Amelia seemed happy to wear it.

Sharaine's choice of A.K. outfit was a little different. She had chosen an elephant mask complete with large ears, a trunk that dipped well below her chin, and a slot for the eyes. It was certainly not a mask fit for battle as it was heavy and awkward, but it was the symbol that Sharaine had chosen to represent her family. She also didn't wear matching armour, opting instead for a bulkier cloak.

Cali was wearing her wolverine outfit, her face visible through the mouth crafted into the mask. Dom still embraced the rooster persona that Kase had given him and was ready with bow and arrow for any long-range threats that might come their way. They had both been tested in many battles, and they were ready to fight many more.

"No gloves today?" Lenia asked.

"I don't think I'll wear gloves ever again," Amelia said proudly. She tilted her wrist to make her mermaid design dance.

"Maybe I should ditch my gloves too," Kase said. The reason he had worn his gloves in the first place was to hide his mermaid design, since no one else in the realm had the sword, fire, and quill markings on their forearm.

Now that everyone knew his identity, were the gloves really necessary? They did protect his hands in a fight, but maybe he could wear something better?

"I like them," Lenia said.

"So I should wear them for our date tonight?" Kase joked.

"Depends." Lenia giggled. "Are you saying that to figure out where we're going, or are you genuinely thinking of wearing your Dandy Lion gloves on our date?"

"Both." Kase squeezed Lenia's hand.

Lenia looked away bashfully, but quickly became serious. "Well, let's not get too ahead of ourselves. They're early."

Kase turned to look in the same direction and noticed a horse-drawn cart in the distance. It was accompanied by a few single riders on horseback. He couldn't make out who was riding yet, but hopefully it was their invited guest.

The A.K. had brought two sets of chairs, one on each side of the barrier facing each other. Inside their dome of safety, Cali and Sharaine sat up front, while Kase, Amelia, and Lenia sat behind them. Dom stood behind everyone, bow in hand. He was technically the lookout, but Kase also prepared his lightning attack by drawing a nearby storm closer. He had plenty of time to 'charge his power,' as Lenia liked to put it. He wondered if lightning would be able to penetrate the boundary.

Kase and Lenia both kept swivelling their heads until the cart and driver were close enough to recognize. Mardious held the reins. He was wearing a tattered, black, hooded cape. Two female heads swirled around him. They were the same illusion Kase had seen when he had brought Sharaine back to life. And now he finally made the connection: both heads looked like Amelia.

Kase felt fingers grip his knee. Amelia had one hand on his leg, and one hand on Lenia's. Kase checked with Lenia. She was looking his way. Amelia's excitement was a little painful, and so Kase grabbed her hand instead. She clutched it tight.

Mardious stopped the cart. Jax was the rider closest to them on Mardious' left. The other three riders remained behind the cart. Kase tried to connect with their horses and felt calmness fill each beast's heart.

Jax took a long look at the A.K. "Do I get paid now?"

Cali stood. "The second half of your payment is already sitting in a secure location. We will give you coordinates once we've transported the hostages."

"The hostages are not his to release," Mardious sneered. The darker, more sinister Amelia was whispering into Mardious' ear. The softer, tiara-wearing Amelia had a blank, empty expression.

Sharaine removed her helmet and stood. "Please, have a seat," Sharaine's voice cracked, but she quickly regained her composure. "This gathering is peaceful. We hope that everyone here obtains the resolution most beneficial to them."

Mardious smirked while the Amelias bounced from shoulder to shoulder. They looked like real demons, with their ghostly, terrifying features. Kase felt like he wasn't the Demon King after all.

"Look, I'm not here to talk," Jax said. "I was asked to deliver. If you give me my gold, then I'll leave you alone to . . . have your fun."

Mardious laughed to himself. The Amelia heads whispered and giggled.

Cali looked over her shoulder to Lenia and gave a slight nod. A moment later, Lenia teleported next to Jax's horse. She stood with her sword drawn, punctured on its tip was a letter that Cali had prewritten with the coordinates for Jax's bounty. Lenia pointed the sword at Jax. It all happened so fast that Jax didn't even have time to reach for his weapon.

"You're right," Cali said. "You delivered on your promise. Now, you may leave."

Jax smirked, took the note, keeping an eye on Lenia as he read it. "I'll be there tonight," he said. "In case you want a rematch." He grinned at Lenia.

Lenia casually sheathed her sword, ignoring Jax's look. She teleported back to her seat. "I have a new date idea," she said to Kase.

Kase couldn't help but smile. If everything went to plan, he'd be spending the entire night with Lenia. For that, he'd gladly support her in a victory over Jax.

Jax turned his horse away from the group and signalled to the remaining riders. They left, leaving Mardious alone. Kase wondered where the rest of the

Brotherhood could be. Were they hiding with the hostages? Were they planning an ambush from the nearby forest? Were the Amelia heads the only illusion?

Mardious hopped off the cart and approached the A.K. The Amelia heads swirled around him, but Kase focused on what Mardious wore beneath his cloak: two straps that criss-crossed over his torn undershirt; both straps held glass vials filled with liquid of various colours. Dangling from Mardious' neck was a silver chain with a butterfly, a gold chain with a scorpion, and a medal similar to the ones the Liberati had won from the Quest Series.

Amelia hugged Kase's arm. Her helmet dipped behind Kase's shoulder, as if she were trying to shield herself from something scary but couldn't turn her curious eyes away. Kase wondered if she was nervous or exhilarated. Maybe she was both?

Instead of sitting down, Mardious grabbed the closest chair, pulled it across his body, and spun it towards the crew. Before the chair could touch down, it bounced back from the magic barrier.

Mardious kept hold of the chair as he watched the blue shimmer where the legs had struck. "New trick?" He grinned.

"Please, have a seat," Cali said cordially. She waved her hand, gesturing for Mardious to take his place for the conversation.

Mardious switched his attention to the barrier. He let go of his seat and held both palms out like he was about to push open a door. When Mardious had been High Wizard Zuke he had always worn gloves. Now his hands were bare, and Kase spied a scar across his palm. With Amelia's obsession with her scars revealed, Kase wondered if she knew how deep Mardious' scar reached.

Mardious pressed against the blue glimmer, but he couldn't go further. He felt his way up and down. The blue glow emanated from every touch but disappeared when the pressure let up.

"How did you get in?" Mardious asked.

Dom fired an arrow from behind Kase, overtop of the seated A.K., through the protective barrier, and into the back of the wooden chair. The chair tipped over softly and landed with a quiet thud.

"Sit down," Dom warned. The rasp of wood and feathers being drawn from Dom's handcrafted quiver were a welcoming sound, even if it was meant as a warning to Mardious.

Mardious reached for the spot where the arrow had escaped the barrier. He tapped his fingers, but the glimmer held strong. The Amelia head with the more evil expression whispered something into Mardious' ear.

"Well played," Mardious muttered. He stepped back, pulled the tilted chair back up, and brushed the seat clean. As he sat down, the Amelia heads vanished.

"Thank you for accepting our invitation," Cali started. "We come to you as allies in this chaotic time of war with a proposal for peace that brings the Brotherhood, Marauders, and New Realm Order back together."

Mardious leant forwards, resting his elbows on his knees. He rubbed his face with his left hand and gave an exaggerated sigh. He rolled his right index finger forward, as if to hurry along the speech that Cali had been practicing.

"As a sign of how serious we are with this proposal, we have brought you what your heart desires most," Cali continued. "In return, we will—"

"Are we really going through with this song and dance?" Mardious rolled his eyes and stared at Cali. "I came here in good faith, expecting you to deliver the doorway. Yet, I don't see it anywhere." He raised his arms and turned from side to side.

"We will take our families home," Cali continued, as if Mardious hadn't interrupted. "We will create an inclusive environment so that all constituents of the realm are respected and appreciated as valued members of our community. We will embrace each other's beliefs and provide open forums so that people with different backgrounds can share their diverse experiences and views. We will introduce actions to proactively reduce institutional barriers and promote equal opportunity for all."

Mardious sighed again and stared up at the sky. "When was the last time you created a policy?"

"We are not policy makers," Cali said off script. "But we will—"

"The answer is never," Mardious interrupted again. "I commend you on your past actions, as the Animal Kingdom collective. When you showed off the power of the doorway and brought back a dragon to destroy the castle of the Triple Crown, you sparked a revolution that will bring about change."

Kase did not want to relive the past, and he did not enjoy Mardious' cheap summary of their intentions. The demonstration of his power was to show the world the corruption of the Triple Crown, and the lengths that High Scholar Sheese, High Warrior Mac, and High Wizard Zuke—aka Mardious Hood—would go to. Removing them from power was the goal, not all-out war.

"We are not responsible for this war, yet we have a voice in the solution," Cali said sternly.

Mardious laughed. The Amelia heads returned and laughed with him as he stood. "Just because you have ideas does not mean that you know what's best for the realm," he said. "You're too young and naïve to understand. To build a stronger community, it first needs to suffer. Violence, destruction, and death are all part of setting the world on fire. I thought that was a lesson I taught you."

Mardious strode a few paces towards where Kase sat. He stared at Kase and grinned. The Amelia heads smiled along with twisted, cruel smiles.

Kase felt nails dig into his knee. "Please get me out of here," Amelia said softly. She tried to wedge her helmet beyond Kase's shoulder.

Kase turned to her instead. He held her hand, softening her grip. "It's going to be okay," Kase said.

"Is there something you want to say to me, Dandy Lion?" Mardious sneered. The Amelia heads echoed Kase's name, emphasizing the 'Dandy' part.

Kase looked to Cali, who gave him a reassuring nod. She'd predicted that Mardious would engage with Kase if things were working in their favour. It was time for him to pitch into the politics, even if he felt like an imposter.

"Yes. You forced me and my friends to risk our lives for the people we care about most," he admitted. "I now bear the burden of bringing the deceased through the darkness and back to the light—even if it sometimes makes me feel like a demon."

Kase squeezed Amelia's hand. Amelia chuckled and moved away from his shoulder.

"Well then," Mardious said smugly. "Allow me to relieve you of your burden."

Kase focused on the Amelia illusions as they glared at him. He felt the darkness that suffused Mardious, and it was like some suffocating cloak around his shoulders. "No," Kase said sternly. "Allow me to relieve you of yours."

Kase turned to the real Amelia. "It's time," he said. He stood, pulling at her hand, but not forcing her to stand. He still sensed her nervousness, but she didn't pause too long. She stood with Kase and they left their row together, and then both of them stepped towards the barrier.

Mardious took a step back. He pulled a vial from one of his chest straps and steadied his thumb on the cork. The Amelia heads swirled around like wolves getting ready for a kill. As strong as Mardious was trying to look, Kase saw emptiness in his eyes.

"I was hoping for a fight." Mardious laughed, popped the cork off his vial, drank the purple liquid inside, and then tossed the empty vial aside.

Now he gripped his dagger tight. He swayed from side to side, the emptiness in his eyes filling with something else, something worse.

Kase stopped. Amelia tapped him on the arm and stepped closer to Mardious, being careful not to break the barrier. She took a deep breath, removed her helmet, and brushed the hair away from her face.

Mardious stopped dead in his tracks. The Amelia illusions disappeared.

Amelia stared at Mardious for what seemed like an eternity.

"You're so . . . hardened," she finally said.

Mardious' head blurred. It was like he was twitching, but it was happening so fast it was difficult to focus on his features. The only things that stuck out were his bright, purple eyes. Was it a new illusion? Kase focused on the area around Mardious to see if he could feel any magic or manipulation of the elements.

"My world isn't ready for you, babe," Mardious said. His words ran together, and they sounded a little higher-pitched.

"Are you going to let those people go?" Amelia tilted her head at the cart while holding fast to Mardious' gaze.

Kase felt the air around Mardious stir. It was as if a sudden rush of wind had blown between Mardious and the cart, kicking up dust along its path. For a brief second, Kase thought he saw Mardious' form blur towards the cart, but then he blinked, and Mardious returned to where he was standing.

"They are free," Mardious slurred.

Just after he said those words, the gate on the back of the cart flung open so hard that it bounced back on its hinges. It didn't seem like magic had opened the door, but Kase didn't trust how easily Mardious had released the prisoners.

"Wait," he said to Lenia before she could teleport away. He held his fist high, signaling a hold position. Sharaine stood, but Lenia stayed seated and focused on Kase.

Kase turned back to Mardious. The gust of wind settled, along with his swirling cloak. Kase had a theory about the liquid that Mardious had just drunk. "What's in that potion?"

"It's not a potion." Mardious' words were still slurring together. "It's an elixir."

"You used it on yourself?" Amelia asked.

Mardious nodded with exaggerated slowness. "If we had enhancements like this, instead of mere potions, we would have escaped." His high-pitched voice held a longing sadness. Tears swelled up in his eyes, reflecting their purple light.

Mardious opened his arms wide and stepped forwards, but the barrier continued to hold strong. When had he sheathed his dagger? Kase wondered.

Despite his worries, Kase dropped his arm. Lenia disappeared with Sharaine, then reappeared beside the cart. Their voices didn't carry far enough, but Sharaine seemed overjoyed to meet the prisoners. After Sharaine greeted the prisoners with smiles and hugs, Lenia teleported them away in groups of twos and threes. Now Sharaine dropped to her knees and hugged her sister.

Cali stood but said nothing. She had discussed how delicate it might be when Mardious saw Amelia, and so their plan was to let things play out naturally.

Kase studied Mardious' elixirs further, noting the different colours. He wondered what other enhancements there might be, and where Mardious had learned of the mixtures.

Amelia moved closer to the barrier and reached out, her attention on the dangling medallions that Mardious wore. Her fingers broke the barrier, pushed past the Quest Series medal, and caressed the golden scorpion.

"You're the one hunting unicorns," she said.

Mardious' hands still rested on the barrier. Kase was relieved to see that the barrier allowed Amelia to touch Mardious' dangling accessories without allowing him to pass through.

"They provide key ingredients for elixirs." Mardious gently took Amelia's hand, twisting it until her mermaid design faced him.

Kase checked on Lenia. It looked like she'd teleported more than three-quarters of the prisoners away. There didn't appear to be any rejects, and so Sharaine's warning of Mardious slipping some Brotherhood members into the mix must not have been Mardious' plan. Had the leader of the Brotherhood really come with only a few magical elixirs for protection?

"Clever," Mardious said, still examining Amelia's wrist. An Amelia head appeared on the side opposite Kase, but her features were blurred.

"Don't squeeze so hard," Amelia said. She released the scorpion medallion and tried to jerk her hand back. Mardious kept his grip tight. The second Amelia head appeared.

Should he intervene? Kase mentally reached for the nearby storm, but he hesitated before bringing down a bolt. Clouds rolled in closer, rumbling with pent-up electricity. Kase looked to Cali. Her brow was furrowed in confusion, but she didn't signal for Kase to act. Dom had an arrow ready but not drawn.

"Yes, Amelia does have a scar," Mardious slurred. "Here!"

Kase turned his eyes back, but Mardious had already drawn and swiped with his dagger. A dark line of blood appeared on Amelia's forearm just below the base of the scale of her design.

"Don't!" Amelia yelled. She yanked her arm back, but Mardious' grip was unbreakable. She stumbled backward and he followed, stepping through the barrier. His free arm, the one not holding Amelia's wrist, moved in such a blur that Kase couldn't see his hand or his dagger.

Kase lunged forwards, but before he could draw his sword, something ploughed into him with such force that he fell to the ground, ribs cracking. It was Mardious; Kase saw the flash of the Mardious' bright, purple eyes as he charged him. Belatedly, he heard the sound of Amelia hitting the ground.

Kase felt the blade of a dagger pierce his chest; the strength of the blow had sliced clean through his Dandy Lion armour.

Amelia gurgled. It sounded like she was having a seizure.

Kase tried to push Mardious off him. He managed to get his right forearm wedged against Mardious' neck, but he still couldn't budge the thin wizard. Between one breath and another, Mardious broke his grip and sliced Kase's arm.

It felt as if an army of ants were crawling inside the cut in Kase's chest. Mardious must have added a potion to his dagger, just like he had with Sharaine. Kase tried to drive back the phantom ant army, but he couldn't control it and the agonizing crawl intensified.

An arrow flew over Kase. It should have struck Mardious, but he had somehow disappeared. The arrow hit the chair outside the barrier with a thud. A second later, Dom shrieked.

Kase's entire left side went numb. He couldn't resist the poison further. He could only hope that his healing powers would kick in so that he could at least suppress it. His head dropped to the side, just in time to notice Dom flop to the ground. Mardious was now holding Cali in the air by the neck.

"Where is the doorway," Mardious slurred.

Cali gripped Mardious' arm. Her legs flailed, but her kicks weren't landing. She struggled to breathe. Mardious showed no concern that she couldn't speak.

Kase's eyelids were falling, and so he focused all his energy on his surroundings. It felt as if he were pulling a blanket down from the sky, thread by thread, wrapping it around his fingers until he had enough of it to tug.

At the sound of Cali hitting the ground and gasping for air, he forced his eyes open. Mardious' arms were limp, and his chest rose and fell as if he'd just completed a morning run. The illusionary Amelias circled around his head once more. The wizard pulled another purple vial from his bandolier. He popped the cork off the top and brought it to his lips.

Kase yanked his magical blanket with all his might. A crackle boomed as a bolt of lightning struck the barrier. Like a rock tossed onto a frozen pond, the lightning rippled across the shield, but it didn't break through.

Kase was disappointed, yet relieved that his magic held strong.

Mardious looked towards Kase and smiled. "Almost," he said. He drank his elixir and threw the vial to the ground. He seemed pleased when it shattered magnificently.

Suddenly, the rampaging wizard disappeared.

Lenia returned and knelt next to Kase.

"Poison," he muttered. He choked as something rose in his throat.

"We're safe," Lenia said.

Lenia lifted Kase's shoulders, as she did, his head to fell to the right. Mardious was lying on the ground outside the barrier where Lenia had dropped him. He pushed himself up and slowly stood. The Amelia heads swivelled to face the barrier; Mardious' glare soon followed.

"Amelia looks dead," Lenia said. "Cali, the hostages are secure. What's next?"

Cali used a chair to pull herself up. She brushed the dirt off her Wolverine uniform and adjusted her helmet. "Let's get out of here and regroup." Her voice was raspy, and she sounded shaken.

Mardious ran to the edge of the boundary. "No!" he yelled. He pounded on the barrier, blue light radiating from his fists. His eyes slowly changed from brown to purple as his fists beat faster, blurring in the air.

Kase's eyelids fluttered down, but he forced them back open one last time and saw that he was back in the caves of Jenim Island. He couldn't feel the right side of his body.

He didn't fight his heavy eyelids anymore. Darkness.

CHAPTER 13

Lost Soul

"It couldn't have been her," The Shadow said.

Mardious stopped twiddling his fingers. His golden levitation carriage landed softly on the ground. He pulled both levers to ensure that none of the mixture that fuelled the flight of the carriage stayed burning.

"She wasn't an illusion though, was she?" The Angel responded. "She could be touched."

Mardious closed his eyes. His head swayed. The voices became louder the longer he stayed awake. They weren't wrong, though.

He hopped off the seat of the carriage and landed flat-footed on the Skyland terrain. He checked over both shoulders, but no dragons had followed him this time. It seemed like the higher he flew, the less likely he was to be spotted.

"Her eyes spit the truth," The Shadow said.

"They didn't have that spark," The Angel agreed.

Mardious grabbed the second-last orange vial in his bandolier. His throat instantly went dry. He hated this elixir the most. He wondered if dragons felt the same way when they blew fire.

He checked over his shoulders again. The warm glow from the rivers of lava surrounding the region provided enough light to see across the barren shale. There were hills of caverns in the distance, but they were too dark to see into. There used to be a cavern where Mardious was standing, but he had destroyed it, leaving only the beautiful, white portal gateway.

Mardious carefully pulled the cork out of this vial. "Can't stop, won't stop," The Angel reminded him. He brought the vial to his lips and tried not to gag as he chugged the bitter liquid.

He fluttered his fingers, imagining he was playing one of Amelia's favourite songs. He already felt the effects of the elixir and jammed his fingers harder on the non-existent keyboard. He inhaled deeply, wanting to get the worst part over with.

The burning sensation deep in his belly peaked. He opened his mouth and screamed as dragonfire escaped his lips. He directed the burst over the portal frame, long enough for the doorway to turn from white to black. Once it completely changed colour, the stone panels within the frame ground open, disappearing into the edges.

Mardious quickly grabbed a blue vial. He poured it down his gullet. Was he swallowing? He couldn't even tell. His mouth felt like he'd taken hot soup, added tea, wrapped it in cheese and spices, and swallowed it all at the same time.

He felt like coughing but forced himself not to. He'd made that mistake before and had ended up spewing a combination of blue liquid and fire everywhere. This time, his breathing slowed as he felt the cool wave of healing reach from the tips of his toes to his now-motionless fingers.

"I wonder if dragonfire would have penetrated the shield," The Shadow said.

How had Garrick created it? Mardious hadn't felt any magic coming from the Chosen Wizard, but maybe his power superseded normal magic abilities. What other secrets had he uncovered? Which ones were left to expose?

Mardious wouldn't need to wait much longer; he knew the power would soon be his.

Fully recovered, Mardious hopped back onto his carriage, pulled the levers, and felt the magical lava mix with the other fuel elements. With a twiddle of his fingers, he steered the levitating platform down through the portal gateway.

As he was teleported to the crypt where the red piece of the doorway had been kept, his eyes went directly to the pen that he had built for his newest pets. It looked empty—that is, until he touched the now-glowing jade gemstone in his scorpion medallion.

The white unicorn stared back at Mardious. She seemed more confident with his presence than before. The two pale-blue unicorns still sulked in the corner.

"Why do they smell so bad?" The Shadow asked.

"Aren't they supposed to poop rainbows or candy?" The Angel added.

Mardious smiled. He let go of his scorpion medallion, exchanging it for Amelia's medal. He couldn't wait to show the real Amelia his pets, discover new things about them with her, and live with her in the abundant world he'd created.

He steered the levitation carriage to a spot beside the unicorn pen. He'd constructed the enclosure out of wooden bookshelves that had been left behind by the ancients, first securing the bases with piles of gold coins that had also been stored in the chamber. The coins had a lion's head etched into one side, resembling those in the stash that Jax had received from the A.K. as payment.

"They didn't get it from here," The Angel reminded him.

There were two other chambers with the same coins: on Jenim Island, and in the Leviathan Triangle. Did that mean the A.K. were hiding in the secret chambers like he was? And in which one were they storing the doorway of life?

"He doesn't need the doorway in order to utilize its power," The Shadow said.

Mardious remembered how Garrick had brought the dragon back to life when they were at the castle of the Triple Crown. He didn't set up the doorway, and the dragon didn't walk through it from the afterlife. The dragon had simply appeared.

"Why did Sheese say it worked differently?" The Angel asked.

Mardious pulled the lever on the carriage to stop the fuel from burning. He hopped off the seat and opened the side door. He dragged out one of the small hay bales that he'd taken from the Garrick farm.

He was already out of breath, but he still had so much to do.

"Your new batch will be ready soon," The Shadow said.

Mardious slid a vial of purple solution from his bandolier, popped the cork off, and chugged the whole thing.

He took a few deep breaths as he waited for his elixir to kick in. Unlike the fire-breathing elixir, he loved the feeling of this one, which he called the Purple Monster. It made him feel like he was on top of the world. Like he could accomplish anything. It also made everything quieter and more peaceful.

The crackle of the fire around the room faded to a hum. The flames stopped flickering. It was as if all the power in the room entered Mardious' body, giving him a boost of strength greater than that of a hundred warriors, and greater than the speed of a thousand horses.

He didn't need encouragement from The Shadow or The Angel to continue.

Mardious grabbed the hay bale he'd dropped and tossed it over the fence. As soon as he let go, it hovered in the air, slowly following the trajectory he'd sent it on. He stepped into the carriage, grabbed another hay bale, and let it fly too.

After the bales were all hanging in the air, he moved on to the ice blocks that he'd collected. He still wasn't used to interacting with a world that was slowed down, and it was a little confusing when he felt no cold when he touched frozen water. The ice was large enough to cradle with his arms, and so his cloak insulated his skin as he ran the blocks out.

Several blocks were placed in the troughs for the unicorns. These blocks would melt to provide the water the unicorns needed to quench their thirst. The other three blocks were for his experiments, as he needed water in both solid and liquid form for his elixirs.

Next he grabbed four needles from his potion tables and returned to the unicorn stable. Only the first of the hay bales had touched down. Mardious didn't like chasing the unicorns around without the elixir. One of the younglings had gotten the best of him before and had kicked him in the shin.

To locate the beasts, he kept his finger on the jade gemstone and used the needles to take two blood samples from the adult unicorn and one sample from each youngling. He deftly avoided the manure in the pen and returned his samples to the potion table. He checked the room for a shovel or pitchfork.

The flames around the room flickered. The younglings shrieked.

The weight of the world fell back on Mardious' shoulders.

"Suck it up," The Shadow said.

"Would they be friendlier if their pen was clean?" The Angel asked.

Mardious would also be happier if it didn't smell like an outhouse in here. Maybe he shouldn't have brought them here after all. If it hadn't taken him weeks to find them, he would have considered hiding them elsewhere.

How did the fake Amelia know he had hunted them?

"More proof she's a trick," The Shadow said.

Mardious walked back towards the pen. He didn't care about the hay bales that littered the floor, or the first ring of fire that had gone out around the room. He focused on the white unicorn, who hadn't moved an inch since he'd arrived.

He leant on the fence post, standing between the piles of gold that kept it secure, and stared into the majestic black eyes of the beast. He could feel it judging him, and he wondered if it truly understood his intentions yet. He gently lifted his finger off the glowing gemstone of the scorpion medallion.

"I'm not going to hurt you," Mardious said.

As soon as he stopped touching the jade medallion, the unicorns disappeared.

Mardious closed his eyes and extended both arms. His fingers danced as he focused on playing a soulful song; something the real Amelia would love. He swayed his head, trying to connect with the beasts around him. The only thing he felt was another ring of fire disappearing.

"Time is running out," The Shadow said.

Mardious opened his eyes. The pen was still empty. He sighed and touched the gemstone again. The younglings still hid in the corner away from him, but the white unicorn had taken a few steps forward.

"Maybe next time," Mardious said.

He headed back to his setup of elixirs and potions. There were forty stations, all set with different ingredients, measuring flasks, cauldrons, and elements for control. Since some of the elixirs took longer to create than others, he had the same elixirs brewing at different stations, all in different stages of development. The recipes that the ancients had left in their texts provided precise details on how to brew each one.

His first stop was his task list, which helped him monitor the progress of his elixirs, identify what supplies he needed for his next trip, and organize his priorities in the precious time he'd been given. It also relieved a bit of stress, knowing that he could leave a project at a suitable stage while he was away.

At the top of his list were his ice blocks and recent samples. To start his healing elixir, he first had to cool the unicorn blood. He did this by carving out holes for the needle vials, double-checking that the levels were measured correctly, and leaving them for an hour or so.

He checked on his latest batch of the Purple Monster and Firebreather elixirs, since they both required a forty-eight-hour simmer in their respective cauldrons. He'd rigged an oil basin underneath each cauldron to keep a flame burning, and each basin still had enough fuel to burn a little longer. He decided to top up each one with a stash of lamp oil he kept nearby just in case.

Next on his task list was topping up his own fuel. He had plenty of a nourishment elixir that had all the essential vitamins and nutrients his body needed for the day. It tasted like dirt due to most of the ingredients being from the roots of common plants, but he liked the efficiency of his nutrition. Not having to cook or eat fancy meals gave him more time to work.

"Do you think a few dates would help wash it down?" The Angel asked.

Mardious tried not to dream of Amelia while he worked, but meeting a counterfeit version of her was almost better than the illusions that he could create. How did Garrick know what she looked like? She was the right height and age. Her voice was almost exactly as he remembered. How were those details right, but all the scars that made her who she was, were missed?

"Only the scarred survive," The Shadow reminded him.

Mardious rubbed his chest. The healing elixir worked like Amelia's magic, able to heal a wound while leaving behind a souvenir. It would have been useful on that fateful day.

"Your eyes spit the truth," The Angel said.

Mardious wiped his tears away. He needed to stay focused. The A.K. were daring, and now they would pay for attempting to fool him. He checked his task list and then started a new batch of the Purple Monster. It was the most laborious, but he'd used up some of the supply, and so it was crucial to get more started.

He sifted through his closest storage piles. He'd used a lot of the old shelving for the unicorn pen and so most of his supplies were strewn about the stone floor. The supplies were organized into appropriate sections, but it wasn't as neat as his previous potion-making laboratories had been.

He grabbed ten cocoa leaves from the vegetation section, and returned to his workstation that had the recipe, the measuring spoons, and a mortar and pestle made of dragon scales. He also collected a couple limes and fresh mint to help make the paste. He never tasted the mint when drinking his elixir. Was it supposed to help ease the flavour? Or was there some magical property to mint?

Another ring of fire extinguished, leaving only two to light the room. He hustled to his carriage to grab his new stock of blue phoenix feathers, centaur hooves, fairy wings, and goblin eyes—he would need all of them later. He brought this haul back to the table, then climbed the staircase to the portal.

He didn't know everything about the portal that led to the cavern, but he understood that the dragonfire that opened the door magically fueled the rings on the surrounding walls. He'd tried lighting the rings himself, but that didn't work. Returning to the surface to blow more fire onto the door seemed the only way for him to avoid being trapped in his secret laboratory.

On the Skyland surface, he was a bit disappointed not to see any dragons. Normally, his presence in the area would attract at least a fly-by or two. Baiting a dragon to blow fire on the portal helped him save his elixirs—plus spared him the pain of the fire-breathing experience. He might even be capable of taking down a dragon with his purple elixir. He could store its body in his laboratory and use its scales, so useful in so many different potions. He still had parts left over from a deceased golden dragon, but he was running low on inventory.

He'd have to hunt dragons another time.

He sighed, drank his orange elixir, and covered the portal entrance with fire again. After choking down his blue healing elixir, he noticed that the jade gemstone on his scorpion medallion was glowing. Was it picking up the unicorns through the portal? Or was there another one in the area?

The Angel and The Shadow stayed silent.

Mardious considered reaching for his Purple Monster elixir—it gave him a clear advantage when capturing unicorns—but he didn't want to make any sudden moves. He curled his palm towards him and ever-so-slightly reached out his index finger until he touched the glowing gem. He kept his head still and strained his eyes to scan the terrain.

There was nothing but dark shale and overcast skies ahead of him. He turned his upper body left, scanning as he slowly spun around. There were no unicorns in his line of sight—no signs of life at all, for that matter. Was the scorpion medallion malfunctioning? He completed a full circle and checked it. The jade gem was no longer glowing.

Did he imagine it? Maybe it was a sign?

"Control the world. Don't allow it to control you," The Shadow said.

Mardious shook his head and returned to his laboratory. He didn't waste any time tending to unicorns, listening to the Angel or Shadow, or dreaming about Amelia. He focused on his task list, and the preparations he had to make. Once he was finished, he could afford to dream.

He started by drinking a peach elixir that would help him stay awake. He then ground his coca leaves into a paste before putting it into a glass vase that hung over a boiling cauldron. He checked on his other purple elixir stations, one stage at a time. At the final stage, he tested his newest batch on a couple of caged mice.

He hadn't been precise. The batch was contaminated. The mice died.

The faulty batch could still be useful. He could sell it to Sheese to ensure that his New Realm Order lost in battle. Or should he give it to Porkchop and the Brotherhood? They were growing richer due to the war, but they were only loyal to him because of his promise to deliver the doorway.

"They may need a reminder of how valuable you are," The Shadow said.

He dropped the beaker into his discarded pile with the intent to transfer it to smaller vials once he had a new plan in place.

He finished more healing elixirs as well as more Firebreather elixirs to enhance his abilities, and then made some classic potions to paralyze his enemies. He also made some more fuel for his carriage with some magic magma that he had stored. After his ninth return to the surface to reset the portal, he had completed everything on his task list. He took stock at the end to see what other materials he'd need for his next visit.

He started a new list.

What did he need for the Everlasting elixir? That was what he needed to figure out first. From his carriage he pulled out the last item he had stored: fake Amelia's helmet. He rubbed the green hair between his fingertips.

"Is it real?" The Angel asked.

"It doesn't appear to be dyed, but that's far from your expertise," The Shadow said.

Mardious tried to remember what he had read about langaras in the ancient texts. They were pets of The Chosen, providing protection to those that wielded the power of the doorway of life. Was it possible that Garrick had brought one back? Were the langaras the natural guardian of the stone pieces, or did they just use the langara to make masks or elixirs?

Mardious set the mask down at an open station and turned to his piles of books. He knew which text had the Everlasting elixir recipe, but where had he read about the langaras? His curiosity gave him a boost.

He flipped through all the texts, looking for keywords and pictures. There were a few moments where his focus slipped as he dreamt about what he and the real Amelia would do with the extra time that the Everlasting elixir granted them.

They would build their dream castle, wear the most luxurious garments in all the land, and rule the world with an iron fist. They would balance the scales, ensuring that no one would suffer from the poverty they had grown up with in the Badlands. They would be the most beloved King and Queen that the realm had ever seen, wiping out all their enemies in a single swoop and embracing a lifetime of peace and tranquility.

"Make sure you have room in your castle for pet langaras," The Shadow said.

"And don't forget about the unicorns," The Angel added.

The unicorns would likely reveal themselves when they saw what wonderful rulers Mardious and Amelia were. In fact, Mardious decided, he would have to find a medallion to keep the unicorns away, so they and their manure wouldn't pester him all the time in his castle.

He tossed his last book on the floor. He'd made a messy pile, but he'd re-organize it another day. He hadn't found any more info on the langaras.

He returned to the station with his recipe book and tore the Everlasting elixir pages out. After reviewing the recipe, he was disappointed to realize he couldn't even start making the elixir. The first ingredient was the bulb of a cosmic rose flower. Luckily there was a coloured drawing of it in the recipe.

"It's as beautiful as a storm," The Shadow said.

"And for some reason, requires lightning to grow," The Angel said.

Mardious wiped away more truth from his eyes. He tried to tell himself that he was close to his dream life, even if he had encountered another obstacle.

Not only did he need to create a special paste with the langara hair, but the elixir he made with it was used alongside the lightning to grow the flower. The second half of the recipe used this specially-grown flower, meaning that even if he found a wild cosmic rose, only one grown in this manner would give him the elixir needed to extend his and Amelia's lives.

Another ring of fire extinguished, dimming the room around him. It felt like the right time to wrap things up for the night.

He glanced around the room and took note of what he'd accomplished that day. He left his next task list but took with him a separate list of supplies he'd need to bring back. He checked the unicorn pen one last time, and then left his laboratory in his levitation carriage. He didn't look back, his only focus being for the future.

He was one step closer to bringing Amelia back, so they could watch the world burn and rule over the ashes together, just like they'd always been destined to do.

CHAPTER 14

Hardships

"Why was he alone?" Kase asked.

Lenia reached up, lifted higher onto her tiptoes, and folded over. Her hands dangled towards her bare feet but didn't quite touch the short grass. Kase followed her lead, feeling the stretch in his hamstrings.

"How do you know the Brotherhood wasn't watching from the woods?" Lenia replied.

"I didn't feel anything," Kase said. Usually a disturbance would have triggered fright from rodents, irritation from birds, or scurrying of certain insects. He swayed from side to side, feeling how his body responded to the stretch. "Did you connect with any creatures while you were teleporting the hostages?"

"No time." Lenia sighed. She reached farther, and then walked her hands forwards until she was face-down on the ground. She pushed her torso up, locked her arms, and looked to the sky.

Kase copied Lenia's moves again. He closed his eyes and let the morning sun grace his cheeks. "He should have brought an army," he said. "If they all drank an elixir like his at the same time, they could end a war in seconds."

"I don't disagree," Lenia said. "But that type of victory would first require discipline, organization, and trust between each warrior. Do you think the Brotherhood is that capable?"

Kase sighed and opened his eyes. He stared at the star shape buried in the ground before him. The doorway of life. He knew how much of an advantage true power was, and how his headfirst plunge through the doorway had changed his life forever.

"You didn't feel Mardious under the power of that elixir. Even if they stumbled, that kind of speed and strength would be too much for all the Marauders to offset," Kase said.

"Marauders, maybe, but not all warriors," Lenia said.

Kase was stretching his neck, but he stopped when he met Lenia's smile. Her green eyes sparkled in a ray of sun.

"Of course." Kase puckered up his lips and kissed her.

"It's too bad you were poisoned, and we weren't able to go on a date," Lenia said. She turned to stretch her neck the opposite way. "But I like our mornates. I'm glad we didn't give them up."

"Me too," Kase said. He faced away from Lenia and saw Talen walking towards the entrance of the castle. "Even if we add night dates, I hope we still keep our morning and day ones too."

Kase rolled to a seated position, facing Talen. "Good morning, Tal," Kase said. He was done with his stretching. "I didn't expect you to be up this early."

Talen veered away from the castle and joined Kase and Lenia on the grass. She sat beside them, her legs crossed, and set her basket next to her knees. The basket was filled with black roses. "I have not been to sleep," Talen said.

Lenia rolled over. "Have you both been awake all night?"

Amelia was morose and depressed after meeting Mardious. The second time Kase had brought her back, her experience before death had been depressing, lonely, and heartbreaking. On the one hand, she'd struggled to believe that Mardious had turned into a monster. On the other, she had completely accepted her fate when the poison was coursing through her veins. She even now wished that Kase hadn't brought her back.

Since her revival, Amelia had been claiming that the man they met wasn't Mardious, but Talen had convinced her to learn about what Mardious had been doing with his life since she had known him. It started with some history lessons, then the sharing of news articles on lesser-known events, and finally the watching of moving images on the giant sage mirror that captured news of Mardious and High Wizard Zuke.

Talen nodded. "She said I could rest, but I told her that friends stick together. The topic has been top of mind ever since I read King Michael's books on voluntary hardships."

"Is it voluntary because you're choosing to go through it with her?" Lenia asked.

"Sort of," Talen said. "The way King Michael put it, living through trauma or hardships together united all of those that travelled the same path because they were familiar with the struggle. When they overcame it, they all shared in the glory and appreciated what it took to get through the obstacles rather than only seeing the end results."

Kase felt a little guilty. He'd had a good sleep and a wonderful morning with Lenia, but it was at the expense of his other friends and responsibilities. "How can I help carry the burden with the two of you?"

"Let me help as well." Lenia tapped her heart, touched her lips, and pointed to the sky.

"It is a little too late to jump in on this one," Talen replied. "But there will be plenty of new hardships for us to tackle together. We have been successful before, and we will conquer everything that gets thrown our way in the future. The tea from these rose petals will help. Would you like some?" Talen tapped the basket.

"Tal!" Amelia shouted from inside the castle. "Tal? Tal!"

"She doesn't call you Shark Knight?" Kase asked.

"Or Demon Shark?" Lenia added.

Talen gave a rare smile, stood, and grabbed her basket. "I told her my friends call me Tal." She turned and followed Amelia's calls into the castle.

As Talen confidently strode into the castle, gently swinging her basket, Kase found himself thinking about what was truly important. He turned back towards the closed doorway in the ground. He remembered King Michael's warning when he accepted his power, about how it would corrupt those who used it. Would he have to choose between his power and his friends?

It felt like an easy choice.

Now, Kase found himself thinking about how quickly things changed. A once-flighty Amelia was now questioning her path. Cali was scrambling for a new way to stop Mardious and the rest of the former Triple Crown. Was it time for Kase to change his ways too?

"Have you ever thought about giving up your trident?" Kase asked.

"No," Lenia said bluntly. "Why would I?"

"There was a time when Mardious stole your power from you," Kase said, remembering how devastated Lenia had been. "But that was when you were still learning how to use it effectively. Would that change with what you know now?"

Lenia furrowed her brow in confusion. "It would be worse," she said. "Why? What are you trying to get at?" She grabbed his hand.

Kase looked at the doorway again. "I thought that I would recognize the corrupting power of the doorway of life, but I only feel the desire to give it away. Am I supposed to feel like it's a part of me? That it's something that would be devastating if it was stolen?"

Lenia shifted closer to Kase and draped her arms around his torso. She tucked her legs in and leant her head on his shoulder. "We obtained special power in different ways," she said. "I created mine and was granted a boost from the Mermaid Queen. You were forced into finding this ancient relic and into using it to change the fate of the world."

Kase chuckled. "You make it sound like I had a sword to my neck," he said. "Yes, I used it to bring everyone back from a terrible fate, but it was still a choice I made. Sometimes I wonder what made me special enough to be put in that position, and for the world to notice."

Lenia squeezed Kase tight. "You've always been special," she said. "It's just taken a long time for the world to catch up. Sometimes I wish I didn't have to share you with them."

Kase wrapped his arms around Lenia. "I know that feeling," he said. "I hope I never live through what Amelia is battling right now. Her world has been turned upside-down."

"It's nice to see she has accepted support from her friend Tal," Lenia said. "When you brought me back, I definitely appreciated the help of the entire Liberati."

"Then maybe we should both help her out too?" Kase asked, knowing that Talen had warned them not to.

"We will, but we don't need to do it all at once," Lenia said. "We have obligations to the rest of the A.K.: like training this morning, checking supplies, and seeing if Cali, Dom, and Sharaine have news on what's next."

"And if Amelia is part of the A.K. now, those plans help her too," Kase agreed.

Lenia and Kase finished their stretches and returned to the Jenim gold mines. With the new threat of Mardious' elixirs, the group was reluctant to do any activities out in the open. Instead they found new, auditorium-sized spaces for training. Dom warned that it wasn't sustainable to stay indoors for long periods, but they'd have to make do until a new plan was formed. Kase suspected Dom hoped they could leave the giant kingdom and journey elsewhere. He and Ashlyn had wanted a vacation, but the war and the new baby had delayed it.

Along with the other warriors-in-training, Kase and Lenia started the training session with a few laps around the area. The peace plans may have been delayed due to their failed meeting with Mardious, but spirits were higher than expected.

Dom led some long-range weapons practice before Lenia taught some new defensive positions for melee combat. Kase wondered if they could upgrade their training practices to mimic an army fuelled by elixirs, but sticking to the basics seemed the best way to keep everyone calm and collected. His grandfather had advised that focusing too much on the unknown added stress to new, intermediate, and superior warriors alike.

Kase was paired with Curtis for the sparring session. Kase wished he could spar with the Unicorn Knight, but she was taking on her brother. He'd have to settle for Curtis, the Kodiak Mountain, who was looking a lot more fit recently. His mouth moved faster than his sword, though.

"Becca likes my drawings, but I can't tell if she's just being nice," Curtis said. "You should see hers, though! The line work, use of color and shadowing ... they're so beautiful. I hope I can sketch like her someday."

Kase returned a combo of his own, but he wasn't swinging hard. He wanted to focus on his footwork, and so he pivoted to get away instead of hitting Curtis with another attack. He also wanted to hear what Curtis was doing for dates. "What other things do you do together?" he asked.

Curtis turned the other way and hit Kase with a spinning attack, which Kase blocked easily. "We've been watching a lot of news lately," he said. "You should hear her Sheese impression. It's hilarious!"

Kase tried a spin of his own, keeping his feet close and using his momentum to deliver a heavier blow. Curtis was knocked back, but he kept his balance. "I'd like that," Kase said encouragingly. Watching the news didn't seem like a very entertaining date, but adding a humorous element could make it memorable.

"It helps filter out all the political speak so I can understand what's going on," Curtis admitted. "She spent a lot of time working with Cali and Sharaine at the Triple Crown, so she's familiar with the language that the former leaders use. She breaks down the deals that Sheese has made, identifies some of his allies, and helps explain the beliefs of the New Realm Order." Curtis took a step back instead of attacking. His smile beamed.

"Sounds like things are going well," Kase said. He kept his wooden sword ready, but he didn't feel like attacking. Curtis seemed caught in more important thoughts.

"I'm all in, Two Times," Curtis said. He dropped his sword to signal a break. Kase nodded and they moved to the edge of the sparring area to grab some water.

"I'm happy for you, Curtis," Kase said. "Hopefully we can get out of hiding so you can build back what you've lost."

"Build back … this is the best-case scenario!" Curtis poured a glass of water for himself and Kase. "Becca was so used to working late hours that she didn't have time to focus on the little things. Looking back on my time as a Guardian, I feel the same. Staying here has helped us both improve our quality of life. Before we were just wasting our time searching for validation while working for someone else's dream."

Kase accepted his water. Was this really Curtis? The same Curtis who had encouraged Kase to be a High Guardian? When the war was over, Kase thought everyone wanted to go back to the same lives that had been taken away, but it was a relief to see new paths being planned.

"What dream are you working towards, then?" Kase asked.

Curtis looked over both shoulders, as if it were a secret. Kase leant in close to play along. "Well, it's not quite planned out yet, but it starts with a garden," Curtis said in a low voice. "Becca's always dreamed of reading next to a flower bed, sipping on fairy juice and eating purple strawberries."

Kase could taste the purple strawberries and tried not to think about lunch. "Sounds lovely."

"I suggested we grow our own fruit," Curtis continued, "which turned into owning an orchard and getting some animals. Before I knew it, we were talking about owning our own farm!" Curtis beamed again. "Can you imagine? Well, I guess you can—you were a farmer, right?"

Was Curtis just looking for a less-challenging life than that of a warrior? Farming, though, was more work than Guardian shifts, even boring ones. "It's hard owning a farm," Kase cautioned. "Are you sure you're dreaming of the right life?"

Curtis chuckled. "Maybe not, but with Becca by my side, I'm up for the challenge!"

Kase glanced at Lenia. He knew they could do anything together. He appreciated Curtis' excitement and felt the impulse to help. "You and Becca should talk to my aunt and uncle then," he said. "They can give you tips on how to get going, what the daily chores are like, and the tricks with different crops and animals."

"Really?" Curtis grabbed Kase and gave him a bear hug worthy of the Kodiak Mountain. "That would be a big help!"

"You're welcome," Kase gasped.

Curtis and Kase returned to their sparring session. Now with more pep in his step, Curtis could give Kase the footwork challenge he'd been looking for. Combined with the stretching, running, and long-ranged weapons training,

Kase felt like he was getting back to peak form. If he could keep on this training regimen, he might have a chance against an elixir-drinking super villain.

Kase was able to connect Curtis with his aunt and uncle at lunch. He didn't have time to dive into the conversation, however, since Cali had scheduled a meeting in the sage mirror room. With Talen busy leading Amelia's recovery, Sharaine had taken Talen's place. Cali also wanted to be more inclusive to wizards and warriors with their strategies, and so Roman, Helena, and Aura also joined the group. Now they were all seated together, facing the sage mirror.

Kase had grabbed a couple sandwiches and fresh veggies and scarfed them down as Cali went through the meeting agenda.

"With our Mardious plan in shambles, we need to switch our focus to defeating Sheese and Mac," Cali said. "We'll start the meeting with updates on both and then move onto mind-mapping solutions right after. We have a lot to get through, but any questions before we start?"

Kase would have asked a question, but his mouth was full.

"What about the Brotherhood?" Lenia asked from the back of the room.

Kase was happy that Lenia had read his mind. He traded two of his celery sticks for a carrot from her plate, but she wasn't paying attention to him.

"I was planning to discuss that after," Cali answered. "Since they're not as readily in the news, we've been unable to gather intel on their operation. We may need to assign that to you, Lenia."

Lenia nodded. She turned to Kase and made a gesture with her index finger and thumb, silently recruiting Kase for her assignment. Kase tapped his heart, kissed his fingers, and threw them up to the sky in agreement.

"Sharaine, would you like to start with Sheese?" Cali asked.

Sharaine stood from her seat at the front and faced the small crowd. Kase stole another carrot from Lenia's plate.

"Mirror, Mirror, show me moving image twenty-five in the Dealmaker folder," Sharaine said. An image of Sheese giving a speech appeared on the main sage mirror.

"They continue to steal everything from us." Sheese banged his fist on the podium. "They've stolen our homes, our jobs, and our livelihood. They've stolen our freedom!"

The crowd erupted.

"Mirror, Mirror, pause," Sharaine said. "We've noticed that Sheese isn't tackling important issues anymore. His platform used to centre on new policies for scholars, health plans for the injured, and tax breaks for his supporters. Now he's bypassing the logic and details of his political plans and focusing on the emotions surrounding the turmoil between scholars, wizards, and warriors. Mirror, Mirror, continue."

"It's time to fight back!" Sheese yelled. "We will rain fire upon the Marauders, drive the Brotherhood back into the hole they crawled out of, and share the power that the Animal Kingdom selfishly keeps hidden!" He raised both arms in the air. The crowd cheered again. "This I promise you!"

"Mirror, Mirror, pause," Sharaine said again. "His supporters are loud, but he still doesn't have the tactical force needed to threaten the Marauders. He may have access to hidden resources, though." She pointed to Sheese's hand.

Attached to Sheese's wrist guard was a clearly visible blue vial.

"New Hawk-eye?" Lenia whispered.

Kase smiled but stopped himself from laughing. He wanted to support Sharaine as a valuable new member of their team.

"Did you find any other evidence of elixirs?" Aura asked.

"Only one," Sharaine said. "It's two weeks before this rally. Did you want to see it?"

Kase tilted forwards in his chair. How long had the rest of the realm been developing elixirs? Did Mardious get them from Sheese, or was it the other way around?

"Do all our enemies have elixirs now?" Kase asked.

Cali looked over her shoulder at Kase and Aura. "We're not sure yet. Let's focus on what we *do* know, and then get into more details." She gestured for Sharaine to continue.

Kase tried to reassure himself that Cali and Sharaine had a plan, but now that Sheese and Mardious were linked, he wondered what that meant for the

A.K. They couldn't fail again.

"Mirror, Mirror, show me moving image forty-four in the Mighty King folder," Sharaine said.

In the image Mac sat in the throne room at the castle of the Triple Crown. Where there had been three thrones, there was now only one.

"The Pledge of Loyalty is the greatest bond that we share as leaders of the new world," Mac said. "Those who abide by it will live. Those who ignore it will be eliminated." He stood from his perch and drew his sword. The image panned out, revealing a kneeling Marauder bowing towards Mac.

"I would like to commend Josephine for her action in Tailsgate," Mac continued. "She successfully eliminated the scholars and wizards that would not voluntarily acknowledge the pledge. For her courage, perseverance, and leadership, I grant her governorship over the land." He tapped the tip of his sword on each of Josephine's shoulders.

"Soon, we will rid the world of those who fool us with their magic and manipulate our minds with lies and deceit." Mac sheathed his sword. He slammed his fist into his chest. "Dragoon!"

The moving image faded.

"As you can see, the Marauders are targeting wizards *and* scholars," Sharaine said. "Combine that with Sheese's new stance on fighting for freedom, and it would appear that we're moving closer to a violent conflict."

"Thank you for presenting, Sharaine," Cali said. She stood and joined her old colleague at the front. "We have failed to convince Mardious to step down, or to thwart him as a powerful threat. Sheese and Mac have their own agendas, and they seem destined to fight each other for dominance. I'm not sure what our next move is, but now that we know the rules of the game, where does that put us as players?"

Kase leant back. He was shocked that Cali hadn't started a plan yet.

"You believe their threats are real?" Roman asked. "If the elixirs are as dangerous as you've described, how will the Marauders be able to claim victory?"

"We aren't certain how Sheese obtained the elixirs," Sharaine said.

"Sheese likely has wizard consults in his circle," Dom said. "They either conveniently discovered the same information as Mardious, or the New Realm Order has made a deal with the Brotherhood, joining forces to go toe-to-toe with the Marauders."

"They have a common enemy in Mac, but it's highly unlikely that Sheese would put his entire platform in jeopardy by even talking with Mardious," Cali noted. "The Brotherhood threatens the freedom and liberty of the New Realm Order. Acceptance of one enemy to combat another is not what an egotistical leader like the Currency King would consider."

"So why don't we focus on Mac?" Helena said. "If the scholars and wizards have elixirs that give them an advantage in battle, the Marauders are vulnerable. If we can get to Mac before the New Realm Order or Brotherhood, we can try to end his tyranny before the fighting begins."

"That would save the most lives," Cali said. "Unfortunately, Mac is the hardest to get to."

"Sneaking into his hideout is different than dressing as Marauders in Kimroad," Dom said. "The old castle of the Triple Crown is a stronghold with surveillance mirrors in every corner, guards at every entrance, and an unlimited supply of weapons. We'd likely be captured or killed the moment we step inside."

"Breaching the walls unprovoked may also lose us credibility," Cali said. "We need a reason for him to listen. Otherwise, we'll just end up caught in an endless battle."

Aura raised her hand. Kase was reminded of when Talen used to do that. She didn't wait for Cali to give her permission to speak, though. "Why should we do anything at all?"

The room went oddly quiet. "Interesting take, Aura," Cali said. "Please continue."

"It didn't seem possible before," Aura said. "Each former leader was playing a role, but now they're at a standoff. If aggression builds past the breaking point, then we could witness a battle where only one king is left standing."

Kase could feel the lava creep into his heart. He knew the consequences of war, and the pain it caused: both to the losing side and to those that experienced retribution. "How many thousands of people would suffer and lose their lives fighting for the power struggle of kings?" Kase asked angrily.

The room was quiet again.

"Healing is what we do," Aura said. "Once the dust settles, we can bring back those we've lost. The A.K. will be in a position to rebuild the realm slowly, remind the fallen about the quality of life, and ensure the war mongers are persecuted for their hardships."

Kase rubbed his eyes. How long would it take to bring thousands of people back? How many times would he dive into the lava each day? How much pain could he handle? "I'm not a backup plan," Kase snapped.

Aura looked to the floor. Cali stared at Kase, her eyes softening in pity. "We must reflect on all the possibilities, brother," she said. "We all understand the burdens you bear, and we're grateful for all you've done for us. We will not put you in a position to rebuild the world following its destruction. Ideally, we'll come up with a better plan to help avoid it."

Kase turned to Lenia. He didn't realize his fists were clenched. "May I be excused?"

"Of course," Cali said. "I have a few more images I'd like to share with the rest of the group. Can I catch you up tonight, over dinner?"

Cali looked to Sharaine. "Maybe we should at least verify that Tailsgate has been overtaken. Lenia, are you willing to report on the claim of Josephine's governorship?"

Lenia stood up. "I've never been to Tailsgate before, but we can plan it out." She tapped her heart, kissed her fingers, and pointed to the roof.

Kase nodded. Lenia grabbed Kase's hand and teleported them back to the Kingdom of Moiras. They stood at the base of the doorway of life, right where they had stretched earlier that morning.

Kase rubbed his face. "I'm sorry for asking to—"

"You don't have to explain," Lenia said. "There's a lot to consider. We'll find the right plan of action though, because we always do." She wrapped her arms around Kase and squeezed him tight.

He felt better already, but he still needed a break. Could they go on a day date knowing that the world was crumbling around them?

"I'm going to head back, though," Lenia said. "I want to poke Sharaine, Cali, and Aura a little more about the elixirs. Why don't you get some rest and join someone else who needs a friend right now?"

Kase hugged Lenia back, and then took a step away before she teleported again. He thought about going for a run to clear his mind. Maybe he could find Maxim and go for a hunt with the pack. He slowly turned to face the castle.

Or maybe he should take Lenia's advice instead.

He entered through the garden, climbed the stairs to the third floor, and followed the laughter through the halls. When he made it into the lounging room that held the giant sage mirror, he was surprised to see Amelia and Talen watching moving images of his Jester Joust.

"Hey, Maxim, ever heard of a breath mint?" Kase said on the image.

Amelia laughed again then, as she reached for her plate, she noticed Kase in the doorway. Her arm escaped the blanket draped over her shoulders as she punched the air. "Demon Jester!" she exclaimed.

"Mirror, Mirror, pause," Talen said and sipped her tea. She was also cloaked in a blanket.

"I'm glad you're awake," Kase said. "Mind if I join you?"

Talen looked to Amelia, who was still giggling. "We're watching the second Jester Joust. I thought this was some of your best work, even though you lost to Dom in the votes."

"Spoilers!" Amelia giggled again. "Your jokes are amazing, Demon King. Would you like a date?" She picked up the plate and held it out.

"Dom played the crowd well that day," Kase said. "I like this crowd better, though." He grabbed a date and tossed it high in the air, catching it in his mouth.

Amelia giggled again and mimicked Kase's toss. It was good to see her in high spirits, and it gave Kase hope that the future was something they could tackle together. But could he truly survive bringing back so many of the thousands who would inevitably fall in an all-out war?

The world had changed for Amelia, more so than it had for any of the others Kase had brought back. If a war broke out, how long would the fallen have to wait? Would they accept the new world they'd return to? Would it be up to Kase to decide who was brought back early, and who would remain buried?

Kase missed the joke on the sage mirror, but Amelia's laughter made him smile. He grabbed another date and tried to stay in the moment. If he had to dive constantly into pain to help others, how could he spend time with his friends and laugh? It would change him. That much he knew.

CHAPTER 15

End of an Era

Talen ruffled the blue tablecloth, creating waves to showcase her surprise. Kase liked the theatrics, but it was weird coming from Talen. Was this another effect of the cosmic rose tea she'd been drinking the last few days?

She yanked the tablecloth away, revealing a triangular metal frame with a black cloth pulled over it. "Ta-da!" she said with a smile.

Kase smiled and clapped politely. Lenia scratched her head. "What is it?" she asked.

"It's a glider," Talen said. "We were watching some old Jester Joust footage and Kase was making jokes about the goblins from Death Mountain. It reminded me of our Quest Series when we built watercrafts to race down the river."

Kase had forgotten that joke, because it didn't get any laughs, but he remembered the event. It was fun, until Mardious Hood interfered.

"So it's for a race?" Kase asked. He thought Talen was going to help them on their journey to Tailsgate.

"No, it's for your mission—unless you want to keep relying on Turanus," Talen said. "Goblins are well known for their extreme adventures, so I researched some of their other traditions. Along with racing through the rapids, they often jump off the top of Death Mountain and ride the air currents to the south. They call it a goblin glide, but I have a new name for our glider: Knightwing."

Kase studied the frame a little more. A purple unicorn horn protruded from the centre of the metal frame. The black cloth stretched in a triangular shape reminded him of Lenia's cape. "The Unicorn Knightwing. Do I get one, too?"

"I only had time to make one," Talen said. "But it's for two people! I'll demonstrate."

Talen got on all fours and crawled through the metal frame. She turned around and laid down on one of two metal slabs that didn't seem attached to anything. Each slab had two leather straps that Talen threw across her back.

"You'll want to make sure the levitation platforms are tight, but you'll be able to steer the glider like this." Talen gripped the bottom of the triangle with both hands. "We don't have enough fuel to keep a normal levitation platform afloat, but the Knightwing will allow you to burn less fuel. When you arrive at your destination, you should be able to unhook the cloth from the frame to teleport the glider back in pieces."

"It's less bulky than a bigger platform, but lasts longer than a smaller one," Lenia said. "I love it, Talen! I especially like the purple touch."

"That was Amelia's idea," Talen said. "She wanted to call it the Demonhawk, but I told her we don't really like birds, and then she talked about wanting one for herself ... she's funny sometimes." Talen looked to the ground.

Lenia raised an eyebrow to Kase. "We'll have to race sometime," she said.

"If we're racing, then I want my own, too," Kase said. "I'll call it the Fireball. It will be all white, but when I win it will burst into flames!"

"Fun!" Lenia giggled. "We should make a bet."

"A championship shirt? Ice cream?" Kase suggested.

"I don't know if you want to bet with Amelia," Talen said. "She doesn't really play by the rules. She does what she wants and says what comes to mind. It's takes so much . . . courage."

"Has she thought of an A.K. name yet?" Lenia asked.

Seeing Amelia and Talen's friendship blossom gave Kase hope that Amelia would officially adopt the A.K. lifestyle, even as she was trying to come to terms with the terrible things that Mardious had done when she was gone. Amelia was a wild card, and it was difficult to predict whether she would revert to her Money Jane ways or adopt a newer version of herself.

"That's a surprise that only Amelia will unveil," Talen said. "With the

Knightwing, you should be able to finish your mission in Tailsgate before she wakes."

"Agreed," Kase said. "What else do we need?"

Kase, Lenia, and Talen gathered the rest of their supplies. The glider couldn't take much weight, and so Kase only took a small sac with a couple of water bottles and some snacks. Lenia strapped her trident to her back so they could teleport out. They both took a sword and a couple sacs of Sleepy Time in case they needed to put someone or something to sleep in order to sneak around.

"You'll want to wear your helmets," Talen suggested. "The cool winds might make it hard to keep your eyes open."

"I'll teleport them back with the glider once we get to phase two," Lenia said. "Our Marauder costumes should help us blend in with the locals if we discover that the town is in fact run by Josephine."

"I'll get them ready for you," Talen said.

Lenia teleported Kase to the top of the Skyland Grind. There they could see the floating islands that led the way up. The area was brown except for a few white dandelions, as if a forest fire had damaged all the grass and trees. There was also a smell of bacon.

Lenia returned with the Knightwing frame, which had been broken down into four pieces: the crossbar, each wing, and the triangular steering piece. Kase and Lenia put the frame back together before stretching the cloth across the top.

When they were finished, Kase steadied himself under the triangular frame so it rested on his shoulders and walked it as close to the edge as he could. Before crawling back to Lenia, he grabbed a couple white dandelions and hid them in his coat pocket.

"How tight should this be?" Lenia asked. She was standing behind the Knightwing, struggling to strap into her levitation device.

Kase raced over to help her out. But when he placed his hands on hers, he realized she'd figured it out already. She looked up at him softly. The setting sunlight made her green eyes nearly glow, reminding Kase of the first time they'd kissed.

Kase wrapped his arms around Lenia, pulled her in tight, and kissed her deeply.

Lenia broke it off, but she kept her nose close to Kase's. "If we keep this up, we're not going to make it to Tailsgate."

"Is it going somewhere?" Kase kissed her again, but Lenia pulled back in laughter.

"I wish we could stay here all night, but the faster we get to Tailsgate, the faster we can get home," she said. "Plus, we don't want to get caught by a dragon out here, do we?"

Kase instinctively looked to the sky. Even with the power of the doorway, he didn't share a strong connection with dragons. The only dragon he'd brought back to life had been occupied with the chaos of High Guardians, and he had found nothing to share with the great beast.

Unlike Turanus, who was staring at Kase from across the field.

Kase sighed. "You're right." He let go of Lenia. "If Turanus can find us this fast, I'm sure dragons will soon follow."

Lenia followed Kase's gaze, just in time for Turanus to teleport within their reach.

"I didn't mean to interrupt," Turanus said to Kase.

"We're taking a trip using our new glider." Kase gestured to the Knightwing. "You're welcome to fly alongside us."

"I tracked the man with the scorpion necklace to a cave in the northeast," Turanus said. "I'm unable to track him further."

"He seems distressed," Lenia said. She reached out and stroked Turanus' snout.

"He's been following Mardious," Kase said to Lenia. "The direction is consistent with our trek to the cache that housed the red piece of the doorway. What did the cave look like?"

"Its door requires fire to open," Turanus said.

"That's the cache." Kase turned to Lenia. "When was the last time you were there?"

"I haven't been there since you started teaching me archery," Lenia said.

The portal of the cache required dragonfire to open. Lenia would lure a dragon to the door by teleporting around the area, and then disappearing once the dragon blew fire onto the portal. She had borrowed a few golden bows and some books for Talen, but there was an entire treasure trove that remained largely undiscovered.

"What else do you think is in there?" Kase asked.

"He leaves the door open when he's there, but it closes when he leaves," Turanus said. "I'm unwilling to enter. Are you?"

"We left a lot behind," Lenia said. "Is that where he found the medallion? What other secrets from King Michael were left there?"

"Maybe elixirs," Kase said. "Do you know if he's there now?"

"The door is open," Turanus said.

"Should we check?" Lenia asked.

"No, Turanus confirmed he's there now." Kase took a deep breath. "What do we do?"

Lenia looked down and tapped her foot.

Kase wondered if Mardious was alone. With the threat of dragons, it was likely that the open door was unguarded, but they could still find cover in neighbouring caverns. Were there members of the Brotherhood in the cache with him? How many would there be? If there were elixirs, what would happen if Kase and Lenia could get their hands on some before Mardious ingested his?

"It appears to be the only entrance," Turanus said. "I haven't found a separate way in yet, but I keep trying to find caverns underneath the island."

"Lenia can't teleport directly into the cache either," Kase said. "The only way in is through the portal, but there's a risk we won't be able to enter stealthily."

"If he has an elixir handy, we're doomed," Lenia said.

There was only one direct way out of the cache. Could Kase and Lenia wait for Mardious to leave, and hit him and his crew with a lightning bolt? How many of the surrounding caverns would they have to scour to either find a suitable hiding spot or possible guards? Would there be surveillance mirrors pointed at the cache?

Kase looked around for surveillance mirrors where they were standing.

"This information is useful, but it feels like we should use it for another day," Lenia said. "If we keep to our main mission, we can get two sets of intel back to Cali and make a plan for our next move."

Kase didn't see any mirrors or disturbances in the terrain around them. Cali had never mentioned any plans of attack before, but would this new information change her thought process? Was it time to make a major move instead of slowly building a plan to take down the kings?

"If we could get to him today, wouldn't we be closer to avoiding further conflict?" Kase asked. "It's a surprise to us that Mardious is here, but we could use the element of surprise to our advantage. Even if he drank an elixir, we saw that it takes a few seconds to kick in. Could you teleport fast enough for a fatal blow?"

"Breathe," Lenia said. Kase hadn't realized he was holding his breath. "I like it because it's bold, but what might it cost? Worst case, we lose and perish. Best case, would it really end a conflict? What would the Brotherhood do without Mardious? Maybe we can come up with something better on our trip to Tailsgate, or better yet, get the help from our leadership of warriors, wizards, and scholars?"

Kase drew air in through his nose and out through his mouth. His heart rate slowed. Lenia was right. A plan that had this many questions right away seemed too important to make in the moment, even if the payoff would be greater. "Turanus, keep an eye on the doorway for us. Find us if Mardious leaves."

"I'll do what I can," Turanus said. He disappeared.

"Let's go." Kase marched to where Lenia had put his levitation platform and helmet and dressed himself with his gear. Lenia skipped along and put her helmet on too.

"How do we get the Knightwing airborne?" Lenia asked.

"The winds swirl around the island," Kase said. He concentrated on the environment, connecting with the air currents that were close to the edge. "If you control our platforms, I'll move the wind to blow us in the right direction."

"Perfect," Lenia said. "Fully open your mixture lever. We'll adjust it when we get settled."

Kase and Lenia climbed into position under the Knightwing. Even though Lenia was controlling mixtures of both magic lava and potion, Kase could feel the power resonate within him. He focused on the swirling winds instead.

Kase closed his eyes and took another deep breath. The winds stirred up his conflict. He wasn't ready to let go of the possibility of going after Mardious, but Lenia's plan to work something out would help them prepare. As much as Kase wanted to run right in and start a battle, victory would likely come easier with a proper strategy.

Lenia lifted the platforms so that they hovered just above the grass. Kase was about to aim the breeze to push them forward, but instead Lenia tilted the platforms and pushed them over the edge.

The horn of the Knightwing pointed down, forcing them into a nosedive off the island. Kase felt his body lift towards the cloth. He almost lost his grip and saw Lenia's right hand flail. "Hold on!" Kase yelled. He grabbed Lenia's hand and steadied it back on the frame.

Lenia was laughing.

The small islands that led up to Skyland passed them by in flashes. Luckily, they were too far away to hit any. The patchwork quilt that was the ground grew rapidly closer.

Lenia's body slammed into Kase's, sending the Knightwing into a spiral. "Woo!" she yelled, her thrilled shrieks muffled by the fluttering of the cloth on the glider.

Kase focused on what a flying beast would do. Maxim flapped her wings to get higher, but then stretched them out once she got to a cruising speed. She kept her head straight and her wings wide, even when there was a rush of air during the flight. Even Turanus had glided through the night after galloping to get airborne.

They needed to steady the glider.

Kase focused on the wind. He brought in a gust opposite to the direction they were spiralling; this steadied them, yet they continued to nosedive.

Kase sent another gust past their feet and towards the front of the glider, which caught the wind like a sail. Finally, the Knightwing's horn pointed forwards and their descent stopped. It felt like they were floating in the air like a cloud.

"That was so much fun!" Lenia shouted.

"Do you think your brother would have wet himself?" Kase asked, remembering the time that Lenia took him and Leland for a quick skydive off of Skyland.

Lenia tapped Kase's arm. "He's gotten better," she said.

"We didn't lose too much altitude, right?" Kase asked.

"Maybe," Lenia said. "Can we get much higher?"

"Let's decrease the mixture in the levitation platforms," Kase said. "I'll try manipulating the breeze to see how this thing handles."

Lenia and Kase moved the levers on their platforms to the same angle. Lenia was able to control the burning in both without a noticeable dip in position. Kase manipulated the wind so they could move left and right, and eventually up and down. The dives were much shorter trips, but Lenia's laughter made them worthwhile.

Lenia even figured out how to steer the Knightwing better. By pushing the triangular frame forwards or backwards, rather than only relying on the wind, it was easier to either stay steady or dip down. Their experience would definitely give them an advantage over Talen and Amelia in a race.

As their gliding became more reliable, the excitement wore off a little. Lenia checked her compass to make sure they were still headed to Tailsgate, but almost dropped it when she put it back in her pocket. Kase checked his own and pulled out a dandelion stem. The white seeds had blown off by the time he presented it to Lenia, leaving only a green nub.

"Make a wish?" Kase said confidently. The slow pace of the glider made it easier to talk as well. He used his power to re-grow the dandelion, rapidly maturing from bright yellow to white. But as soon as he let go of his connection, the white seeds blew off the flower's head.

Lenia grabbed Kase's hand. "Tell me a story," she said.

"Once upon a time," Kase began. He didn't have a story ready, but he knew an idea would come to him on the fly. He returned the dandelion stem back to his pocket.

"Classic!" Lenia said.

"Once upon a time," Kase repeated, "A beautiful Demon Queen ruled the land of the afterlife, protecting lost souls from further peril and pain."

"Like me?" Lenia giggled.

"One day," Kase said and tried not to laugh, "an evil wizard known as The Pigeon Master broke through the magical barrier that protected the land of the afterlife. He wanted to feast on the Demon Queen and devour every last soul. Because, as we all know, pigeons eat souls for breakfast, lunch, and dinner."

"All birds," Lenia said. "Not just pigeons."

"Sorry, all birds," Kase said. "The Pigeon Master commanded his army of birds to attack the Demon Queen, but she was ready for him. She had trained vigilantly for years, waiting for this moment. Not only did she destroy every bird that breached the barrier she also collected their feathers to construct a flying platform for her lost souls to enjoy."

"Ruthless," Lenia said. "I love it."

"Without a winged army, the Pigeon Master was unable to chase the Demon Queen," Kase said. "For no matter how powerful the wizard was, he would never bring the Demon Queen down from the new heights she had reached. The end."

Lenia lifted a hand off the glider and snapped her fingers. "That's the best story yet!"

"Thank you, thank you," Kase bowed his head, but wasn't willing to let go of the glider frame to exaggerate his gesture.

"I admire her courage in that story," Lenia said. "I don't think the real Demon Queen would face an army of birds by herself."

"I disagree," Kase said. "I admire the real Demon Queen's courage. It's why I think we can take on the real Pigeon Master tonight. We've been in so many battles together. It's a great opportunity to get a big win."

Lenia put her head on Kase's shoulder. The Kinghtwing tilted to the right.

"It's easy to look back in hindsight, but how many of those battles actually went according to plan?"

Kase rested his head on Lenia's helmet. Their glider shifted back on course. At the battle of the Triple Crown, Kase had been stabbed by a dragon-handled sword, which had been painful, but it did lead to the crumbling of the High Authority. Before that, Lenia had been crushed by stone pillars that Mardious had demolished with dragonmite. Although they were alive right now, they had lost a few battles.

"Does the Quest Series count?" Kase asked.

"I guess," Lenia said. "But the only consequence of losing the Quest Series was not receiving a medal. It's not like we would get captured, tortured, or lose our lives."

"Those were the days," Kase joked. "Sometimes I wish we could go back."

"Do you mean go back and graduate, drop-out?" Lenia giggled.

Kase technically hadn't finished the warrior program at The Academy; he'd been promoted to his High Guardian task force after serving a short work term in his third year. He felt like he'd accomplished what he needed to, though, even if he didn't have the credentials to prove it.

"If I did go back, I think I'd apply to the wizard program," Kase said. "Do you know any former professors that could give me a good reference?"

Lenia laughed. Her helmet shook so much, Kase had to lean away from her, steering the glider off course. "You're the most powerful wizard in the realm! What are you going to learn at the Academy?"

"I'm not the most powerful at everything," Kase admitted. "Potion making is probably my weakest skill. I mean, I can read a recipe, but I can't identify all the ingredients like you and Aura, nor do I have an instinct for it like my mother does."

"Fair." Lenia righted their course. "Potion making is a bit of an art."

"The best part about going back would be the Quest Series," Kase said. "I could enter it all four years and become a six-time champion. I'd be the greatest of all time!"

"Do you think six championship medals makes you the greatest?" Lenia asked. "What if I entered again, and you only won five?"

"What?" Kase laughed. The glider swayed a little more. "You'd train as a warrior just to enter the Quest Series for one year, and you'd compete against me?"

"I'm already a trained warrior," Lenia replied confidently. "I'd enter the scholar program."

"So you'd become a wizarilar? A schorriard?" Kase asked.

"It's pronounced Triple Threat," Lenia said. They both laughed.

"All right, Triple Threat, first quiz: how would you attack Mardious Hood in the dragon cache?" Kase asked.

For the rest of the flight, Lenia and Kase discussed their plans to infiltrate Mardious' hiding spot. They talked about how they would sweep the area around the cache for surveillance and, if they found none, install their own mirrors to watch the area. They'd find out who else accompanied Mardious on his trips, how many Brotherhood members there might be, and what their schedule was like.

Given any opening, they'd attempt to get into the cache when Mardious wasn't there. Lenia would bait a dragon as she'd done before to open the door. Kase could even practice connecting with the dragon. He'd had no luck before, but maybe he'd find what was missing and create a new magical ally.

A quick trip into the cache without Mardious and the Brotherhood there should give them an advantage. They could scour the area for hiding places, determine what weapons Mardious might have stashed, and develop a strong defense when it was time for attack. They could leave traps, install more surveillance mirrors or, if they were lucky, they could find elixirs to use against him.

Their plan wasn't foolproof, but at least it was more logical than an impromptu, surprise attack. Talking it through with Lenia gave Kase confidence in their victory, but it also helped him get in the right mindset for battle. Was there a future where he could also become a Triple Threat?

"What if I joined you as a scholar at the Academy?" Kase asked. Tailsgate was finally in view. From the air, they could see a giant bonfire in the middle of town. The glow from the flames outlined the skyline of the surrounding buildings, but the smoke plume was shadowed by the night sky.

"Are you really interested in becoming a scholar, or are you just trying to get on my Quest Series team?" Lenia joked.

"Both?" Kase asked. He could feel a storm brewing in the distance. He couldn't tell if it was just rain clouds, or if it was a thunderstorm.

"I'd like that," Lenia said. "But we're going to have to train hard. Just because we won the Quest Series in the past, doesn't guarantee that we'd win it one—let alone four—more times. Our past victories have only prepared us to continue on to the future."

Kase felt a flash of lightning in the distance. He smiled. "Spoken like a true scholar," he said. "Are you sure you can't teach instead? Educate scholars, wizards, and warriors as a Triple Threat Professor?"

"We'll figure it out." Lenia pointed ahead. "We should probably land before we reach the bonfire. We don't want the light to reveal our shadow."

"Should we even breach the town?" Kase asked. "It might be easier to sneak in on foot if there's an event happening. We could change before we enter."

"It's safer from the sky," Lenia said. "We should have just enough fuel to get us there. If we can land on a building, we'll likely avoid any pedestrians, Marauders, and surveillance mirrors."

"Okay, Captain Two T's," Kase said in his best Curtis impersonation. "Steer us to the right roof and we'll survey what's next from a safe spot."

Lenia giggled. They flew the rest of the way in silence, their minds now on their mission. Kase wondered how many Marauders would be patrolling the streets, what kind of cavalry they'd have, or if there would be any visible captives.

When they reached the town's edge, the Knightwing dipped. Kase peered through the darkness to see if they'd been hit by anything. He noticed Lenia grip the frame a little tighter.

"Hold on," Lenia said.

Kase turned his attention to the fuel. He felt the last bit of magma burning, and wondered why Lenia hadn't given him more warning. He braced himself for whatever they needed to figure out next.

"Straight ahead, four stories," Lenia said.

There was no one near the town gate, but there was a crowd on the main strip. It was still too difficult to see exactly what was causing the commotion around the bonfire. Kase hoped it wasn't wizards being burned at the stake.

The levitation platforms gave out. Kase and Lenia both swung down, dangling from the frame. The Knightwing angled to the right under Kase's heavier weight. He tried to shift to the centre, but almost lost his grip as the glider dipped suddenly.

"We're almost there." Lenia had tucked her body up in preparation for landing.

The buildings below them seemed to pass by at lightning speed, but they were still on course to land on the rooftop that Lenia had identified. Kase tried to think of anything but his grip.

"Just a little farther," Lenia said. Her legs were swinging. "Now!" She grabbed Kase's arm and teleported them to the rooftop.

Kase's feet hit the ground, and he instinctively crouched. Lenia helped him keep his balance. "That was an easy landing," he said.

The Knightwing soared just above their heads, dipped abruptly, and crashed into the roof. The ornamental unicorn horn broke and flew into the parapet. The frame bounced a few times, sliding to a stop against a closed door that likely led down into the building.

Kase looked around to see if anyone had noticed, or if there were any visible surveillance mirrors.

"Poor Knightwing." Lenia teleported to the edge of the roof and picked up the broken unicorn horn.

Kase crouched and hurried to the far edge of the roof. He ignored the glider, although he heard music coming from behind the door. He crouched behind the parapet and peered over the edge. A rustling signalled that Lenia had teleported next to him.

Down the street, a few blocks from where they had landed, a crowd of Marauders danced around a giant fire. They were tossing objects to fuel the flame.

"Are those books?" Lenia asked.

The objects did flutter open when the Marauders threw them, but it was difficult to see. What looked like tree limbs were piled at the base of the fire, but they could have been tables, chairs, or bookshelves.

"Should we get a closer look?" Kase asked.

"Study the crowd first. I'll clean up Knightwing and grab our Marauder gear," Lenia said.

Kase didn't notice anything peculiar about the Marauders. They seemed to be in celebration mode, happy with their destruction of knowledge. They clearly had no ambition of becoming Dual or Triple Threats. He tried to figure out how close the storm was. Not only could he bring rain to ruin the fire dancing, he could also use the lightning to clear the crowd away.

He felt a lightning bolt scatter across the sky and saw a glimmer of it in the distance. He waited for the thunder.

A clash behind him caught his attention instead.

"You little . . . " Lenia was rubbing her knee.

"Are you okay?" Kase asked. He was about to stand, but Lenia put her arm out and laughed.

"Don't worry, I'll win this battle," she said. She disconnected a frame piece and disappeared.

Kase returned to the storm. It was easy for him to reconnect to the wind currents; instead of pushing the Knightwing along, he was pulling the dark clouds closer. The rain would have likely missed Tailsgate tonight, but his manipulation of it would quiet the crowd and allow him and Lenia to sneak around better.

Another bang broke Kase's concentration. He took a deep breath and turned again, but this time Lenia and the Knightwing were gone. Standing just outside the open door were two Marauders.

"It's him!" one shouted.

Kase stood. He glanced back over the edge, noting how far of a fall it would be. He'd likely survive but would need some time to heal. And if he ran, he'd have no way of telling Lenia where he had gone.

"Are you sure?" the other Marauder said. "Isn't he supposed to be ten feet tall?"

Kase needed to buy time for Lenia to return. Was she having trouble storing the Knightwing? Had Talen not found their Marauder uniforms?

"He's not a giant," the first Marauder said. "He used to be one of us."

The first Marauder was bigger than Kase. He seemed poised and ready for battle. If he had once been a High Guardian, he wouldn't hesitate to attack. The second one was shorter and fatter but did not seem shy of an altercation. Was he a former High Guardian, too?

Kase raised his hands. "It's okay, I'm not here to harm you," he said in a low voice.

The Marauders looked at each other. The big one unsheathed his sword, while the other grabbed a horn and started blowing.

Kase drew his sword, too.

"Drop your weapon," the first Marauder shouted.

Kase felt for the lightning again, but it was too far away. He didn't have time to move the entire storm, but he'd try to bring some 'dry lightning,' as King Michael had called it. A strike would be devastating to everyone on the roof, so Kase wouldn't use it unless he was out of options.

He thought about emptying a potion from his beltline but settled on a different tactic.

"I came to talk," Kase said. "Who runs this town?"

A couple more Marauders stumbled out the doorway. They were shorter and scrawnier, and they hesitated before drawing their swords. But even nervous warriors were still a threat.

The second Marauder handed his horn to one of the new ones. "Keep blowing," he commanded. He drew his sword and stepped beside the first.

Kase needed a shield. A magical dome would have been nice, but a ring of fire might be intimidating enough. He didn't have his fire starter with him, and the bonfire down the street was too far away, but an illusion would likely do.

"Bring your commander to me." Kase traced a semi-circle between him and the Marauders with the tip of his sword. An illusion of fire followed, flickering up to knee height so that Kase could still see the warriors.

The Marauders fanned out. Two more joined from the stairway. A total of six Marauders now faced Kase. They didn't cross the fire barrier, but the horn still blew.

"Surrender now and we'll take you to her," the first Marauder said. He raised a fist and kept his sword pointed low. The other Marauders stopped moving, gripped their swords with two hands, and positioned their feet in an attack position.

Where was Lenia?

"What is your name?" Kase asked, trying to stall further. Would Professor Triple Threat try to reach a diplomatic solution like a scholar, or go on the offensive like a warrior? Should he sneak a potion out from his beltline, or would that movement cause the warriors to panic?

None of the Marauders moved.

The first Marauder pulled his fist to his chest, but the classic 'Dragoon' battle cry never followed. Instead, Kase felt two sharp pains: one in his back and one in his shoulder. Kase reached behind him. An arrow stuck out of his jacket.

"Get him!" the first two Marauders shouted at the same time.

Kase didn't know which one jumped through the fire first, but his illusion disappeared. He was heavily outnumbered. With archers on the rooftop across from him, and likely more Marauders on the way, he needed to move. He aimed left and swung his sword at the first warrior he saw.

His sword clanged off the Marauder's sword, but Kase didn't need to engage any further. He just needed to keep circling the roof to dodge arrows and swords until Lenia returned. His dry lightning was almost in range; it was too late to try a Sleepy Time potion now. He was struggling to keep track of the Marauders, and so controlling the flow of powder *and* moving lightning into place wasn't an option.

His back tingled where the arrows were sticking out—his body attempting to heal itself. His magic was all over the place.

One of the hesitant Marauders swung at Kase. It was a weak, overhead strike that Kase easily parried. Kase slid his foot and tripped the young warrior, then kept moving towards the far end of the rooftop.

"Block the door, Thumper!" a Marauder yelled.

The horn blower stopped the alarm and drew his sword. He stood in front of the doorway, but Kase wasn't looking to escape down the stairs. Kase took a swipe at the horn blower, which was easily blocked, before moving back across the rooftop.

Another two Marauders charged at Kase. When the closest one swung, Kase spun to his right and slashed at the Marauder's knee. His comrade caught Kase on the shoulder with a slice, but at least Kase had immobilized one of them.

Kase's jacket was in pieces. He thought about taking it off. He had more Marauders to contend with, but an arrow hit him in the chest before they could attack. He stumbled back, clutching at his jacket. It was hard to breathe. Black spots clouded his vision.

The closest Marauder brought his sword up for an overhead strike. He swung it down hard at Kase's neck. Kase braced for the death blow and the lava pit.

It never landed.

Lenia stood tall, blocking the blow with her sword.

Kase pulled the arrow out of his chest and felt his body healing. His vision cleared. Lenia kicked the now-exposed Marauder in the gut, forcing him back.

Kase pivoted to find a Marauder charging them from behind. He engaged with the attacker, this time deflecting a few hits before landing a swipe at the Marauder's knee. Two down. Kase turned to see Lenia drive the hilt of her sword into the jaw of another.

The horn blower had stepped past the door's threshold and was yelling down the stairs. With no one in melee range, Kase scanned the opposing rooftops. He noticed three archers on the tallest building beside them, readying their bows.

Kase felt a stir in the clouds above. He pointed his sword just past the archers and delivered a dry lightning blast to the rooftop. The lightning destroyed the bricks on the opposing parapet, knocking the archers back onto the roof.

Everything seemed to stop.

Lenia used the opportunity to spin back towards Kase. She grabbed his hand and teleported them back to the castle.

Kase dropped to his knees. He was exhausted.

"I guess you got your battle after all," Lenia said. She pulled the last arrow out of Kase's back.

Kase flinched and then laughed. "Barely escaping danger, using a combination of warrior skill and wizard magic, and making me laugh while you tend to my injuries: classic Kase and Lenia date."

Lenia giggled. "Not the outcome I was looking for, but we figured it out, didn't we?"

Kase took a few more deep breaths. Another failure. They confirmed the Marauder presence, but what else could they have discovered if he hadn't hesitated so long, deciding how to act?

CHAPTER 16

A New Purpose

Cali rubbed her eyes. "What did you do?" she asked with a sigh. She was still in her sleepwear, and her hair was a mess, but she seemed more disappointed than tired.

"We got caught," Kase said bluntly.

"They sneak into our town. They use magic to destroy us. They are a menace to our way of life!" Mac screamed overtop a stationary sage mirror image that showed Kase's lightning attack.

"It's my fault, Cali," Lenia said. "We should have swept the area before—"

"This shines a light directly on us," Cali interrupted. "Mirror, Mirror, switch to Scholar Stage." The surface of the mirror swirled, and when the cloud disappeared it displayed the live news segment hosted by the New Realm Order.

The reporter sat at a desk, but her focus was on a family across from her. They were in a small auditorium, gathered on a stage in front of an audience of about one hundred. The father was rubbing the shoulders of his wife while she held their baby. All members were dressed in ragged clothes and had soot on their faces.

"I tried to reason with the Marauders, Cali," Kase said, even though he knew he'd been cornered. "They have orders to capture or kill. I'm certain that doesn't just apply to us."

"They took everything," sobbed the father in the mirror.

The reporter reached across her desk and held the father's hand. "The Currency King will save you and your family."

"We need damage control," Cali said. She stared at the sage mirror with a frown.

"Or we could attack," Kase said. "We learned from Turanus that Mardious is hiding in the dragon cache. If we ambush him when he's least expecting it, we could take him out of the equation. It should have the same ramifications as pairing him with Amelia, even if it's riskier to engage with him aggressively."

Cali stared at Kase for a moment. "I need to think." She turned her attention back to the report. "Mirror, Mirror, stop moving image."

"If we wait too long, we might miss our shot," Kase said.

"Our shot at what?" Cali asked. "Failing? Mardious got the best of us, *again*, and now we've caused more harm by being blamed for an attack on the Marauders. We're fueling the conflict instead of stopping it."

"Our past failures do not predict the future," Kase said, remembering his talk with Lenia. He looked to her for support.

"We'll learn from our most recent mistakes," Lenia said. "We can sweep the area before heading into the cache, thereby reducing the risk while you and the other leaders create a more detailed plan."

"No, you're wrong," Cali said. "We can't afford to make any more missteps. The scholars are marching towards an inevitable war. The realm will soon be cut in half unless we can stop either Sheese or Mac, not Mardious."

Even though Cali was focused on the Marauders and New Realm Order, Kase thought Mardious could be the key to unlock both sides. If they knew what he was up to in the cache, it could provide them with the defenses needed to save countless lives in a battle.

"How much time do you need to make a decision?" Kase asked.

"Well, I'm up now," said Cali. "Once the others wake, I can call a meeting. But I don't see us coming to a quick solution that satisfies warriors, wizards, and scholars. If our enemies are also taking the day to fast track their plans, any decisions we make will need to resolve things quickly."

"Okay." Lenia gave Kase a nod. "We'll return to the castle and rest."

"No, I'd like to stay here with Cali," Kase said. "I want to be involved in the research and planning. We can do more than just await orders. Right,

Triple Threat?"

"How about both?" Cali said. "It's been a long night. Go take a quick rest and be back for breakfast. I'll inform the others first thing, and we can all research together—like the old days of the Liberati."

Kase wondered what time it was. He didn't feel tired, but they'd been up all night so far. Maybe he did need a break in order to come back stronger tomorrow. That way they could find a solution, not just talk about it.

"To the library," Kase joked.

Lenia grabbed Kase's hand and teleported them to the Kingdom of Moiras. But instead of their room at the castle, they ended up at the watering hole. The sky was cool purple with the approaching sunrise.

"Beautiful spot," Kase said. "Might be tough to sleep once the sun's up."

"Clean yourself up," Lenia said. "I'll grab us a change of clothes before we head to Skyland."

"Really?" Kase asked. "What about Cali?"

"In hindsight, we probably should have scouted the cache instead of travelling to Tailsgate," Lenia said. "We know Mardious is there, we'd have thousands of caves to hide in, and I can teleport around the area already, rather than us gliding in on the Knightwing. Plus, Turanus has our back. When was the last time he failed?"

Lenia had good points, but Kase still wanted to give his sister the benefit of the doubt. Was there a way to satisfy both? "If we had more information, it might help us convince Cali and the rest of the A.K. leaders to consider alternatives rather than making another educated guess. Do you still have energy for a stakeout?"

"I happen to know someone who brews tea that helped her stay awake for three days," Lenia gloated. "I'll go see if she can make us some." She disappeared.

Kase was impressed with the Triple Threat. He took a sniff of his armpit, and found out she'd been right about that, too. He stripped to his undergarments. His Dandy Lion outfit could use a clean dip as well, and then a dry in the sun.

He jumped in and instantly regretted the move; the water was ice cold. He wished his healing power could keep his body warm, but he eventually adjusted. He waded deeper and now floated, watching the purple sky slowly turn to orange.

"You're back!" Maxim said.

Kase stood, but the watering hole was deeper than he had thought; his head was the only thing that remained above water. He heard Amelia's shriek first, then saw Maxim dip and land at the water's edge.

"You always know how to find me," Kase said to Maxim. "And you brought a friend?"

"Demon King!" Amelia laughed.

"You're up early," he said.

"I'm actually up late," Amelia said. "I thought I'd grab something for Tal to eat when she woke up, but we got side-tracked. Is this a special pool or something?" She slid off Maxim and walked to the water's edge.

"Is she helping you hunt?" Kase asked Maxim.

"No, I just like her ear scratches," Maxim said. "Thanks for the reminder, though. I need to get back to the pack. Are you offering to help?"

"I have plans," Kase answered. "Maybe tomorrow?"

Maxim purred, spread her wings, and took off.

"Hey, wait for me!" Amelia said. She opened her arms up, but Maxim was already flying away.

"She's hungry too," Kase said. "But I can help you find breakfast for Tal. Did you have anything specific in mind?"

Amelia crept closer to the water's edge. "Not really." She slipped out of her boots and waded in the shallow end. The bottom of her dress floated on the water's surface. "Does she have any favourites?"

Kase couldn't remember if Talen had a favourite breakfast food. She had enjoyed treats from Co.Co. in Kimroad. She also liked all the meals they shared together at the A.K. base, but what would she prefer over anything else?

"She's a bit of a wildcard," Kase said. "I don't recall her mentioning an outright winner, but I also don't remember her avoiding any foods. Maybe eggs and toast would be nice? Or pancakes and fruit instead?" He was starting to get hungry, too.

"I could go for some pancakes." Amelia smiled. "I haven't had any since Mardious and I . . . " Her smile faded. She slumped down and sat in the water. She played with the tiny waves she created.

Kase felt like he'd been punched in the stomach. He remembered how easily he had been reminded of Lenia after her death. "I'm sorry," he said. "I didn't mean to bring him up." He waded to the shallow area. His undergarments clung to his skin, but he ignored the discomfort. He crawled to the shallows and plunked himself beside Amelia.

"Don't be sorry," Amelia said. "It's not like we should stop talking about him or avoid saying his name. Mardious was my life, but things have changed. After seeing some of the things he's done, it's clear he's not the man I remember."

Kase tried to be careful with his words. He was interested to know how Amelia felt about the modern Mardious, but he didn't want to push her into another downward spiral—she'd been in a good mood lately. What would the Triple Threat do?

"Do you regret viewing him through the sage mirror?" Kase mustered.

Amelia sighed. "I don't understand why I was brought here," she said. "I missed my opportunity to grow with Mardious, get into trouble together, and overcome the constant battles that would have helped us climb out of the gutter. He went through so much without me, and it hurts to miss out on it, but I'm also proud to see his accomplishments."

Kase had been so focused on the tyranny that Mardious had exemplified that he'd dismissed how long Mardious, a street kid from the Badlands, had lived as High Wizard of the realm.

"But the thing that hurt the most was seeing the spark fade from his eyes," Amelia said. "He wears a mask to hide his pain, just like we wore masks to hide our identity as thieves. He removed it for a brief second when we met again, but it disappeared just before he attacked me. He's lived so long with the mask on, that I think it's taken over. He's constantly lying to himself."

Kase appreciated Amelia's perspective. But was she a Triple Threat, too, he wondered. He also thought about his Dandy Lion mask, and how it was a part of his identity. Would it eventually take over, and he'd only be seen as a powerful wizard?

"Are masks that bad?" Kase asked.

"In general, no," Amelia said. "But when you use it to hide from those you love, there's nothing worse. I think that is why I'm here. That's why I've been brought back. I need to save him from himself."

Kase hadn't considered saving Mardious, only defeating him. Amelia's perspective was interesting, but could she actually do it? "Do you have a plan?" he asked.

"Planning was always Mardious' thing," Amelia said. "I'm more of an improviser. We had so many loving moments together. I know that all I need is one more to make a difference in his life."

Amelia's plan may have lacked specifics, but Kase liked her heart. "I'll help you get there," Kase said with a smile. He tapped his heart, kissed his fingers, and pointed to the sky.

"Real ones die for what they love, Demon King," Amelia said. "If we make it that far, promise you'll let me rest. Promise me you won't bring me back again." Amelia tapped her heart twice, kissed her fingers, but kept her hand outstretched. She tilted her it back and forth.

Kase remembered her pain when he'd brought her back the second time and understood her viewpoint, but he didn't agree with it. "I promise." Kase rested his hand on his heart. "Is that your own salute?"

Amelia took a deep breath. "Tal told me that pointing to the sky means great, and pointing to the ground means trouble, but what about things that fall between the two? Sometimes bad things have an element of good, and good things have unintended evil. It's a balanced salute that signals that everything will be okay." She flipped up her wrist to display her mermaid design.

Kase liked how the A.K. salute continued to evolve in greater ways. "Is it all right if I use that too?"

"All demons can use it." Amelia returned his smile. "But if you want to help me in return, I could use some demon training. Can you teach me how to sword fight? Or summon a dragon out of thin air?"

Kase smiled. He was glad to have Amelia on his team. "Let's start with the basics," he said. "Have you ever controlled the elements?"

"Controlled what elements?" Amelia asked.

Kase reached out towards the watering hole. He twirled his finger and shaped the water into a snout that poked up from the surface. "Water, air, and fire are the ones I started with," Kase said. "If you can clear your mind, feel everything in your heart, and focus on your goal, you can manipulate the elements to your will."

"Why would I want to do that?" Amelia asked. She was fixated on Kase's creation.

"Maybe for fun?" Kase said. He manipulated the water so that the snout turned into a dragon's head rising from the watering hole.

He remembered encountering the purple dragon on Skyland and how it revealed itself from the misty waters. He allowed his water creation to follow the same path. The dragon stood and spread its wings out wide. It leaned its long head back; bubbles now formed in its mouth.

Amelia shifted closer to Kase; he didn't want her to shy away. He manipulated the dragon to blow water, covering them both. Amelia shrieked and then laughed as they were doused. Kase laughed, too, and rubbed water from his face.

"You're such a troublemaker." Amelia giggled. She splashed more water at Kase, and he fell back, laughing. When he stood she was combing her wet hair away from her face, curling it around her ear. Her blue eyes glowed in the morning sunrise.

Lenia cleared her throat. "Having a good time?" she asked.

"Demon Queen!" Kase said. Lenia held a teacup and saucer in one hand, and a change of clothes for Kase in the other, but she didn't seem impressed. Did she miss the show?

Amelia turned towards Lenia. The water had made her dress nearly see-through, the fabric clutching her skin. Kase looked away bashfully, and then realized his garments were also skin-tight.

"Want to join?" Amelia asked.

Lenia glared at Amelia instead of responding. The teacup rattled on the saucer.

"Amelia was gathering breakfast for Tal, but Maxim dropped her off early," Kase said. "She's also looking for a professor to teach her some tricks. Would you be willing to help her, Professor Triple Threat?"

Lenia's cup stopped shaking as she softened. "Of course, but not in my undergarments," she said. She took a few steps and handed Kase the teacup. As he reached for it, she bent over and kissed him.

"Tal showed me some moving images of you fighting High Guardians," Amelia said to Lenia. "Did it take you long to master your craft?"

Lenia handed Kase his clothes. "I'm still learning," Lenia said. "I can show you how to build good habits, though. Think of using magic and practicing battle techniques as feeding your skillset. You need to feed it every day to grow. If you miss a day, you may lose your energy and starve your talents. Stay disciplined, and you'll grow big and strong."

All the talk about eating was making Kase even hungrier. The tea tickled his taste buds, too.

"Can we start tonight?" Amelia asked. "I still need to make Tal breakfast before I go to sleep."

"Works for me." Lenia smiled. "Talen was in the kitchen helping me with this tea, so let's go see what she'd like." Lenia touched Amelia's shoulder and they both disappeared, leaving Kase alone in the shallows.

Kase slammed back his tea and changed into his clean clothes. He wondered if he'd have to walk back to the castle, but Lenia returned for him. She also took a quick dip and changed into some new clothes before they joined Talen and Amelia for breakfast.

Amelia told some jokes while they ate, trying her hand at appropriate material for the next Jester Joust. A lot of her references were to the Badlands, though, so Kase and Lenia could only politely laugh. Talen laughed harder than Kase had ever seen her do, and he wondered if she'd gotten some background from Amelia prior to the joke telling.

Kase was surprised to realize he didn't feel any different because of the tea: there wasn't an energy boost or magical feeling. He felt normal, just like any other day.

After Amelia left for bed, Lenia and Kase quickly went over their plan with Talen. She was happy to go with them to check out the cache.

Lenia first teleported them to the same spot they took the glider to see if Turanus would meet them there again. Lenia's instincts were correct; the unicorn appeared shortly after they'd arrived.

"He left just before sunrise," Turanus said. "He's currently at your school."

"Really?" Kase asked.

"Really what?" Lenia asked Kase.

"Mardious is at The Academy," Kase said. "Which is good, I guess, but why would he go there?"

"That's where Sheese has been calling the shots for the New Realm Order," Talen said. "Controlling the portal gateways there gives Sheese's people enough authority to limit travellers, as well as provide a viable escape route. It's susceptible to attack, but the Marauders would need to march a long way."

"That also means Mardious can get here within a few hours," Kase said. "If he can use the portal gateway to get close to Skyland, he can make the hike up the islands and through the volcanic stretch."

"He has a floating, golden box," Turanus said.

"Sorry," Kase said. "Turanus just told me he has his levitation carriage."

"That would give us," Talen tapped her chin, "about thirty-two minutes, assuming he travelled at full speed."

"That's plenty of time," Lenia said. "Once we're in the cache, I can do routine ten-minute check-ins with Turanus. We can get in and get out."

"What about surveillance mirrors?" Kase asked.

"We can't check all the caves," Lenia said. "We can do a quick sweep inside, but with only thirty-two minutes to spare, we should just focus on a quick survey."

"I brought two surveillance mirrors of my own," Talen said. "One for outside, and one for inside. That is, assuming it will work on the inside of the cache."

"What if Mardious has someone standing guard?" Kase asked. "What if they're hiding in one of the caves with some elixirs? They could attack us before we have a chance to defend ourselves."

"I have not seen anyone else," Turanus said.

The group agreed on the plan of action. Turanus disappeared to keep an eye on Mardious. To help their escape, Lenia grabbed some cuffs and bound herself to Talen and Kase. Talen was in the middle so that Lenia and Kase could use their free arms to attack. Lenia was confident that even if someone had the power of an elixir, she could teleport away in a flash, giving them time to recover.

Lenia first teleported Talen and Kase to a safe cave to mount the surveillance mirror. They scanned the area and didn't see any movement, not from guards, not from dragons. They approached the white portal gateway with extra caution. After standing before it in silence for a short time, they realized they were safe. Getting to the outside was easier than they thought, but how would they get in?

"Well, this is a problem," Kase said. He tried searching for dragons in the area. Although he'd never connected with a dragon, he thought he'd at least feel their presence.

"It was hit or miss when I came before," Lenia said. "Sometimes I'd luck out and they'd find me here right away, but other times I'd have to teleport along the path that leads to the cache, slowly baiting a dragon the whole way."

"How long would that take?" Kase asked.

"A couple hours or so," Lenia said.

Kase wondered if Mardious had scared all the dragons away from the area. But then how did he get in if it was this hard to bait a dragon to blow fire onto the portal?

"Look for bones," Talen said. "Remember the dragonmite?"

"Brilliant, Tal," Kase said. A golden, three-headed dragon had originally guarded the cache that held the red piece of the doorway of life. Mardious had used a platform of dragonmite to defeat the dragon, spraying its remains all over in the explosion.

"Learning from the past, figuring out our future," Lenia added. She teleported the group quickly around the site, until Talen spotted a claw the size of Kase's torso.

Kase held it in both arms and focused on his breathing. "The last time I did this I destroyed a castle," Kase said.

"And this time, we'll rebuild one," Lenia said.

Kase closed his eyes. He felt the dragon stir inside him.

Lenia stroked Luna's snout while Kase rubbed the necks of youngling unicorns. They had sandwiched him in their hopes of being rescued.

"We'll survive," Luna was reassuring Kase. "The Scorpion gives us food and water. His stings are quick, but not deadly. It's the mice you should save first."

Kase glanced to the tables of experiments. He felt the exhaustion of the mice in the cages on the far side of the cache. They were not getting fed, and so they remained still to conserve energy.

Talen's sage mirror flashed as she documented everything.

"I still say we should take everything." Kase said. "If we do it all at once, how would Mardious know it was us?"

"Who else would it be?" Talen shouted from across the room. She angled her sage mirror to capture images on all sides but was careful not to disturb any of the apparatuses, liquids, or elixir recipe pages.

Lenia scanned the room. Another ring of fire had disappeared, signalling that the portal gate would soon close. "Even if we had the time, I can't teleport everything." She stroked Luna's snout again. "I wish I was strong enough to carry you, Luna."

Kase considered lifting one of the younglings to see if they were heavier than the two-person maximum that Lenia was able to teleport. But it might be worse if they were only able to save two of the unicorns. If they left Luna behind, Mardious might take his anger out on her.

"You don't think Mardious might be suspicious of a golden, three-headed dragon in the area?" Kase tugged at his collar. He hadn't relived the moments of the dragon's death before bringing it back to life, but he had felt a reversal of the lava that flowed through his mouth and burned him to the core. It was like he had blown fire three times.

"Skyland is home to many dragons, so it is reasonable to assume that another golden dragon exists," Talen said. "This cache is not home to anything, which is why we need to ensure that we leave it as we found it: no tracks, no evidence of movement, and no teleporting anything away."

"At least, not until we come up with a better plan," Kase said.

"Learn from the past, adapt for the future," Lenia said. "We'll come back for you, Luna."

"Be strong, young ones," Kase said. "This will be over before you know it." He patted their necks, but he still felt their nervousness rise. He plucked a hair from each of their manes. If Mardious changed his mind about their survival, Kase would be able to bring them back.

Talen captured a few extra images of the elixir notes while Kase and Lenia said their goodbyes to the unicorns. Kase hoped Talen's notes would be detailed enough for them to develop their own elixirs. It wasn't as successful a trip as they had hoped, but it was enough. They understood the madman a little more and maybe, just maybe, they had what they needed to destroy his advantage.

CHAPTER 17

Rally Cry

Amelia focused on the pile of sand. She held Kase's Quest Series medal, but no matter how tight her grip was, she couldn't seem to move the bits of sand from one plate to another. "It's not working," she said.

"It seemed like a logical substitution." Talen rubbed Amelia's shoulder. "I am sorry it does not replace your lost medal but thank you for trying."

Kase tried to focus on measuring the ingredients for their first elixir, but he found this kind of potion making boring. It was a lot of prep work, and a lot of waiting, but not much action. Lenia was busy comparing the notes they'd found to some books in King Michael's library, which seemed even more boring.

He triple-checked the amount of cooled unicorn blood before adding the last ingredient. He didn't want to waste any of their blood. After confirming that Luna and the younglings were okay, Turanus had been quite willing to donate some blood if it meant stopping Mardious Hood.

He stared at the candle that kept the purple liquid bubbling. "Was the medal the only source of power you're familiar with?" he asked.

Amelia stretched her hand out and moved her fingers. "Mardious mimicked playing the piano to focus," she said. "Could that do it?"

Kase had always thought it strange that Mardious tickled the air when he was showing off his illusions or manipulating the elements. Now he realized there was a musical meaning behind it.

"A wizard's magic belongs to them, and anything they use to amplify that power requires a connection that cannot be forced or mimicked," Lenia said, looking up from her notes. "You can twiddle your fingers all you want, but unless that helps you clear your mind, open your heart, and feel the magic with everything you have, you might just be stuck playing an imaginary piano."

"Thanks, Demon," Amelia said. "I have an appreciation for music, but I was never a player. I guess I'll just have to wait for Mardious to return my medal to me." She leant back in her chair and crossed her arms.

Lenia snapped her book shut. "That would be the easiest, but you don't strike me as an easy-way-out type." She looked to Kase. "I need to pick up some fairy tears." She disappeared.

Amelia huffed and sat up straight. She gripped Kase's medal and focused on the sand pile. Amelia glared hard at the plate but nothing happened. Kase remembered his struggle with fire control, and how frustrated he felt when he had no clue what to do, and then how uninspired he felt when Lenia showed him how simple and easy it was.

"I think finding another source of power may work better," Talen said. "For instance, Lenia used to rhyme words to focus her magic before she created her trident. I wonder if her power would have grown if she had not levelled up her power source. Do you know, Kase?"

Kase thought about the discipline that Lenia showed at improving all her skills, not just as a wizard. "She would have found a way," he said.

"Did you change sources, too?" Amelia asked. She stopped her sand-moving practice.

"Yes, as a matter of fact," Kase said. "I started with Lenia's trident, but my power grew when I fell into a pit of magic lava. My skin melted away from my bones, my insides were burnt to a crisp, and then my skeleton turned to mush. After that, I didn't need a focus tool at all."

Amelia raised her eyebrows while her jaw slowly dropped. She shook her head and returned to her sand pile. "That's why you're the Demon King," she said.

"We all find our way," Kase said. "You've already lived through difficult obstacles of your own. Maybe the easy part is next. Is there anything new that you've connected with that feels different from your old life?"

Talen met Amelia's gaze, and then looked away shyly. Amelia turned her left palm up, but instead of tickling the air with her free hand, she ran her fingers across her mermaid design. She focused back on the sand, but nothing happened.

Amelia crossed her arms. "This sucks," she said.

"Maybe we missed a step," Talen said. "Instead of focusing on too many new things, we could combine something familiar with something new. Is there any magic you enjoy performing?"

Amelia's fingers moved up her arm. "Healing," she mumbled.

Kase was hoping for something else. Since he could heal himself, he doubted it would help Amelia to practice on him. He checked the room to see if Lenia had returned, so she could help Amelia try something else.

Talen decided not to wait. She reached into her pocket and pulled out one of the tiny spikes that she used as the Shark Knight. Without a word, she gripped the spike and jammed it into her wrist. She let out a tiny squeal, but kept her wrist extended towards Amelia.

"Tal, you didn't have to …" Kase stood up to help, but Talen raised her healthy arm.

"It's okay." Talen winced. "Amelia's got it." She aimed her shaking arm at Amelia.

Amelia stared at Talen's oozing wound. Blood had streaked from the penetration point down towards Talen's elbow. A few droplets hit the floor. Amelia seemed more fascinated by the wound than disgusted.

"You'll need to remove the spike for me," Amelia said. She put her left hand gently on Talen's elbow and then readied her right hand near the wound.

Talen nodded. She gripped the top of the spike, squealing again as she wiggled it. It didn't seem that deep.

"Quickly," Amelia instructed. Her voice lowered with confidence, like she was in control.

Talen yelped as she pulled the spike from her wrist. She crumpled, but Amelia covered the wound with her right hand before too much blood squirted out.

Kase reminded himself not to intervene, but he fought the urge to help.

Talen's arm was shaking. She looked away and stomped her foot.

Amelia closed her eyes and took a deep breath. She let go of Talen's elbow and pressed her mermaid design to the hand covering Talen's wound. As soon as she exhaled, her hands started to glow.

Talen squealed again, but Amelia giggled. Kase didn't know if Talen was shaking her arm faster, or if Amelia was moving it for her. Amelia tilted her head back and screamed so loud that Kase covered his ears.

Amelia let go of Talen's arm and relaxed back into her chair, breathing heavily.

Talen raised her arm and studied her wound. She ran her fingertip over the scar that Amelia left. "You did it," Talen said.

"I missed that." Amelia shook her head and then stared at her hands. There was dried blood on her right wrist, but her hands and the mermaid design were clean. She twiddled her fingers like she was playing a tiny, upside-down piano.

Kase was happy to see Amelia's perseverance. It gave him hope that he could learn something new, rekindle his plans, and have faith that they'd figure everything out.

"What happened?" Lenia asked upon her return.

Talen was wiping the excess blood off her arm with a cloth. Amelia was still staring at her hands, while Kase was searching through the notes that Lenia had left behind.

"She's back," Talen said.

"I never left," Amelia answered. She placed her elbows on the table and refocused on the sand. She touched her wrist as she concentrated.

"Where are your fairy tears?" Kase asked, noticing Lenia's empty hands.

"I thought your mom could help, but I ran into Cali instead," Lenia replied. "There's been a new development that requires an emergency meeting. She's requested our presence in the dining hall."

Kase checked the elixir, but it needed time to simmer anyway; a meeting wouldn't interrupt its brewing process. He put Lenia's notes down. "Let's go," he said.

"All of us," Lenia said. "Even the newest member: Demon Knight."

Amelia stopped staring at the sand. "Everybody?" She curled back into her chair. "What will I wear?"

"It's not that formal," Lenia said. "We should probably clean up the blood, though."

Lenia teleported Talen and Amelia away. Kase didn't need to change, and so he was left alone to review Lenia's notes for a little while longer. It looked like Mardious had multiple kinds of elixirs they could find useful, provided they could make them correctly. But with super wizards like Lenia and Aura on their side, Kase was confident they'd figure it out.

Lenia returned alone and teleported Kase to the dining area of the A.K. hideout. Kase stood beside Amelia and Talen in the back and surveyed the scene.

Family and friends were seated facing a giant sage mirror, which had been moved from the command center. Tables filled with snacks and tea flanked the sides. Both Kase's grandparents were fixing a plate.

Amelia had found a new black dress with matching gloves, an outfit that suited her new name: the Demon Knight. Unfortunately, Talen's mask for her wasn't ready yet.

"Here, Kase, take your brother," Ashlyn said as she entered. "I need to grab some water."

Kase turned and accepted Vance. "Good to see you too, Mother," he said. Ashlyn kissed him on the cheek and rushed towards the closest table of goods.

"That's your mom?" Amelia asked. "She looks so young," she mumbled.

"Well, she was dead most of my life," Kase said. "Would you like to hold him?" He cradled Vance and bent lower so Amelia could easily grab him. "His name is Demon Baby," he joked.

Amelia didn't respond. She carefully took Vance from Kase, held him close, and gently rocked him. Usually Vance fussed around newcomers, but he seemed fascinated with Amelia, staring at her as she made cooing noises.

"Please have a seat!" Cali yelled from the front.

Most people were already seated and talking, but now they fell silent and focused on Cali. The few stragglers at the refreshments table rejoined the group, except for Ashlyn. She rushed back and took Vance away from Amelia.

"Thank you so much," Ashlyn said. "You have a gentle touch for being the Demon Knight." She snuck away before Amelia could respond.

"How did she know?" Amelia asked.

"Legend travels fast," Talen said. "I see some dates at the table. Should we grab some and sit?"

"Can we stay here instead?" Amelia took a step back. "I'm more comfortable in the shadows."

The room was dimly lit, but it was nice to be relatively unnoticed in the back. Kase grabbed Lenia's hand and hoped she didn't teleport them to a seat.

Instead of waiting for everyone to sit, Cali played an image on the giant sage mirror.

"The time has come," Mardious said. He was dressed all in black and sitting on a throne in the middle of the woods. The back of the throne was split, and the red velvet that once covered the seat was scratched and frayed. There must have been a campfire in front of him, because the darkness of night covered the treetops behind him, but his face remained illuminated. He looked menacing despite the lack of vials, necklaces, and swirling Amelia heads.

"The Brotherhood will not sit idly by while the New Realm Order wages war with the Marauders. We will take back what's been stolen. We will destroy the foundations of any system that continues to oppress outsiders. And we will exact our revenge on those that have hurt our families. We are the true leaders of tomorrow, and if it's a fight that the world wants, then it's a fight that only we will win!"

Mardious laughed. The image panned out to reveal Brotherhood members in the background chanting 'Oliyeah' and waving their weapons in the air. Only the closest angry faces could be seen hollering, as the rest looked like only shadows.

Kase recognized Porkchop and D'Angello in the crowd behind Mardious. He checked on Amelia to see how she'd react. She'd taken a step back, her eyes on the ground.

"Stop moving image," Cali said. The image froze with Mardious in the middle of a maniacal laugh. Cali turned to the crowd. "The New Realm Order has identified Kimroad as their chosen battleground. Considering Mac won't leave the old castle of the Triple Crown, it seems logical that Sheese would attack him in his stronghold. Sheese has promised to rain fire on the Marauders, but it seems like the Brotherhood will also join the fight."

"This is the first time that all three leaders plan to converge," Sharaine said. "If we want to make a real impact, this may be our only shot. The reason we called this meeting is to agree on a plan of action that suits everybody."

"Mirror, Mirror, show Mind Map A," Cali said. A cloud appeared on the sage mirror, followed by a parchment inscribed with random words and phrases. Kase noticed 'voluntary hardships' in the top right corner, and 'avoid war' circled on the left, but the biggest phrase was 'share the doorway of life'.

The crowd murmured. Cali and Sharaine stood tall and waited for questions, but no one stepped forward.

"Should we come clean about the elixirs?" Kase asked.

"I don't think it would make a difference," Lenia said.

They didn't even know if the elixir recipes worked yet, and it would take time to mass-produce them for the A.K. Since they were extremely outnumbered by the New Realm Order, the Brotherhood, and the Marauders, the elixirs wouldn't give the A.K. a significant advantage. Kase surmised they would be best used in a defensive situation to counteract any enemy elixir use.

"This is a big decision, Cali," Roman said from the front. "Are we supposed to decide tonight, or do we have time to review and reflect?"

"The sooner we make a decision, the quicker we'll be able to react," Cali said. "The march continues whether we have a plan or not, so people's lives are at stake if we fail to act at all."

"What does failure look like, Cali?" Dom asked. "Is it continuing to live in this hole? Is it losing the people we love, again? Is it ignoring the safety and security of all residents of the realm?"

The crowd murmured again. Cali smiled at Dom, seemingly pleased with the conversation and turmoil they were producing. "Failure can be defined by each of us, in many different ways, and I encourage you to answer that for yourselves." Cali said. "For me, failure is letting a few supposed leaders make decisions for the masses. Failure is taking for granted the lives of those who are supposed to be served, rather than enriching their quality of life and respecting those who may disagree. Failure is continuing to follow the same orders expecting different results."

Some crowd members nodded. Curtis looked over his shoulder, as if to check with what others were saying. Kase wondered how his recent failure to hit Tailsgate with a lightning bolt applied.

"How do you define success?" Talen shouted from the back. "Is it the opposite of failure? What happens if we follow different orders, but get similar results?"

Cali's smile disappeared. "Thanks, Tal," she said. "Does anyone have an answer?"

The crowd went eerily silent. Some were thinking. More were looking around. Kase looked down as he thought, catching sight of his mermaid design in the dim light.

"The answer is unity," Kase said without thinking.

Cali shielded her eyes from the light of the sage mirror. Roman turned in his seat and did the same. Everyone in the crowd shifted to look back at Kase.

Lenia ignited her trident, so everyone could see him. She squeezed his hand.

Kase took a deep breath. "Some of my best memories involve time spent with warriors, wizards, and scholars together, and that still continues in little moments today." He looked to Lenia, Amelia, and Talen. Amelia was staring past him at Lenia's trident. He was glad to see she was not backing away into the shadows.

"Success to me would be sharing that feeling with the realm," Kase said. "With Mardious calling the Brotherhood to arms, we now have the former High Wizard, High Scholar, and High Warrior fighting against one another. Their hate is bleeding into everything else, further dividing scholars, wizards, and warriors in the best-case scenario, and utterly destroying each other in the worst. It's up to us to stop them from allowing the world to close itself off from the beautiful differences among us."

Kase looked back to the mind map on the sage mirror. "There is one element that I've been wrestling with for a while, and that is sharing my power with the world. It's been a gift and a curse to bring back those that have perished, but if one leader shouldn't be responsible for the deaths of thousands, then one also shouldn't be responsible for the lives of those who have fallen. I understand that giving it up will put us all in danger, but it's the only thing we have that differs from those in power. It's a piece of magic that sets us apart."

Kase's revelation was met with only attentive silence. He extended his arms, palms up, and made a not-to-scale illusion of the doorway of life. Instead of a portal leading into the ground, he shifted it so that the crowd could see the coloured pentagram. Even though the majority of the A.K. reaped the benefits of his power, they were never told how it came to be.

"This is the source of my magic," Kase said. His illusion split into coloured pieces, just like it had been before Kase had reassembled it. "Remnants were scattered throughout the realm by an ancient king, but we were able to finish what Sheese, Mardious, and Mac had secretly started. If we were to give the pieces back to the leaders of the people, showing the world its capabilities rather than hiding it, they would be forced to come together to use the power for themselves."

"Or convince their followers to tear their enemies apart to keep it," Cali said from the front. "It's a risk to trust the doorway of life to others . . . but it might be the only way to avoid chaos."

Kase moved four pieces—blue, red, green, and yellow—away from the centre. He allowed the rest of the doorway to disappear, leaving the pieces floating in a circle. "We would keep a piece for ourselves," he said. "That will allow us to retain our voice and share in the world that will come from a united people. We can only hope that our wisdom and experience gained from wielding this power is of value to those who would use it next."

Kase's illusion disappeared.

"It's a decision we'd have to make anyway, down the line," Cali said.

"Making it now will give us a chance to save lives, rather than just bringing them back in a desolate future. Anyone accepting this power must agree to equality as the basis of all things. That is the only way the power can lead to inclusion for all."

Kase grabbed Lenia's hand. It felt good to get his ideas off his chest. He finally felt like a Triple Threat himself.

"We!" Curtis shouted.

"We!" a few of the new trainees replied.

"We are!" Curtis shouted again.

"We are!" everyone responded, other than Amelia.

"We. Are. The!" Curtis said.

"We. Are. The!" Amelia caught on this time.

"We are the A.K.!" Shoulders rose and fell like waves in the sea as people danced in their seats. Ashlyn was rocking Vance. Leland was rocking Lenia's niece. Lenia bounced into Kase and pumped her fists at shoulder level. Amelia had even joined in by the end.

When the chants subsided, Cali pointed back to the sage mirror. "We don't need to decide right now, but I urge you to reflect on the ideas presented. We all have a vote, an opportunity to shape the future, and we need to agree on a plan of action together if we expect the realm to do the same. We will meet again tomorrow night to tally the votes."

Kase, Lenia, and Talen stuck around the compound to chat with their families and friends, to introduce Amelia, the Demon Knight, to those she hadn't met, and to eat some snacks. Even though Kase had laid his truth out, no one seemed concerned about the pending decision Cali had presented. Everything seemed ... okay. He even shared the Demon Knight's new salute to drive it home.

When the party died down, Lenia returned Kase, Talen, and Amelia back to the castle. Kase and Lenia were still feeling the effects of the cosmic flower tea but didn't want to spend their time mixing elixirs or studying strategies. Instead, they lay next to the doorway of life, the stars glittering above them.

"Your speech proved how great a leader you are," Lenia said.

"I was surprised to have support from Cali," Kase said. "You didn't say anything to her before, did you?"

"No, I don't get many chances to speak when she's in meetings with her scholars," Lenia said. "Maybe when I'm a Quad Threat like you: warrior, wizard, scholar, and leader."

Kase chuckled. "I'm also a Demon King," he joked.

Lenia laughed. She rolled closer to him. "So you're a Quintuple Threat?"

"Not if you unite them," Kase said.

Lenia laughed harder. "You should save that one for the next Jester Joust."

Kase put his arm around Lenia and laughed with her. He knew only one person would find what she had said funny.

Maxim landed next to them and settled into the grass. It was late for her to be out, but Kase was glad that she'd heard their laughter and decided to join.

"Where's the crazy one?" Maxim asked.

Lenia nestled into Kase, but Kase's attention was now on Maxim. Would he have any more conversations with her if he distributed the doorway of life? After all, he'd only been able to communicate with her and the other langaras after he'd fallen into the magic lava of the doorway.

"The crazy one? She goes by the Demon Knight now," Kase said.

"You have such strange names for each other," Maxim groaned.

Kase didn't know how to break the news of the doorway to Maxim, so he decided not to sugar-coat it at all. He told Maxim of the proposal he'd made with the A.K., the possibility of others wielding the power of the doorway, and Kase's fear that he might not be able to chat with her for much longer.

"Will you still stay at the castle?" Maxim asked.

"Anything is possible," Kase said. "That's the exciting part, but also the scariest. All I'm certain of is that things will be different."

"If we can't talk to each other, how will I know that everything is okay with you?" Maxim asked.

Kase thought about the different ways that he communicated with his friends. He knew of one sign that they used for respect, hope, happiness, and unity. He sat up to show Maxim but ended up disturbing Lenia's comfortable embrace.

"What are you doing?" she asked.

"Maxim wants to know our salute," Kase said.

Kase stood tall and instructed Maxim to follow his lead. He tapped his heart twice, kissed his fingers, and wavered his hand back and forth. Maxim leant back so she was sitting on her hind legs, tapped her heart with her paw, licked her claws, and reached forwards.

"Perfect," Kase said.

"So now you're a langara professor too," Lenia said. "I'd say you're a Sextuple Threat, but you're just going to unite it."

Kase looked over his shoulder and smiled at Lenia. "Don't steal my jokes," he said.

He sat back down and cuddled Lenia some more as she laughed. She picked a white dandelion from the grass, lit her trident, and moved a flicker of flame to create a flowery fireball. Kase revived the white dandelion a few times so Lenia could make more wishes.

Maxim lay next to them until they all fell asleep. Kase drifted off, knowing his next conversation with Maxim would likely be in a dream.

CHAPTER 18

Too Good to Be True

Cali's fingers gripped the edges of the square blue stone Kase handed her. The stone was the shape of a sage mirror, but thicker. She ran her free hand across the etchings and then flipped it over and felt the smooth side. "Why is it so small?" she asked.

"It was more challenging than I thought," Kase admitted.

After the A.K. had overwhelmingly voted in favour of splitting the doorway of life into four pieces, Kase summoned a few lightning strikes to shatter the portal in the Kingdom of Moiras. Since it was the most powerful act he could summon, they'd all assumed that it would work instantly. But after multiple failed lightning strikes, they ended up with something new.

"How did King Michael get six-foot slabs?" Cali asked.

"Talen wasn't able to find any clues in the library," Kase said. "They're not the same size as before, but it might be better this way. They're a lot easier to transport."

Since all the new pieces were hand-held, Lenia could teleport them to a proper rendezvous point. It would eliminate the possibility of an ambush during transport.

Cali looked out the castle window to the field. Some of the grass was blackened by Kase's lightning strikes. "How do you feel?" she asked.

Kase didn't feel any different. It wasn't like he was expecting a reversal of his experience when he was melted in a pool of lava. He did anticipate that something would be missing, but it hadn't happened yet. "I feel exhilarated, but nervous," he admitted.

Cali grabbed Kase's hand. "Me too," she said. "Let's show the rest of the A.K members our blue piece and transport the others to the appropriate leaders. The faster we act, the more lives we might be able to save."

"Before we execute our plan, Cali, there's something you should know." Lenia gave Kase a nod.

Kase was reluctant to confess to Cali, especially when she was in such a good mood. "We have a proposal on how to get the red piece to Mardious," he said. "Since we know he's hiding in the dragon cache, we were thinking of returning the red piece while he's away. This would eliminate another conflict with the Brotherhood or any mercenaries in the Badlands."

"I trust Turanus' intel too," Cali replied. "But how do we know the Brotherhood isn't guarding the cache?"

Kase reached into his pocket and pulled out a vial that was filled with purple liquid. "We've been there," he said.

Cali took the vial from Kase. She held it up to the window and studied the elixir. "Great work," she said. "When did you go?"

Kase explained his, Lenia's, and Talen's excursion to Mardious' hideout and what they had discovered there. Their surveillance mirror inside the cache didn't work, but they could still track Mardious' movements from the one outside. After spending two days testing elixirs of their own, they now had a small stash of the purple, blue, and orange elixirs, the same ones that Mardious had been focusing on.

"I'm sorry we ignored your orders, Cali," Kase said. "Hopefully our success outweighs our punishment."

Cali opened the vial and smelled the elixir. "I was trying to protect you," Cali said. "If you're safe, I'm proud that you took ownership of something you believed in and could level the battlefield with this magic. It works the same?"

"We think so." Kase looked to Lenia. She gave him a shrug and nodded along.

"It enhances my teleportation," Lenia said. "If we were ever in a situation where we needed to evacuate fast, the elixir would give me the ability to teleport hundreds of times in what others would feel as an instant."

"How much is there?" Cali asked.

"Of the purple?" Kase asked. Cali nodded. "We have thirteen vials. It takes longer to make than the healing and fire elixirs."

Cali checked the purple elixir again. "These last few nights, I thought you two were spending some much-needed alone time together. I didn't realize you were working on a plan of attack."

Kase looked to Lenia and shared a smile. "Sneaking into caches, teasing dragons, and practicing magic are good dates," he said.

"When our work is done, we'll have fun with normal date stuff too," Lenia added.

"Cheers to that." Cali put her cap back on her vial and raised it.

"You should try it," Kase said. He pulled another sample from his pocket. "It might help you understand what we're up against." He popped the cap off the vial and raised it to Cali.

Kase and Cali drank their elixirs at the same time and waited for the power to kick in. Lenia teleported away, leaving Kase and Cali in the room alone. Cali tapped her fingers on the table nervously; then Kase noticed her eyes turn purple.

Everything went quiet.

The first noise Kase heard was a tap from the table, but it didn't match the rhythm of Cali's fingers. "This is weird," she said. Her lips also moved before her speech reached him.

"Think of it like a dance," Kase said. It was advice he'd received from Amelia when she experimented with the elixir, but he'd take credit for it for now. "Feel your surroundings and react to your instincts instead of focusing on each individual note."

Kase glided across the floor of the large parlour. He sped up and leapt over one of the loungers near the fireplace, twisted in mid-air, and curtseyed upon landing.

"Increased strength is a nice bonus to the speed," he said.

Cali stretched out her fingers. "I can feel it, but I don't think I'm stronger. I haven't even been practicing my warrior skills, so how would it help me?"

"Well, if our plan works, you won't have to fight," Kase said. He took a step, jumped up, and landed in the lounger.

Cali made her way across the room and sat in the lounger perpendicular to Kase. "How long does it last?" she asked.

"A minute or so of real time," Kase said. "To us, it will feel like ten times that. You might feel tired after, so you can use this if you want." Kase reached into his pocket again and pulled out a blue vial.

Cali accepted it. "It's kind of nice to have an escape like this," she said. "I can't remember the last time I had a few minutes to waste." She stood up abruptly. "Want to play the cloud game?"

"Of course," he said with a smile. He rolled off the couch and followed Cali to the balcony. Cali opened the door carefully, as per Kase's advice, so it wouldn't swing open and shatter under her strength. They leant over the railing, but Kase looked down at the doorway of life portal instead of up to the sky.

"It's like they're not even moving," Cali said.

Kase glanced up. The clouds indeed stood still. The breeze felt light on his skin; he tried to connect with it. He hadn't tried any magic while testing the elixirs, only his speed, strength, and battle skills.

"That one looks like the Demon Knight's mermaid design," Kase said. Three clouds connected with streaks, symbolizing the balancing of scales.

"I'm jealous," Cali said. "Do you think Anastasia would make one for me?"

"Of course!" Kase said. "Do you have a design in mind?"

"Well, I *am* the Wolverine," Cali said. "Just like that cloud." She pointed to a giant blob that was next to the scale. Kase couldn't make it out, but when he and Cali had met a wolverine, it was just as misshapen and ugly.

"Perfect," Kase said. He suddenly realized he hadn't had a conversation with Cali lately about anything besides plans.

"Tell me about your new idea for the red piece," Cali said.

Kase must have jinxed the conversation. "It's the same as the Badlands plan, but we don't have to entrust anyone with the relic and the note. We simply leave it in the cache for him to find—after we empty his supply of elixirs and save Luna, of course."

Cali folded her hands together and leant her elbows on the balcony. "That's definitely easier," she said. "If we take all of his inventory, it will be less for the Brotherhood to use."

"After Lenia takes the purple elixir, she can clean out the entire cache in no time," Kase said. When Lenia had teleported under the effects of the elixir, she had found she could teleport bigger objects than usual. The elixir would help her carry more items. More importantly, it would help teleport Luna and the younglings away.

Cali turned to Kase and smiled. "I'm proud of you, brother, for what you've accomplished." She opened her arms and gave him a hug.

As he hugged her back, he felt the breeze return. "I'm proud of you too, Sis. For what you've done, and what you will continue to do."

They returned to the cloud game until Lenia teleported back to the castle. They agreed on the new plan for the red piece before Cali returned to the A.K. caves. The first piece of the doorway would be to Mardious, because it was easier for just Kase and Lenia to drop it off. Sheese and Mac would follow, but other members of the A.K. were needed for those missions.

Since, like Amelia, Mardious worked nights, it was better to travel to Skyland during the day. After checking the surveillance mirror and confirming the dragon cache portal was white, they set off to their first destination.

They tried to check with Turanus first, but when they arrived at the edge of Skyland he didn't appear. They waited a few minutes, and then decided to keep moving. They needed their surveillance mirror to survey the terrain in private and mitigate any surprise, and so Lenia teleported to the cave where they had stashed it. The portal was still white. And no dragons were around.

With the orange elixir, they wouldn't have to bait any dragons out to blow fire on the portal. Lenia teleported and used the elixir to open the portal. She returned to Kase in pain, but he healed her. It felt like when he'd swallowed lava from the doorway of life.

When they had both recovered and entered the portal, Kase's heart sank.

"It's all gone?" Lenia asked.

"Not everything," Kase said. He noticed Luna perk up, but the younglings remained huddled in the far corner of the pen.

There were still some piles of treasure on the floor, but the bookshelves were bare, the tables were clean, and the piles of ingredients were gone. All the elixirs were missing. Kase assumed that they wouldn't even find a drop on the floor.

"Do you think he set any traps?" Lenia asked.

"Can you feel any?" Kase stretched his fingers and tried to connect to any danger. There wasn't any dragonmite burning. There weren't any animals hiding in the corners. He didn't sense any illusions.

"No," Lenia said. "We don't need to wait to find them, though. Let's get the unicorns out of here and report to Cali."

"Should we still leave the stone?" Kase asked.

"I can always come back and get it," Lenia replied.

Lenia drank one of the purple elixirs and waited patiently for the magic to kick in. Kase placed the red stone and note on the empty podium where they'd originally found the doorway piece. He didn't know how to display it, but he had little time to think about it before Lenia teleported him to the A.K.'s main strategy room.

Cali was sitting with Sharaine, reading some notes and enjoying lunch. Cali almost chocked on her sandwich when she realized Kase was standing at the opposite end of the table.

"Back so soon?" she asked.

Two plates appeared before Kase, both with sandwiches and an assortment of veggies. Lenia was sitting next to where Kase stood. Her eyes still glowed purple.

"We were too late," Lenia said slowly. Her voice sounded higher pitched than normal.

Kase sat next to Lenia. He placed his hand palm up so she could grab it. Her hand vibrated as she gripped him tight.

Kase explained what they'd found—or didn't find, for that matter. By the time he'd finished, Lenia's hand had stopped vibrating. They both took a bite of their sandwiches.

"If he's transported his entire inventory, that can only mean one thing," Cali said. "He's getting ready for war."

"No," Sharaine said. "They're ready now. They're attacking today."

This time Kase almost choked on his sandwich. He watched as Cali and Sharaine searched the giant sage mirror for news of war, but nothing came up on any of the moving images except old reports and interviews with Sheese in his stronghold at the Academy. Lenia watched intently.

"There's nothing mentioned," Cali said. "Although, if I were going to war, I wouldn't be announcing it, either. There's only one way to know for sure." She looked to Lenia and Kase. "We need to enter phase two. Now!"

Kase thought about drinking a purple elixir so he could eat his lunch in peace, but they were down to ten vials, having retrieved none from Mardious' stash, and they needed to conserve every drop.

Cali's phase two plan was to play to Sheese's vanity. By surrendering to him directly, he'd welcome the stage to take credit for their failures, but also lecture them to show his superiority. If Cali kept him talking long enough, there was a chance that Sheese would come up with the idea of peace on his own and then force Mardious and Mac to unite for the betterment of the realm.

Kase thought Cali was being a little too hopeful, but boosting Sheese up was better than tearing the world apart.

Unlike the Marauders, who would attack first and ask questions later, The New Realm Order would assume that Kase still had his power and likely accept surrender. So rather than bring the entire A.K. with them, Kase and Cali would venture out on their own, and Lenia would watch from the rooftops. With the added power of the purple elixir, Lenia's stealth would be heightened, and she could get inside before anyone knew she was even there.

Kase also had a contingency if the New Realm Order used elixirs, too.

"We should carry swords," Cali said as they got ready. "It will make them feel like they're doing a good job when they search us."

"Potions too?" Kase asked.

"Yes, dress normally," Cali said. "I'll grab my wolverine helmet."

Lenia teleported Kase and Cali to their respective quarters to dress in their A.K. uniforms. Aided by the cosmic rose tea, Talen had been busy creating new outfits, so Kase had a shiny new chest plate waiting for him. It had hints of gold, but still had its trademark slash from the langara. He had matching gauntlets and girdle, but his upper arms were left bare.

Kase hadn't restocked his potions, but they could afford to lose them. He didn't strap any elixirs to his belt, though. Instead, he emptied a vial and held it in his mouth. He slipped on his golden Dandy Lion helmet with its red tint and mane and then double-checked that he had his potion belt and sword.

Once Cali was ready, Lenia teleported her and Kase to the quad of the Academy. She left without a trace. Kase didn't want to give away Lenia's position, and so he avoided looking to the rooftops. Instead, he scanned the common area, where children were running, playing, and enjoying some food, and some senior citizens played games of their own. The contrast of the old and the young, of the joy and the severity, all surprised Kase. But it also reminded him of his first visit to the Academy.

"This doesn't look like a stronghold," Cali said.

Kase noticed a few elderly couples near a fire pit. Behind them was the portal gateway hub. The keystones had ironclad locks covering them. He tapped Cali and pointed. Did that mean that the portals couldn't be used?

"It's the A.K.!" someone shouted from behind.

"That's better," Cali said.

Cali and Kase both turned to see a mother shielding her kids. A few more parents scurried children away. No one seemed like they wanted to battle the infamous Dandy Lion and Wolverine.

"Wait!" Cali raised her white flag. "We're here to surrender!"

A few of the adults spoke into sage mirrors. Others stared at Kase and Cali. No one made a move towards them.

Kase peeked at the castle skyline. The Academy banners still hung as they had when he'd first entered. The midnight owl marked the scholar castle, the unicorn marked the wizard castle, and the three-headed dragon marked the warrior castle. The peach tree flew over the administration castle—the largest given its vast auditorium.

Lenia used to sneak up to the wizard castle to watch the sunset, but he assumed she would now be on top of the scholar castle; it gave a better view of the common area. He wondered if she was close enough to hit him with a grape.

A few men and women rushed out of the administration castle. Kase was surprised to see Grand Master Carter leading the pack and carrying a quill and notebook. He still wore his administration uniform, as if he hadn't stopped working during the war. His entire group stopped before getting too close.

"Miss Garrick." Grand Master Carter's eyebrows furrowed in disappointment. "Why are you here?"

Cali removed her helmet. Kase followed suit, trying to show that he wasn't there to battle. He checked the group behind the Grand Master for elixir vials, but their robes were bulky and could be hiding anything.

"We come in peace," Cali said. "Would you be able to assist us in a sit-down with Sheese, the Currency King?"

The group behind the Grand Master whispered to each other. One of them spoke into his sage mirror, but Kase couldn't make out what he was saying. The Grand Master seemed unconcerned by the commotion behind him and focused instead on writing notes in his book.

"And you, Mr. Garrick?" Grand Master Carter asked. "Why are you here at the Academy?"

Kase had been asked this question before: he had wanted to be a great warrior like his grandfather. He looked to Cali. Should he swallow his elixir to answer? It seemed too early. Should he pound his chest instead? Or give the A.K. salute?

"He's here to help end the war," Cali said with a smile.

The Grand Master made a note in his book. He seemed intrigued, but relaxed. He turned towards the man speaking to the sage mirror. "Satisfied?"

"Grab their weapons," the man behind the Grand Master instructed. "They shall pass."

Other members patted down Kase and Cali, removing their swords, potions, and inspecting their helmets. They paused when they found Cali's relic necklace. Cali's prediction was perfect; Kase was especially glad they didn't check his mouth, even though he'd almost swallowed the elixir when one of the men inspected his beltline.

Grand Master Carter led the group into the administration castle and down the main hall to the auditorium. Kase was relieved to see the balcony was empty—Lenia would easily watch from above—but he was disheartened to see the madness on the auditorium floor. It reminded him of the last event in the first Quest Series, but instead of championship trophies standing on podiums, sage mirrors stood on desks.

A commander sat at each desk. Some were shouting orders, while others watched intently. Each sage mirror had a different angle of the city of Kimroad. A few showed the city on fire.

At the front of the auditorium was a stage. Sheese and a few other commanders had a larger desk with even more sage mirrors. Sheese struck a regal pose as he watched his new prisoners being led to his station. He sported a grin as wide as a child celebrating their birthday.

Kase and Cali were led up to the stage, which was eye-level with them, while Sheese stood over them haughtily. Their escorts returned to their stations, all except the Grand Master. He stood at attention with his notebook open and his quill ready for scribing.

Kase knew the Grand Master was a dedicated note-taker, but he was surprised that his role in the New Realm Order wasn't more prestigious.

"Good afternoon, Sheese," Cali said. "We've—"

"Call me Your Majesty," Sheese sneered.

Kase tried not to roll his eyes. He thought about swallowing the elixir to give a snide comeback, but he was stumped for a clever comeback. What would he demand Sheese call him besides Dandy Lion or the Demon King? He wished the Triple Threat were there to come up with something.

"Sorry, Your Majesty," Cali said, bowing her head. To play his part, Kase bowed his head too. "We've—" she began.

"Supposedly, you've come to surrender," Sheese said sarcastically. "Not sure how much of that I believe. Shall we forego the pretenses?"

"We brought you a gift," Cali said sternly.

Sheese laughed. "A peace offering? You should have led with a deal. Everyone else did." He waved his arm to the sage mirrors on stage. "Tactically, we are in the strongest position, and it is with that strength that we will bring about our future utopia. If you want to be a part of this New World Order, just name your terms, and I will offer you a price."

Kase tried not to swallow the elixir again. He was amazed how easy it was for Sheese to deflect the responsibility of the realm's collapse, considering the lies of the High Authority were the reason for it in the first place. He scanned the stage and wondered how many of Sheese's soldiers believed the lies that he fed them. All they seemed to be focused on were the images of burning buildings, broken walls, and bloodied corpses.

"I agree," Cali replied. "I believe that the realm is strongest when it includes everyone: scholars, wizards, and warriors. Which is why we've come here today: to offer equal share in the power that can create the ideal realm."

Cali reached under her neckline and pulled out a gold-colored stone that dangled from a matching chain. She held it up for all to see, but only Sheese seemed to recognize what it was.

Sheese leapt off stage. Kase noticed several chains tucked under His Majesty's robe. Did they hold scorpion medallions or elixirs? Sheese wasn't wearing a bandolier, but his robes extended past his wrists, and were baggy enough to hide multiple secret pockets.

"You couldn't be that stupid." Sheese snatched the chain from Cali and held it closer for inspection. He felt the etchings carved into the stone, smiling as it met his approval.

Kase got ready to swallow the elixir.

"We've given a piece to each leader, but have kept one for ourselves," Cali said. "My terms are as follows: call off the war, and we can work on a plan to unite the realm, together."

Grand Master Carter started scribbling in his notebook. Sheese's laughter stopped when he noticed the efficient note-taking. "No need to record that one, Carter. You're dismissed."

The Grand Master looked to Kase but bowed towards Sheese. "Yes, Your Majesty." He turned and headed towards the auditorium exit. Kase tried to peek at the Grand Master's book. He wondered what other secrets were inside.

Sheese lowered the chain and pulled out his sage mirror. "Mirror, Mirror, connect to High Wizard Zuke," he said.

Kase wondered why Sheese still used Mardious' alter ego, considering the entire realm knew that Mardious had posed as the High Wizard for years. No one on stage seemed to notice or care. Maybe it was difficult to change old habits.

"What," Mardious said.

"Did the Animal Kingdom give you a piece of the doorway of life?" Sheese asked.

"No, why?" Mardious replied.

Sheese grinned. "They've surrendered," he said. He turned the sage mirror towards Kase and Cali. Mardious' face was so close it seemed pressed against his sage mirror. His eyes were bloodshot, but not coloured by elixirs.

With the action, Sheese's robe slid down his wrist, revealing a wristband with a blue elixir. "By tomorrow, we'll have everything we ever wanted," Sheese added. "Mirror, Mirror, end connection." The sage mirror clouded over, and all Kase could see was his own reflection.

Sheese pocketed the sage mirror and studied the stone again. He ran his fingers over the etchings one more time and then tapped it until it swung like a pendulum.

"Who do you trust more: us or the Underground King?" Cali asked.

Sheese grinned. He stopped playing with the chain and stared at Kase. "You are cunning, Cali," he said. "I taught you that nothing comes free and easy, especially the greatest power the realm has ever seen. But you, young warrior, went through the darkest night to taste this glory. I know this, because I orchestrated your journey. Why would you revert to your old ways and give up this gift?"

Kase looked to Cali, who gave him a reassuring nod. He tried not to swallow too hard. He took a deep breath before staring back at Sheese. He focused on a speech that he'd prepared with Cali.

"Why should one person hold this power, Your Majesty?" Kase asked his question loudly so that anyone in the auditorium could hear him. "Should one person dictate how others must act and feel? Or is inclusion the answer to a unified realm?"

Some of the commanders on stage perked up, even though most kept their attention on their sage mirrors.

"The realm doesn't need questions, it needs leadership," Sheese snapped. "It deserves a king the way a lion pride deserves a great lion with a mane. Your inability to hold onto your power shows how weak of a leader you are."

"And your lack of empathy shows your inability to do what is right," Cali snapped back. "Real leaders have the courage to trust. They are the first ones to risk it all. They put others in a position to succeed, not to submit."

"Wrong: leaders do what they must to win." Sheese lifted the chain up to get a better look at the stone. "I have a counteroffer. Give me your piece of the doorway of life, and I'll allow you to serve me in the new realm."

Kase looked to Cali. Goosebumps raced up his arms.

Cali nodded towards Sheese. "I'm not offering this deal to you," she said. "I'm offering it to the leaders in this room: those who signed up to make a real difference, instead of just fulfilling a promise created by unjust circumstances. This is for everyone trapped in a cage, wishing for—"

Cali's jaw stayed open. Kase looked around as the elixir flowed through his veins. Sheese looked shocked as he reached for his wrist.

Kase ran towards the self-appointed king, tore off his wrist guards, and smashed the blue and purple vials he found. Seeing no other threats, he ran past Cali and searched for the Grand Master.

He made it ten rows towards the exit before he thought about Cali. He turned back but was met by Lenia. "Where are you going?" she asked. He couldn't see her lips behind her unicorn helmet.

"The Grand Master has a notebook," Kase said. "If he has a list of the deals Sheese has made with his followers …"

"I'll find it." Lenia grabbed Kase's hand and teleported him back to the kingdom of Moiras.

Cali stood next to him in the library of the castle. Kase was glad she was safe, but he was a little sad that he had to wait for her reaction. It felt like a waste of elixir to threaten Sheese and leave right away. If they had planned better, Lenia could have just teleported them away at any time.

Kase sulked over to the lounger and sat down. Cali turned to face where he had stood, then found him at his seat. She took a slow step towards him.

Lenia appeared on the lounger across from him. He was relieved. Cali was taking forever. It was boring to watch her walk in slowed time towards them.

Lenia held five notebooks instead of one. She handed the top one to Kase. "This is the one he was using today," she said.

"Why the others?" Kase asked.

Lenia removed her helmet. "He gave them to me. He had already pulled them out of his desk when I found him." Her lips moved faster than her words. "We didn't have time to talk—well, I didn't have time to wait for him to talk—but I think he planned on giving them to you before you left."

Kase looked to Cali, who had only taken two steps more. "Good call," Kase said.

"I also placed a surveillance mirror in his office too," Lenia said. "I had one left after securing the ones in the auditorium."

Cali started talking, but Kase and Lenia still had time to flip through the notebooks. "Great job, you two!" Cali said slowly, her voice a few octaves lower than normal.

Kase was disappointed. The only thing he found after his scan was a balance sheet of numbers and shorthand notes in the logbook. It would take time to discern their meaning.

"I liked your short speech," Lenia said. "You'd make a way better king than Sheese."

"I am the Demon King, you know," Kase joked.

Lenia smiled. "And I am your loving Demon—" her voice sped up before she could finish.

The elixir had worn off.

Cali raced beside Kase and sat down next to him. "What are these?" she asked.

"They're the Grand Master's. They may be a way to figure out what kinds of deals Sheese owes," Kase said. "Do we debrief, or go to the next phase?"

"We need to divide and conquer on this one," Cali said. "Let's finish what we started."

CHAPTER 19

Surrender?

Lenia pointed her trident at the sage mirror. Talen had drawn a map of the castle of the Triple Crown with Cali and Sharaine's guidance. The blueprint of the second floor showed all the rooms, doorways, and staircases, but Sheese's old office was highlighted with an X.

"We'll enter here," Lenia said. She would clear the room first using an elixir and then teleport everyone else. "Rooster, you'll take point at the windows to evaluate possible ground attacks out front or archer positions up high."

"I will-a-doodle-do," Dom said. He tugged at the strap of his quiver.

Kase was glad his helmet hid his eyeroll.

"We have to assume that every area of the castle is under surveillance, and so we'll need to move quickly," Lenia said. "The Bull will lead us from Sheese's office to the stairs here," Lenia tapped the closest stairway. The moving image changed to the fifth floor. "We go up three flights, down the hallway to the left, and into the throne room."

"The hallway is tight, but we should be able to push forward if we outnumber our enemies," Roman said. "It's the stairway that worries me. We'll be vulnerable to arrows from both directions."

"I will handle the path forwards," Lenia said. "The Dandy Lion will have our backs."

Kase tapped his heart, brushed his mask, and pointed to the sky.

"The throne room has multiple entries and exits," Helena pointed out. "Have we identified the weakest point?"

"We're making our own." Lenia pointed her trident to the western wall.

"Per the Shark Knight's calculations, we have enough dragonmite to blast a six-by-six entrance. This will help us avoid any additional guards at the doors. Better yet? It will give us an element of surprise."

From what Kase remembered of the inside of the throne room, there were statues and tapestries along the outer walls. Cali had provided her best guess as to the location of the pillars, but they needed a little bit of luck to hit the right spot.

"It draws attention, but if we stay aggressive, we should be able to meet any resistance quickly," Roman said. "I like it."

"We also have these," Lenia lifted her left arm to show off her armband, which held two purple elixirs. Her right had blue ones.

"Will we have enough, Two Times?" Curtis asked, fiddling with his own elixir band. Talen had made matching armbands for everyone, and another small batch of elixirs had finished brewing. Of the A.K., Roman and Helena had been the most excited to try them out.

"For this mission, hopefully you won't have to use any," Cali said. The group turned as Cali entered the room.

"We couldn't stop Sheese from launching his attack, but with Grand Master Carter's notes we could poach some of his followers," Cali continued. "Thank you, brother, for thinking quickly and giving us the tools we were waiting for."

"I had help from Professor Triple Threat," Kase said.

"A nice reminder of adapting on the fly," Lenia added.

"It wasn't an instant win, as these negotiations with members of the New Realm Order will take time," Cali said. "But for this mission, if we can convince Mac to surrender, it may stop the onslaught. If we give him the green relic, it will allow a future for the Marauders. They've lost so many."

"If he's been a High Warrior of the realm, he won't surrender," Roman said.

"We have to give him the option," Kase said. "If we don't try, then Mac, the Marauders, and any innocents caught up in the warfare will die to protect an old ideal."

Helena smiled at Kase. "You're right, grandson. People can change, even the most stubborn, tough, and hot-headed warriors." She playfully shoved Roman.

"Takes one to know one." Roman shoved Helena back.

The team of eight donned their helmets and made one last check of their elixir bands. Lenia's helmet made her look taller, but the point of her unicorn horn barely reached higher than Dom's rooster crest. Neither were as imposing as Roman's bull-horned helmet.

Lenia teleported Dom and Roman first so they could secure Sheese's office.

The next two to teleport were Helena, who wore her freshly polished Ram helmet, and Curtis, who wore his fur pads, adding bulk to his Kodiak Mountain armour. Curtis' brother, Paul, kept the theme of the bear family by sporting a blue Kaber bear mask. Aura rounded out the group with her Zebra Lily armour.

Aura's research was critical to their final mission. After studying the poisons that had been used against the A.K., she had developed a more potent Sleepy Time potion. Instead of a powder that their enemies had to inhale, Aura created a liquid potion that could be applied to arrows, darts, and daggers. Her Zebra vest was covered in blades that would spread a sleepy toxin over anyone who touched them but, unlike Mardious' daggers, the blades would not critically endanger them.

Kase was the last one to go. He had on his gold-plated vest that matched his helmet. He wore an elixir band on each forearm, but also had his potion belt with his standard wizard tricks. His sword was sheathed, and his arrows, coated in Aura's potion, were bundled in his quiver. He carried a bow in one hand and a nutmeg in the other. The nutmeg was a short club with a weighted end. It worked far better than a sword when disarming enemies in a narrow hallway, in Kase's opinion.

Talen came through the doorway, wearing what was, for her, an excited expression. She held one of the Grand Master's notebooks, reading as she walked. She had made a note on his map. She wasn't dressed for battle, but she gave Kase Amelia's salute that everything would be okay.

"Good luck," Cali said.

Before Kase could respond, Lenia returned for him. "Ready?" She looked around at the four of them. For a moment, the old Liberati were gathered again in the library, doing what they did best.

Kase's heart beat a little faster. Their plan was going well—too well. They hadn't seen a soul, nor even trails of blood, discarded weapons, or other signs of attack. Kase tried to ignore the anxiousness and focus on their goals, visualizing their path to victory.

A gust of wind from Lenia's dragonmite explosion tickled the back of his neck, and a dust cloud wafted out from behind him. He left his position of rear guard and followed the group into the throne room.

As he stepped through their makeshift entrance, he drew an arrow back and surveyed the room. The dust was settling near the blast hole. The front door was wide open, but no one was escaping the room, and no warriors were rushing in to inspect the commotion. The only signs of life were an array of fifty sage mirrors that were like a more-condensed version of Sheese's battle room. No one was monitoring them.

"What now?" Roman asked. The point of his sword dropped down.

"Secure the room." Lenia pointed her sword at each exit point. "Kase, Dom, and I will take the sage mirrors."

Roman shouted orders. Paul guarded the hole in the wall, while Curtis and Aura each went to the rear of the throne room. Roman and Helena rushed to the front entrance.

As Kase focused on the sage mirrors, he realized what a different view the Marauders had. Their surveillance mirrors were mounted on the castle, looking out towards the city. The New Realm Order focused on the city from the outside. Compared to when he had seen them last, there was heavier destruction in the city, more buildings on fire, and heavier casualties in the streets.

"Would Mac flee?" Dom asked.

"The castle has secret rooms." Kase leant closer to the sage mirrors, scanning for any sign of the Mighty King in the mirrors that displayed the halls. "Where would he hide?"

"I'll check with Cali and Talen," Lenia said. She disappeared.

Kase focused next on the mirrors showing the outskirts of the castle. Nearly the entire neighbourhood adjacent to the castle was on fire. Smoke billowed towards the sky. At the rear, a group of ragged brutes fought against the shiny armoured Mauraders. Was it the Brotherhood joining the war? Kase searched for Mardious Hood, but wondered if the surveillance mirrors would even register him given his elixir-enhanced speed.

"Found him." Dom pointed to a sage mirror that showed the front courtyard.

Mac was wearing a distinct purple cape with a white ruff around the collar. His helmet was gold, like Kase's, but much shinier. He was shouting orders at the Marauders in the courtyard and pointing his sword to the guard towers at the gate.

Instead of hiding like Sheese, Mac was at the frontlines with his warrior brethren.

"He's a sitting duck," Kase said. A sage mirror with a higher vantage above the courtyard showed a series of trebuchets getting rolled down the street. The New Realm Order weren't even using horses to pull the wooden carts that held the missile-launching weapons. He couldn't tell, but he assumed that elixirs provided the pushers with the required strength.

Lenia appeared beside Kase. "Cali suggests aborting the mission," she said. She peered at the sage mirror that Dom was pointing to.

"If we do, Mac is finished," Kase said. There wasn't enough time for them to go back, make a new plan, and try to get Mac the means to live another day. If the A.K. really wanted to give everyone a chance, they couldn't let the New Realm Order destroy the Marauders completely.

"Do you have a new plan?" Lenia asked.

Kase nodded grimly. "Huddle up!" he shouted.

The A.K. left their posts and rushed over to the sage mirrors.

Kase pointed to the moving images of the front and rear gates. "The castle is about to fall," he said. "Our only chance to save the Marauders is to deliver the relic to Mac so that he can escape before the New World Order and Brotherhood breach the gates."

"And if he doesn't escape in time?" Roman asked.

Lenia grabbed Kase's hand. "We have to try," she said.

The A.K. tapped their hearts, moved their fingers to their lips, and pointed to the sky. Lenia teleported away to grab more of Aura's weapons, including daggers, throwing knives, and arrows. The crew would split up to try and slow down the attack at the gate: four to run interference on the New Realm Order, and four to separate the prize, Mac, from his dwindling army.

The team rushed to secure their new weapons. Kase put more arrows in his quiver, while Roman and Helena took the extra throwing knives and daggers. All except Kase and Dom downed a purple elixir—arrows didn't travel faster when fired from an elixir-bearing archer. It made sense, but was it the right move? Would Dom and Kase be exposed in a battleground?

Kase reminded himself to stay confident. They didn't have time to fail.

Everyone huddled in a circle and waited for the elixirs to kick in. Kase watched Roman since his bull helmet was open-faced. Once Roman's eyes changed colour, he pulled an arrow and readied his bow. Dom did the same. A few moments later, Lenia teleported everyone to their marks.

The shouting and explosion booms hit Kase faster than his ability to survey the landscape. Archers on the wall towers fired arrows down past the metal gate. Some warriors had made a wood and brick barricade to support the gate and were now firing more arrows through the barrier. Countless other Marauders raced around with additional ammunition, that is, until one of them noticed the A.K.

The Marauder grabbed his horn and put it to his lips, but before he could blow it, it was snatched away. He shook his hand, noticing a gash across his forearm. He panicked, but then fell to the ground, asleep.

Kase looked to Dom. They both lowered their bows and raced towards Mac.

"Mac!" Kase yelled over the screams and explosions. It would have been nice for someone to blow their horn after all.

"Mac!" Dom shouted. His feet tapped quickly down the short, cement steps that ran parallel to a large fountain. Water shot out like a steam spout; the fountain was broken in half.

The purple caped Mighty King turned. He had a personal protective unit that consisted of eight guards. They all wore silver-plated armour with gold highlights and green capes. They took their battle stances, gripping their swords and aiming their shields towards Kase.

"Protect the King!" one of them shouted. Kase recognized the voice of Shay, a member of his old taskforce.

"We're here to help!" Kase glanced around. Good. No one to strike him from the sides or behind. He lifted his bow high in surrender.

An explosion outside the front gate boomed so loudly the sound echoed off the walls of the castle. Hopefully it was from Lenia and crew destroying the New Realm Order's supply, and not from an attack on the perimeter. Either way, the gate remained intact—for now.

Mac pointed his sword at Kase. "Kill him!" he yelled.

Kase dropped his bow and unsheathed his sword. He reached back and pulled the nutmeg from his quiver. A shield would have been better, but he'd try to steal one of the Marauders' shiny gold-and-silver ones.

The protecting Marauders spread out to try to encircle Kase and Dom, but one by one they were knocked down. They had no time to react as their swords and shields were beaten out of their hands and their limbs sliced. Now they all slumped to the ground. Some of them flopped a bit, but they soon fell fast asleep.

"You have the dark magic?" Mac's sword drooped towards the ground as he looked up to the sky. "Strike me down, but know that it will only make our cause more powerful."

Marauders within shouting distance heard Mac's plea. They stopped what they were doing and rushed over to help, swords drawn. Kase wondered how much longer Roman and Helena would be able to fend off the growing circle.

"You're right," Kase yelled. He stepped closer to Mac, not wanting to engage in battle. "We've adapted our defense to match what the Brotherhood and New World Order have created. We've come here to level the playing field and stop the carnage that they've brought to your doorstep."

"You cannot fool me, wizard." Mac pointed his sword at Kase. "But if you surrender now, I'll give you my word that your death will be quick and honourable."

Surrender seemed like a ridiculous option, considering it was Kase who was trying to convince Mac to give up the fight. Would he gain favour by dropping his weapons to show Mac respect, or should he stay the aggressor and force Mac to his knees?

"Air attack!" Dom yelled. He pointed his bow to the sky.

Kase checked the sky where Dom had pointed his arrow. He saw a flock of birds flying high, but as they dove towards the courtyard, Kase made out levitation platforms. And riders. Though instead of standing on square platforms, it looked like they were riding tiny, metal dragons.

He couldn't tell what side they were on, but it didn't matter: they were dropping dragonmite charges from above.

"I'll handle them. Cover the courtyard," Kase said.

He took a deep breath and focused on the mixing of the potion in the winged platforms. If he could adjust the intensity of the reaction, the wizard riding the platform would likely lose control, much like when he used the Knightwing. He didn't want them falling out of the sky and smashing to bits, though, and waited until they were closer to the ground.

The charges would be easier to control. Once activated, Kase would be able to feel the magic of the potion and send it away from any potential victims. An explosion in the sky wouldn't hurt anyone if he kept it away from the flyers.

Dom's bow rattled on the pavement. He drank an elixir and drew his sword. "What about Mac?" he asked.

"Are you too afraid to face me, Chicken Knight?" Mac shot back.

Kase noticed a few charges drop to the north. For a moment, he worried that he wouldn't be close enough for his power to work. He ignited one early because the levitation rider had already flown out of range. The other he sent into the castle wall. Its explosion sent a few bricks tumbling to the ground, but no one was around to be caught by debris.

One rider dipped towards the guard towers, dodging Marauder arrows from below. Kase pushed more magma into the compartment of the levitation chamber, causing the rider to speed up. The wizard tried to fight Kase's power, but lost control of the platform and slipped off. He fell to the ground and landing on a Marauder.

A few winged platforms steered Kase's way.

"Why did the Chicken Knight cross the road?" Dom asked Mac. He twirled his sword like a practiced warrior. "No one knows, but the road will get its vengeance."

Kase wasn't in the mood for a Dom joke, but he liked the stalling tactic. He hoped Dom would tell more. Any delay would help his elixir kick in at the right time.

Kase sent another rider crashing to the ground. This rider wore a pouch with a stash of charges. None of the charges had been activated, but for Kase to manipulate so much dragonmite at close range might cause too much destruction if detonated together.

"The riders have sacs of explosives," Kase yelled to Dom. "Try to gather them."

Dom nodded. He picked up his pace and circled Mac, as if getting ready to engage.

Kase couldn't decide whether he should target the levitation platforms or the charges. There were only five riders left, and he could manage their attacks if they continued to fly around. But if the Marauders picked up the fallen charges and turned them against Kase, it could spell disaster for the A.K.'s attempts to talk to Mac.

"Are you really going to fight me, Chicken?" Mac laughed.

"No," Dom said. His eyes turned purple. "I'll save that for The Bull."

Dom charged at Mac, but before he or Mac could swing, he disappeared.

Mac swung around frantically. When he realized Dom wasn't within range, he turned his attention to Kase. He let out a battle cry and charged, but Kase didn't need to break his own concentration as The Bull had grabbed Mac's cape and held him steady. Mac's legs churned a few times before he turned and swung his sword back. Roman blocked the attack.

"Did my grandson explain the situation clearly?" Roman asked. His voice was steady and his eyes were back to their natural colour.

Kase sent a few charges flying up and away to explode in the sky. Something shiny moved in the distance. He squinted at the large, floating object. It was too big to be a bird, but too rectangular to be a dragon. It didn't appear to have wings.

It was Mardious Hood's golden carriage.

"You're … High Warrior Garrick?" Mac asked. He pointed his sword downwards.

Kase slipped an elixir from his wristband and drank it. He had to clear the area before Mardious attacked. Did the riders also have elixirs? How many more Brotherhood members would be coming from the air?

Helena appeared beside Kase. She gripped her sword with both hands. The tip was dripping with blood.

"Do you understand the consequences of your aggressive behaviour?" Roman asked sternly.

"My behaviour?" Mac asked. "We're under attack! I'm defending the bricks that were laid by generations of masons, labourers, and warriors before me, *before you*. The history of the realm is suffering because of the wild ideas of your grandkids, the selfishness of the High Scholar, and the impulses of a deranged lunatic! If you were in my position as High Warrior, what would you do?"

Kase was glad that Roman had caused Mac to elaborate, but they were still a long way from saving what was left. How many of the bodies lying on the ground were sleeping. How many unconscious? And how many deceased? No one was left to pay attention to the standoff with Mac. The focus within the courtyard had shifted entirely to the gate.

Kase checked the sky. Mardious was getting closer.

"When I was young, I would have done exactly what you're doing," Roman said. "I would act first from a position of strength, and fight till the death to protect those I'd sworn to serve. But as a former High Warrior, a father, and a little bit of a wiser man, I understand that I can't choose to protect certain groups over others. Patience, empathy, and love are stronger than sword or shield."

Goosebumps ran along Kase's arms. He wondered how long Roman would need to get through to Mac.

An explosion sent the barrier on the front gate flying.

Mac and Roman both turned in surprise, but the flying planks, bricks, and warriors abruptly entered slow motion for Kase. Instead of inspecting the gate or trying to stop debris from hitting anyone, he raced to the first levitation rider that had crashed to the ground.

The man was dressed like a Brotherhood member, but something about his clothes was inconsistent. Kase understood what Amelia meant about an imposter trying too hard. The shirt seemed intentionally ripped, the black cape wasn't faded, and the boots looked polished. Was this a new member, or was The New World Order pretending to be part of the Brotherhood?

It didn't really matter. Kase slid the sac of charges from around the unconscious man's shoulders. The rider was still breathing. Kase assumed a healer could help his wounds. Kase checked the rider for elixirs but found none. Like archers, it was possible an elixir wouldn't benefit them.

Kase surveyed the gate again. The planks and Marauders that flew through the air had almost landed. The bars of the gate itself had warped away from the centre of the explosion at the bottom. He couldn't see what was on the other side yet because the dust and debris had formed a cloud.

Lenia appeared beside him.

"The New World Order is about to breach the gate," she said.

Kase pointed to the sky. "Mardious is on his way," he said. "If he lands, we'll need to escape."

"I'll get Curtis, Paul, and Aura back to the mines," Lenia said.

"Wait!" Kase reached out to touch her hand. He caught her before she disappeared. "Take my extra elixir. Roman is talking to Mac right now. Hide and wait until the last possible moment before we leave."

Lenia accepted the purple elixir. "Understood. I have a couple ideas, too." She disappeared.

Kase hustled to another rider, but along the way he stopped beside a few Marauders who had been knocked down by the explosion. He reached into his quiver and grabbed a couple arrows. He stabbed both of them in the arm so they'd fall asleep instead of coming to Mac's aid.

He grabbed another sac from the next fallen rider before rushing to Dom. As he approached, he checked Mardious' carriage. Kase was still under the influence of the elixir and to him the carriage looked to be gliding at the speed of an ordinary bird, which meant it was travelling at full speed. And it wasn't showing signs of slowing down.

"Mardious is about to hit the castle!" Kase yelled to Dom. He couldn't see who was actually controlling it. He assumed it was Mardious, but it could have been someone else.

Dom stabbed a Marauder with an arrow. "We still have elixirs," Dom said. "All things equal, we win in combat against him."

"He never fights on equal ground," Kase said. "Let's protect Mac as long as possible. Lenia will get us out. She has my last elixir."

Dom pulled his purple vial from his wristband and held it to Kase. "You might need this more than I do" he said.

Kase was already holding two sacs of charges, and so Dom slipped the elixir into Kase's pocket.

They both rushed back to Mac. Dom's elixir ran out halfway, but Kase stayed with him until he made it to Helena. There was still a large gap between Mac, the struggling Marauders, and the rest of the battlefield.

Kase set the two sacs gently on the ground. He picked one charge up and held his nutmeg in the other hand. His elixir was still working, and he watched while the carriage in the sky above glided into the fifth floor of the castle. Stones flew in slow motion under the force of the golden vehicle crashing full-tilt into the castle wall, creating a hole bigger even than the one that Lenia had made in the throne room.

"There is nothing left here," Roman said. Kase's elixir had worn off. "It's time to rebuild. This relic gives you a seat at the table." He held the necklace with the green piece of stone towards Mac.

Kase held his breath as he waited for Mac to accept it. Stones rained down on the courtyard from the carriage crash above, but this did not bother Roman and Mac.

"You believe the Currency King will accept a truce?" Mac asked. "He only worries about himself, and he will not agree to terms that don't favour him, let alone ones that are fair."

"Old deals can be broken," Mac said. "If the people fight his wars, sacrifice their lives, and give up their homes for a better future, then the people should have direct influence over the new realm that we're rebuilding."

Mac sheathed his sword, took a step forward, and accepted the chain. "Thank you for believing," he said. "I've been alone for—" Mac dropped to one knee and screamed in pain.

Roman grabbed for an elixir at his wrist, but they were gone. Helena dropped to her knees in pain, just like Mac had. Kase felt his arm get yanked away, his blue elixirs and weapons disappearing in an instant. He waited for a strike to land, but instead heard Roman scream as he fell to the ground.

Mac screamed once more. A sword thrust out of his chest. Mardious stood behind Mac, his one hand gripped the sword hilt, his other gripped the green relic. He smiled at Kase. His purple eyes glowed bright.

Kase stood frozen. His blue elixirs were gone. Did he still have a purple one in his pocket? He couldn't afford to reach for it, or for any other potions or weapons. What is Mardious waiting for? he wondered.

Where was Lenia?

CHAPTER 20

Can't Lose

Mardious' purple eyes glared at Mac. "Hello, old friend." His voice was slow and exaggerated, but the words were clear. Kase was impressed with how well Mardious communicated with the normal world while enhanced by the elixir.

Mac reached for his beltline. He grabbed the hilt of his dagger. "Die, traitor," he said.

Before Mac could swing, his weapon was gone. In a flash, Mardious had stolen the dagger, moved to Kase, and dangled it in front of Kase's face. Mac groaned as he flopped to the ground.

"Can you make a dragon appear?" Mardious laughed. While his words were steady, his maniacal laugh was high-pitched and quick. The dagger fell to Kase's feet.

Kase noticed dust floating over the faces of the Marauders that Roman and Helena had hurt but not subdued. He checked his beltline and realized that his potions were now missing, too. Mardious must have dumped their contents on the struggling warriors, because they were falling asleep. Roman and Helena were also covered in powder.

Mardious stood near the front gate of the castle. Another figure stood next to him, and Kase recognized Porkchop's burly frame. His movements stuttered and blurred, clearly sped up by an elixir.

Kase scanned the area for any other blurry battlers or unexplainable chaos. The battle at the front gate took up everyone's attention, but Kase did spot flashes here and there.

He hoped Lenia was working on a strategy. He reminded himself to work on his own, too.

Kase discreetly lowered his hand to the outside of his pocket and found the elixir bottle. Pulling it out would be noticeable, and so he rubbed the lid of the vial until it popped free. With it open, he could use his element control to move the liquid from the bottle, under his helmet, and into his mouth.

He thought about his first element control lesson with Lenia and Professor Bright. He'd moved water from one bowl to another, but it had looked more like a liquid snake slithering through the air. When Amelia had tried it during her practice sessions, her water flows had been much smaller than his, and it had taken her a long time to move the water, but she had persevered.

Kase decided to copy her style and run multiple tiny streams from the elixir bottle to his lips.

Porkchop and Mardious were still beside the gate. They were arguing, but their words were too fast and high-pitched for Kase to make out. Above them, levitation platform riders in Brotherhood black dropped charges on the New World Order's troops who stood on the other side of the gate. Explosions quickly followed. Alliances were shattering right and left.

Innocents were dying. The only way to escape was for the leaders to call for surrender.

Kase's element transfer was complete. He swallowed the purple elixir. Would Mardious keep him alive long enough for it to take effect? He checked for weapons in the area, and saw that Helena still clutched her bloodied sword.

The green doorway piece dangled a few steps away.

"Where are the others?" Mardious asked slowly. Porkchop was now nowhere to be seen.

Kase needed to slow his answer down long enough to buy time for his elixir, but he also had to finish before his speech sped up. "Sheese has the golden piece," he said. "Cali has the blue piece. The red one is on Skyland, where only you can access it."

"And the rest of the frame?" Mardious asked.

Considering the original pieces were bigger, Kase understood Mardious' concern. There was no evidence that the old leaders knew about the portal in the Kingdom of Moiras, but a larger doorway was consistent with their philosophy. Kase tried to stir up the conversation, the way Talen might. "Would you believe we've entrusted it with Amelia to guard?"

A rush of wind surrounded Kase, but when it settled, Mardious had returned to his original position. He was too far away for Kase to reach, but he wasn't armed. Kase would have time to attack him once his elixir kicked in.

"How did you make the Amelia illusion?" Mardious asked.

Kase wondered why Mardious still refused to recognize Amelia. Maybe explaining how the doorway worked would help Mardious accept the real Amelia and buy Kase more time. Kase felt goosebumps rise on his arms.

"The doorway is not a physical barrier to the afterlife," Kase said. "It amplifies a wizard's healing power. Rather than simply closing a wound, it brings a deceased body back to life. I visited Amelia's grave, dug up her bones, and healed her."

Mardious started shaking just as Kase's elixir kicked in. The illusionary Amelia heads were back, swirling around Mardious, but their voices were muffled. Mardious drew his sword.

"You've become a better liar," Mardious said in his normal voice. He stepped towards Kase and raised his sword above his head.

Kase dropped, rolled to his side, and grabbed Helena's sword. He knelt on one knee and held the sword in a defensive position at head height, but Mardious didn't swing. Instead, he sprinted the other way.

Kase chased after him.

Mardious ran for the gate, screaming. Kase couldn't hear what he was saying, but it got the attention of the nearest Brotherhood ally: Jax. Mardious hid behind him.

"Get him!" Mardious yelled.

Jax let out a battle cry as he blocked Kase from getting to Mardious, who was stumbling backwards. Another Brotherhood member stepped up to join him. It was D'Angello. Both Jax and D'Angello wore glittering armor, but the colours weren't consistent with any allegiance. Jax wore red; D'Angello wore yellow.

Should Kase wait until the Brotherhood's elixirs ran out, or engage them in battle? He must have been the last to take one, right? All of his and King Michael's notes had showed a limited timeframe, but maybe Mardious had been experimenting with prolonging the elixir.

Kase couldn't risk waiting it out. He swung at Jax, who parried Kase's attack easily and then countered with a swipe. Kase blocked the attacked and kicked the side of Jax's knee hard. Jax knelt in pain.

Kase quickly slid to his left. D'Angello changed the angle of his sword, opening his side up for an attack. Kase stabbed him in the arm, spun, and hit him with a long slice to the back of the legs. The big man went down.

Kase looked back to Jax, but he was as still as a statue. His elixir must have expired.

Kase dropped his sword, pulled two arrows from his quiver, and jabbed them into Jax and D'Angello's shoulders. There was a gap in their shoulder guards that made them look bigger, but provided no protection.

Mardious continued to back up. His sword wriggled as if he were nervous, but he was laughing. "How much longer do you have?" he prodded.

Lenia appeared behind Mardious. She had her sword in one hand, rope and shackles in the other.

"More than you," Kase answered. He tapped his heart, kissed his fingers, and pointed to the sky.

Lenia slashed Mardious' arm above the wrist. He dropped his sword and grabbed his wound. Lenia kicked the back of Mardious' knees while he was distracted. Mardious fell to the ground in a heap, his head bouncing off the pavement.

Kase rushed to kneel beside Mardious. Rather than remove the straps from around Mardious' shoulders, Kase removed elixirs from Mardious' bandolier, and as fast as he could. Mardious groaned and didn't resist, dazed from the fall to the stone. Lenia used the opportunity to secure Mardious' wrists with shackles, and tie his boots with rope, completely immobilizing him.

"New plan," Lenia said. She touched Kase's shoulder and Mardious' arm. Before any others in the Brotherhood could interfere, she teleported them to the Kingdom of Moiras where the doorway of life was imbedded in the ground.

The greenery of the Kingdom was welcoming compared to the fiery mess, broken bricks, and chaos at the castle. The sun was warm on Kase's damp neck. He thought he noticed some langaras flying high, but they could be some terrifying birds instead.

"Take a blue elixir to Mac." Kase held out one of the vials he'd taken from Mardious' bandolier. "This, too." He pulled the green relic from Mardious' pocket.

"With all of these elixirs, I could teleport others to safety." Lenia continued to pull more off Mardious.

Kase helped her, but he soon felt the breeze on his neck. He saw the blur of Lenia beside him. Before he knew it, the elixirs in his pile were gone, along with Lenia.

He heard metal hitting stone and turned around.

Amelia stood with her hand open. Her sword finished rattling on the stone portal. She wore a black mask that looked like a skull, its mouth covered by a veil. White flowers were painted across the mask. She also wore a long dress that was black as the night sky. Matching silk gloves that reached to her elbows.

"Is he …" Talen stopped herself.

Talen, wearing her Shark Knight outfit, was beside Amelia. Her new silver mask had a tiger-striped plume and a blue visor covering the shark's open smile. She lowered her crossbow-style wristband—she still wasn't that good at aiming her needles. It was the first time that Kase had seen the full outfit, which consisted of chainmail, silver armour, and a blue cape.

"What's next?" Kase asked.

Amelia rushed to Mardious' side and knelt down. She lifted his shackles and quickly dropped them. Mardious struggled to open his eyes. Blood dripped down his forehead.

"Do we have a key?" Amelia asked.

"I'll get one," Talen said. Her cape swung wide as she spun. She hustled back into the castle, but it looked like her armour and heavy boots were already slowing her down.

Kase retrieved Amelia's sword, but he leant on it instead of giving it back to her. It didn't matter—she was focused on Mardious' wounds. His head was in her lap.

Amelia removed her black gloves and caressed his arm. She focused on the gash that Lenia had made.

Mardious squirmed. His eyes fluttered open. They weren't purple anymore. It took him a few seconds to orient himself. Once he did, his Amelia illusions swirled around his head and then fixated on Amelia. Still tied up he pushed himself off her, using his elbow and hips to flop away.

Amelia slapped Mardious so hard the illusions disappeared.

"Stop that," she said.

Mardious went still. He faced away from Amelia, but his eyes were locked on her helmet. His eyebrows raised as he let out a sigh. He softened.

"Can I heal you?" Amelia asked.

Mardious sat up and turned towards her. He nodded but didn't answer.

Amelia held Mardious' forearm with her left hand and placed her right wrist with her mermaid design over his wound. A few moments passed, but a glow soon appeared around her hands. She dropped her head back and screamed and then collapsed to the ground.

Mardious studied the scar that Amelia left behind. He didn't seem concerned with his head wound, even though Amelia had healed that, too.

"A beautiful souvenir," Mardious said. He leant over onto his elbow and got more comfortable. "What happened to yours?"

Amelia sat up and removed her helmet. She brushed the sweaty hairs sticking to her face. "Consequences of being brought back as a demon," she said. Her eyes locked onto Mardious' eyes. "But the deep scars remain."

Kase finally understood why she had cherished her scars so much. They were reminders of her life with Mardious.

"Will you dance with me?" Amelia asked.

Mardious smiled. "What song?" he asked.

Amelia smiled back. "One that hurts, of course."

Amelia quickly got to her feet. She pulled Mardious up by the shackles, helping him stand. She dipped her head through his restrained arms, and he rested them around her waist. She hugged him tight as they slowly wobbled back and forth.

Lenia appeared next to Kase. "Mac is safe, and with the piece," she whispered.

"And the others?" Kase asked.

"The A.K., Marauders, and Brotherhood survivors are safe too," Lenia said. Her eyes locked on Amelia and Mardious. "The New Realm Order have Kimroad, but they haven't won everything."

Kase grabbed her hand. Lenia put her tired head on his shoulder. Her unicorn horn almost blocked his vision and nearly poked his eye. Good thing he was wearing his own helmet, he thought.

Mardious' eyes were closed. He rested his forehead on Amelia's. "I'm sorry," he said.

"It's not your fault," Amelia replied.

"If I hadn't fallen …" Mardious sniffled but didn't stop his slow dance.

Amelia dipped under Mardious' grasp. She held his shackled hands and stared up at him. He slowly opened his eyes. A tear streamed down his face.

"It's not your fault, babe." Amelia reached up and wiped the tear from his cheek. "What happened was unfortunate but look at what you've accomplished! You rose through the ranks and became the most powerful wizard in the realm. You developed enhancements that obliterated warriors and puzzled scholars. You gave the Badlands something to believe in, and they rose up to fight for the dreams that seemed so fragile when we started."

Kase wondered where Amelia was going with her rant; it seemed to validate all of Mardious' dishonest, delusionary, and murderous actions. He tried to judge Lenia's reaction, but she hadn't moved her head off his shoulder. He trusted in her calm nature and let Amelia continue.

"I'm grateful that you're finally here to witness it." Mardious' lips curled into a wicked grin. "We have the rest of our lives to continue balancing the scales."

Amelia looked to her wrist. "No, we don't," she said.

Mardious' smile faded.

"You have the rest of your life ahead of you," Amelia said. "However long that is as a captured criminal. I might have a future I can't even imagine. But we …" She looked back at Mardious and sighed. "*We* don't have a life together in this world."

Mardious closed his eyes again. Kase thought his illusions might return, the way they had when he turned on Amelia at the farm, but they didn't.

"In the short time I've been back, I've changed." Amelia looked down. "I've learned how to use my magic in new ways. I've made new friends. I even met a mermaid. You might think that you can relate because you know me, but I feel like you don't know me at all anymore."

Mardious stopped swaying.

Amelia sighed and looked back up. "And I don't know you."

Mardious stared at Amelia. His tears returned. "I did what I had to," he said. "If you were here, I could have been different, I would have been … happy."

"The reason we're together today is because of the strength, courage, and wisdom of others." Amelia nodded to Kase and Lenia. "They can continue what we started and rebuild what has been destroyed. I trust them to bring peace to everyone in the realm—including the Badlands."

"You don't like the world I've created for you?" Mardious asked.

"This world … it doesn't make sense to me," Amelia said. "I've been gone too long. I've already lived my life—with you." She let her head fall to Mardious' chest. "I've sensed your pain. There's only one place we can go to escape this nonsensical world. It's dark, and there's no coming back, but it's peaceful. There's no one chasing us. There's no one to fight. There's nothing to accomplish."

Amelia pulled Mardious' dagger from its hilt. Mardious let out a few heavy breaths, but his breathing slowed when he met Amelia's eyes again.

"We can rest there, together," Amelia said.

Mardious and Amelia stared at each other in silence, in what felt like an eternity. He finally turned his palms towards her. His scarred hand looked dirty. "I'll wait for you," he said.

Amelia sliced the dagger across Mardious' scar. "You won't have to wait long," she said. She sliced her hand right after.

Amelia dropped the dagger. She lifted Mardious' hands back above her head and let them drop around her neck. She hugged him again, and they returned to their slow dance. She made eye contact with Kase, tapped her heart twice, kissed her lips, and wavered her hand.

Kase didn't know what else to do, except return the gesture.

Mardious' body slumped forwards onto Amelia. She held him steady for a few seconds, but she, too, soon crumpled to the ground. They shook together, before finally settling peacefully.

"No!" Talen yelled.

Kase hadn't realized Talen had returned.

She sped past him, threw her helmet off, and slid on her armoured knees when she reached Amelia. She leant down, but then hesitated, turned away, and started sobbing.

Kase took a step forwards, but stopped when Maxim flew over him. She crashed to the ground on the other side of Amelia. The sudden thud of her paws hitting the stone didn't phase Talen, whose shoulders continued to shake.

Maxim sniffed Amelia and Mardious and then let out a whimper. She bowed her head and looked to Kase. Her eyes were glistening, but she managed to sit tall. She brought her paw to her chest, and then to her fangs, but instead of finishing the salute, she put both paws on the ground. She gave a crippling, painful roar.

Kase bowed his head respectfully. He thought about the promise he made to Amelia. "Real ones die for what they love," he said.

Lenia squeezed Kase's hand. "We live for it, too."

Talen slumped. Kase and Lenia moved to comfort her, and they wrapped their arms around her in a group hug.

CHAPTER 21

See You Around

Kase reached his hand out.

"Don't touch it!" Lenia slapped his hand away.

Her swipe caused Kase's finger to dab the cupcake icing. He quickly licked the chocolate from his pinky. He felt a little guilty that he'd ruined the pastry artwork, but he wondered why Lenia had presented the cupcakes to him if they weren't ready for dessert.

"Are there more?" he asked.

Lenia giggled. "How many do you need?" She swiped some icing from the unicorn cupcake. It was vanilla flavoured and had a green horn, while the chocolate cupcake had a blue one.

Kase waited patiently instead of answering. Lenia turned back to the picnic basket, snuck her hand under the lid, and pulled out a red-and-gold fire starter. When she presented it to him, he saw the lion etched into the square face.

He shrieked like Talen had when Lenia presented her with her shark fire starter.

"Where do you find these?" Kase asked. Lenia had previously given him a fire starter with a trident on it. She'd also found one with a cloud for Cali. He hadn't thought fire starters with different shapes on them were that common.

"There's a hobbyist in my hometown that does custom engraving," Lenia said. She reached into her picnic basket again and pulled out two white dandelions. "The tough part is finding the right color of fire starter. With stores opening again, it's been a little easier to shop around."

Although the realm wasn't back to normal, every discovery was another step in the right direction. Whether that was old shops opening back up, outcasts returning to their homes, or new owners repairing what was lost, it all meant that scholars, wizards, and warriors were uniting again.

The A.K. weren't the only ones that were able to come out of hiding. The Marauders opened the gates to the cities they'd conquered. The New Realm Order left the Academy so it could return to educating the youth instead of offering refuge to the vulnerable. And the Brotherhood left their wilderness camps. There were still challenges to sort through in the aftermath, but Cali and the other leaders were outlining judiciary, executive, and legislative policies that would help the realm heal.

One of the benefits that Kase and Lenia enjoyed was the return to Uncle Eowin and Aunt Anna's farm. Kase was surprised how much he'd missed lounging at his favourite lake, and he was happy to spend his first day off with the person he loved the most.

Lenia stuck the stem of one dandelion into each cupcake. She pulled out her own purple fire starter from her pocket, which now had a unicorn knight mask etched into it. She grabbed the cupcake with the blue icing. "Should we each make a wish?"

Kase stared at his langara-etched present. His shoulders slumped. "This is amazing," he said. "I thought we agreed on small gifts. Something we made?"

Lenia giggled. "It is small, and I got it made. That counts!"

Kase reached into his pocket and presented his card. He reluctantly handed it to Lenia. On the front, he had drawn a mermaid. His drawing skills hadn't improved much from when he had made 'Get Well Soon' cards during a volunteering quest.

"Is this a fairy?" Lenia asked. She giggled again and opened it.

"Almost." Kase smiled. He flicked his fire starter. He lit his dandelion after making a wish.

Lenia opened the card to reveal the message inside. Kase had written *Happy Birthday*, but had crossed it out in favour of a more appropriate celebration.

"Happy Uni-date, Love, Kase," Lenia said. "Don't you mean 'mornate'? Or 'day-date'?"

"They're not separate if you unite them," Kase said proudly.

Lenia laughed. "Hopefully this is the first uni-date of many." She leant over for a kiss. "I love you, too."

Kase slipped his fire starter and dandelion into his pocket. He set his cupcake down, wrapped his arms around Lenia, and kissed her. She pulled him down to the blanket, but their moment was disrupted by hooves clopping down the path.

Kase connected with the horse but stopped himself from controlling its path and sending it the opposite way.

"Whoa," Talen said, pulling up on the reins.

Kase lifted his head. Cali sat behind Talen on the saddle. Cali dismounted first and steadied the horse for Talen. Lenia tilted her chin up and looked back.

"You're a natural, Talen!" Cali said. "Now, just like you mounted with confidence, keep the same composure, but reverse the steps."

Talen nodded to Cali and took a deep breath. She leant forwards, and her hands shifted as she tried to grip the pommel. She swung her far leg back and over the cantle, but her hands slipped from the momentum. She fell sideways, rolling as soon as she hit the rough trail.

The startled horse backed away from Talen. "Easy, Death Hammer." Cali tried to sooth the horse by stroking his snout.

Kase jumped to his feet. He took a few steps, but Lenia had already teleported to Talen's side. He jogged down the lakefront and knelt as Lenia helped Talen sit up.

"It is okay," Talen said. She was staring at the scrape on her elbow.

"Are you sure?" Lenia checked Talen's hairline, but Kase hadn't noticed her head hit the ground when she tumbled. Talen wasn't bleeding or bruised other than her arm.

"I need to toughen up," Talen said. She pushed herself away from the trail, stood, and brushed off her dirty trousers. "I am sorry to interrupt your uni-date, but I have come to say good-bye. My best friends deserve that."

Talen had taken Amelia's death the hardest. She didn't know how Amelia could logically connect death with peaceful slumber. With the increased acceptance of pain and rejection of help from her friends, was Talen headed down the same dark path? Kase wondered.

"I made a promise to Amelia not to bring her back," Kase said. "I won't make the same promise with you, Tal." He opened his arms and hugged Talen. Kase felt Lenia join the group hug.

Talen squeezed Kase tight. "It's not like that," she said. "I have decided to go travelling. I do not have much of a plan, but I am certain that the only way to find what I am looking for is to take an adventurous path. If anything happens, I wanted to make sure that you know how much I love and appreciate both of you."

Lenia tapped Kase's back. "Are you not taking a sage mirror?" she asked.

Kase let go of Talen. He grabbed Lenia's hand as Talen collected her thoughts.

"I would like to request that you don't contact me," Talen said. "If I return to the castle for more research, I will make sure to give you advanced notice, and we can catch up then. I am prepared for a lonely journey, but I know I have the courage to discover something new. Amelia taught me that." She tapped her heart, kissed her fingers, and tilted her hand back and forth.

Kase and Lenia both returned the gesture.

"Are you going to show them your salute?" Cali asked.

Kase noticed Lenia raise her eyebrows. They waited patiently as Talen kicked the dirt.

Talen kept her head down. She tapped her heart twice, kissed her fingers, and flashed an open palm. Her index, middle, and ring fingers were together, but her pinky pointed down while her thumb pointed up. She dipped her hand down, wiggled it a bit, and then lifted it to the sky.

"Is that a dance?" Lenia asked.

"No," Talen said. "It's a shark."

"Can it be both?" Kase asked. He moved both his arms like Talen had, and thought about a lively jig. He tapped his heart but continued to move his hips and feet in rhythm.

"Why not?" Talen responded. She moved both her arms, matching Kase's steps.

"C'mon, Cali!" Lenia said. Her elbows flailed a little more, but she closed her eyes as she danced with no music.

Cali left her horse and joined the group. She giggled as she jumped sideways, waved her arms around, and spun. Kase was glad that Cali was able to get away for a day as well. It had been a long few months of planning, reconciling, and rebuilding.

After the smoke cleared from the Battle of the Capital, new leaders had worked on terms and conditions to bring the realm back together. The holders of the relics represented the leadership: Cali held the blue piece, Mac defended the green, Porkchop was given the red, and Grand Master Carter took the yellow. They agreed that they would reconstruct the doorway of life once everyone in the realm was back on the path to prosperity.

Sheese would have represented the New Realm Order, but evidence of his deals were made public. It wasn't the number of false promises he made that was incriminating, but the expectations of those who had fought for him and won, and the families of those that were lost. When it was time to pay up, he simply could not settle his end of the bargain. He had promised things that belonged to the realm, not his personal wealth or influence.

Grand Master Carter had been the scribe for the transactions and helped them to identify those that had been hurt by Sheese's fraudulent dealings. Rather than being hunted down by the masses that he'd angered, Sheese surrendered himself to the judiciary. He remained in the dungeons of the old Triple Crown castle. Grand Master Carter had agreed to represent the New Realm Order until a vote could decide a new representative.

Mac had taken responsibility for the destruction caused by the war, even though he wasn't the only aggressor, and spearheaded the rebuilding. His open acknowledgement of his wrongdoings helped the Marauders change their collective tone on discrimination, but the hatred and disrespect could not be changed overnight. The learning, understanding, and education to support unity would have to climb higher than the new walls and homes being erected.

Porkchop remained a key leader for those in the Badlands. Instead of being segregated from the rest of the realm, the holder of the red relic was included in the rebuild—a position aided by his ownership of one of the realm's largest property companies. The same resources that were allocated to rebuilding Kimroad were also applied to cities in the Badlands, like Camptown. New trade routes would bring prosperity to the region as well, so that after things were built they could continue to prosper.

Along with this responsibility, Porkchop agreed to help drive out the addiction to Rosebud that his community had suffered from. Led by his daughter, Robyn, a foundation was created to help volunteer centres care for those that struggled. With the redistribution of wealth, the Brotherhood no longer had to rely on the addicting substance to bring money into the community. The A.K.'s donation from the Kingdom of Moiras, given on behalf of Amelia, helped solidify new policies in the Badlands.

Talen slowed her dancing. Tears rolled down her cheeks.

Kase stopped moving his arms. He wondered if Talen's scrape had finally broken her pain tolerance. "Are you still bleeding?" he asked. He reached out for her wrist and tried to look at her arm.

Talen swatted his hand away and wiped her cheeks. "I am fine," she said. "Sometimes memories of Amelia hit me out of nowhere."

Kase rubbed his hand. He wondered if Amelia had influenced Talen's strength too, since he'd never seen her lash out like that. No matter what her next adventure was going to be, he'd miss seeing her change and grow even more.

"I liked Amelia's courage," Lenia said. She'd stopped dancing. "She reminded us that it doesn't matter how small you are, or what support you have, one person can make a difference. I don't know if I can pull off silk gloves like she did, but I might try them if we find the right event." She grabbed Kase's hand.

"Could I wear them, too?" Kase joked. He squeezed Lenia's back.

"I liked how Amelia wore her emotions on those sleeves," Cali said. She was still bouncing around a little, but no longer waved her arms around. "There was no guessing at what she felt when something new came up. If it made her angry, she lashed out. If it made her happy, she'd flash her smile. She didn't hide behind uncertainty or pretend to be something she wasn't."

Talen smiled as she wiped away another tear.

"I admired her heart," Kase said. He checked his mermaid design and thought of her scale. "She was willing to serve others without asking for anything in return. She wanted the less fortunate to succeed, so they didn't have to live through the suffering that she did. She faced her demons so that others could be free."

Talen sniffled. "I loved everything about her," she said. "On the one hand, I wish that it could have lasted a lifetime; but on the other, it proves that I can find it again. I hope we can all share in that feeling together."

"We will." Kase squeezed Lenia's hand again and moved closer to Talen. He embraced her. "So don't be a stranger."

"We're in each other's lives for a reason," Lenia added. "Thank you for showing up."

Cali joined the group hug. "It's not good-bye, it's more of a hard maybe-see-you-around type of farewell."

"I love you all," Talen said.

The group disengaged. Talen strode over to Death Hammer and mounted him with confidence. Cali hopped up behind Talen and they rode off together, giving Talen's new salute until they were out of view

Kase connected to the horse. It picked up speed as it trotted down the path. He lost his connection when he realized he was sitting in a tree with Lenia.

"Was the blanket too public?" Kase asked. He stared at the lakefront through the leaves. Their picnic set up was just below them, with Lenia's trident still standing against the trunk.

Lenia leant her head on Kase's shoulder. "I just wanted to be reminded of this moment," she said. "Any tree house moment with you is worth a lifetime, but I forgot what this one felt like. Do you think it's better than our other spots?"

Kase put his arm around Lenia. "Good question," he said. "We might need to visit all our special places before I make that decision, though. If these moments are each worth a lifetime, I hope we have a lifetime of special places like this one."

Lenia giggled. "I can't wait to have a lifetime of lifetimes with you," she said.

Kase pulled out the dandelion stem from his pocket and presented it to Lenia. He took a deep breath and focused on the flower until the white seeds reappeared. Lenia's eyes widened.

"Want to make it official?" Kase asked.

Lenia pulled out her purple fire starter. "I don't have to wish on it," she said. "I already have you in my life. But I'll never turn down an opportunity to set the world on fire." She sparked her unicorn knight piece and watched as the dandelion burst into a tiny fireball.

Kase brought the dandelion seeds back again. They took turns setting it aflame as they made plans for the rest of their uni-date. He didn't want the moment to end, but at the same time he was excited to see what new adventures they'd create together: in the moment, on the uni-date, and in their lifetime together.

The End.